"Don't flatter

Skylar gave him a once-over, then continued speaking. "Gossip in Cooperton is like ivy and blackberry briars—it's everywhere. You can't get away from it."

Aaron crossed his arms. "Maybe you should try harder."

"Maybe you should remember how impressionable teenagers are."

"Oh, right, you're a fine one to talk, Skylar."

She stared, wondering how he had the gall to say that. "As I recall, you're the one who did the talking."

He had the grace to look uncomfortable. She had to wonder...how much did he remember about the past? Was she just one of many girls who'd succumbed to his charm and good looks? If so, she probably *was* a stranger. Who knew how many of them he'd discarded like yesterday's newspaper.

It was reassuring in a way; she didn't actually want him remembering too much.

Dear Reader,

While on a vacation hike along the ocean, I began thinking about how children would be affected by a playboy father infamous for marrying and divorcing on a regular basis. Would they follow in his footsteps? Would they ever want to get married themselves? What sort of people would they be? Thus, Those Hollister Boys were born, sons of Sullivan Spencer "Spence" Hollister, known in the tabloids as "S.S. Hollister, the man with an ex-wife in every port." Spence has children and ex-wives all over the world and is a hedonist who survives on charm and an enormous fortune.

And who better to team with Spence's marriage-wary eldest son than a feisty redhead? I love writing strong-willed heroines, and Skylar Gibson is one of my favorites. Aaron and Skylar have a history together, including a teenage daughter he knows nothing about. Or does he?

Classic Movie Alert: If you love old movies the way I do, take a look at *Hobson's Choice* (1954), directed by David Lean and set in Victorian England. Starring Charles Laughton, Brenda De Banzie and John Mills, this romantic comedy is about another strong-willed woman who determinedly makes her own future.

I hope you have fun reading *Winning Over Skylar,* the first book in my series Those Hollister Boys. I enjoy hearing from readers and can be contacted c/o Harlequin Books, 225 Duncan Mill Road, Don Mills, ON M3B 3K9, Canada.

Wishing you all the best,

Julianna Morris

JULIANNA MORRIS

Winning Over Skylar

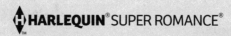

HARLEQUIN® SUPER ROMANCE®

Recycling programs
for this product may
not exist in your area.

ISBN-13: 978-0-373-60839-3

WINNING OVER SKYLAR

Printed in U.S.A.

ABOUT THE AUTHOR

Julianna Morris has an offbeat sense of humor that frequently gets her in trouble. She has also been accused of being interested in everything. Her interests range from oceanography and photography to traveling, antiquing, painting, walking on the beach and reading (mysteries and most other fiction and nonfiction). Julianna loves cats of all shapes and sizes. Her family's feline companion is named Merlin, and like his namesake, Merlin is an alchemist—he can transform the house into a disaster in nothing flat. And since he shares the premises with a writer, it's interesting to note that he is particularly fond of knocking books onto the floor.

Books by Julianna Morris

HARLEQUIN SUPERROMANCE

1713—HONOR BOUND
1864—THE RANCH SOLUTION

SILHOUETTE ROMANCE

BABY TALK
FAMILY OF THREE
DADDY WOKE UP MARRIED
DR. DAD
THE MARRIAGE STAMPEDE
*CALLIE GET YOUR GROOM
*HANNAH GETS A HUSBAND
*JODIE'S MAIL-ORDER MAN
MEETING MEGAN AGAIN
TICK TOCK GOES THE BABY CLOCK
LAST CHANCE FOR BABY!
†A DATE WITH A BILLIONAIRE
†THE RIGHT TWIN FOR HIM
†THE BACHELOR BOSS
†JUST BETWEEN FRIENDS
†MEET ME UNDER THE MISTLETOE
THE HOMETOWN HERO RETURNS

*Bridal Fever!
†Stories of the O'Rourke family

Other titles by this author available in ebook format.

To the memory of my wonderful Uncle Don who put marriage, family and church first in his life. When I think of you, I always see the smile on your face.

PROLOGUE

EIGHTEEN-YEAR-OLD Skylar Naples held the blanket-wrapped infant in her arms and stared down at the tiny, scrunched-up face.

Holy cow.

This was her kid.

She winced as she shifted in the hospital bed. Giving birth sucked, but the result was kind of awesome.

"I'll try to be a good mom," she said. "Honest."

The baby yawned and closed her eyes. She'd have to be fed again soon, and Skylar felt a twinge of worry. There were so many things a baby needed—doctors, food, clothes…roller skates. She'd never had roller skates herself, but her daughter was going to have them. She wanted her kid to have everything she'd never had. It wouldn't be easy to do it working as a cashier at a hamburger stand, no matter how nice the owners were being to her.

Still, she'd have to find a way.

Mr. and Mrs. Gibson had thrown her a baby shower, so she had some stuff to start. She'd also picked up things at garage sales. She hadn't liked doing it at first, but Mrs. Gibson had said that babies and toddlers grew so fast they didn't have time to wear clothes out, so she may as well get them secondhand for a while.

Skylar carefully adjusted the bundle in her arms. She was renting a room from an older lady who'd offered to watch the baby in exchange for yard work and housecleaning. Mrs. Bealer was sweet and kind and a Sunday school teacher at her church, so it should be okay to trust her. *Hopefully.* A fierce protectiveness had filled Skylar the moment she first saw that tiny red face; she wasn't sure she trusted *anyone* with her child.

"Karin Grace is Mrs. Gibson's name," Skylar whispered. "I like it. So if you don't object, that's what I'll call you. Only she goes by Grace, and we'll use Karin. Okay?"

The baby's mouth worked sleepily. It might be silly to ask, but Skylar didn't know much about being a mother and a name was awfully important.

"Karin," she said, to see how it felt on her tongue.

The baby's eyes opened and looked at her. It seemed like a good sign.

Skylar rested her head on the pillow and continued making plans. She'd have to do this alone. She didn't want anything to do with her own messed-up parents or Karin's father.

Her eyelids drooped. She was so tired. Her last thought before drifting off was that she wished she'd met Jimmie Gibson before she'd gotten herself in trouble and that Karin was his daughter.

SKYLAR WOKE WITH a start.

The baby.

She panicked before realizing her daughter was still in her arms, even though she'd fallen asleep holding her. Jeez, at the very least she should have put Karin on the bed first.

"Hello, hello," called a voice from the door.

At first the only thing visible was a huge bunch of balloons, and then she saw Mr. and Mrs. Gibson… and Jimmie.

"Hi," she said awkwardly. Jimmie had been so sweet to her since she'd moved to Trident to work for his parents, but now the baby was here and the whole thing was much more real than before.

Jimmie grinned merrily and her awkwardness disappeared. "Hey, Sky. You look great."

He put a bouquet of flowers on the bedside table and tied the balloons to the chair in the corner. His parents piled gift bags on the end of the bed, but when Skylar tried to tell them they'd given her too much already, Mr. Gibson waved her concern away.

"Nonsense. Just a few small items." He pulled a toy koala bear from his pocket. "Let's see your big production," he said. "I've been waiting months to meet her."

"Me, too," Jimmie and Mrs. Gibson chimed in unison. They crowded around and made cooing sounds as she pulled the blanket away from Karin's face.

"May I hold her?" asked Mrs. Gibson.

Skylar nodded and watched as the three of them inspected Karin, counting fingers and toes and calling her the prettiest little girl they'd ever seen. Her eyes stung, and a funny sensation came into her throat. She hadn't known there could be people like the Gibsons.

She'd grown up in a neighboring town, and all her life she'd been the daughter of "that drunken Naples couple." They were the family that everyone detested, with weeds and trash and broken-down cars surrounding their shabby house. Once she'd planted a flower bed, but her father had stomped it down in a whiskey-soaked rage, knocking her halfway across the yard when she tried to stop him.

"Sky, have you decided on a name?" Jimmie asked.

"Karin Grace, if it's okay with you, ma'am," she said quickly, looking at Mrs. Gibson.

Mrs. Gibson blushed pink. "Oh, my… I'd be *honored*. Imagine having this lovely child named after me."

Mr. Gibson beamed and seemed pleased, too.

As for Jimmie…he smiled and squeezed her hand. If Skylar hadn't known better, she'd have thought he liked her as a girl, and not just as a friend. But it was dumb to get her hopes up. Jimmie had lots of girlfriends. He didn't need one who already had a baby.

CHAPTER ONE

"I'LL HELP, MRS. GIBSON," said Melanie Hollister as Skylar carried a bucket of soapy water to the eating area outside the hamburger stand.

"Me, too, Mom," Karin added.

Skylar hid a smile. "Thanks, but study comes first." She didn't have any illusions—the girls were doing their geometry homework. According to Karin they had a bunch of "dumb-ass postulates" to learn and an equally "lame-o" set of problems to solve. They'd do anything to get out of the assignment, even scrub dried ketchup from tables and benches.

Well…Skylar looked at Melanie and changed her mind. The teenager was solemn, sincere and eager to please—she probably *did* want to help. She was a junior and high schoolers could be cruel to younger students, yet the two girls had formed a close bond since Melanie's arrival in Cooperton, despite their age difference. Melanie had turned sixteen in August, and Karin would soon be fourteen, but they were in several classes together because Karin was in an accelerated program, a year ahead of her classmates, while her new friend had fallen behind from having moved around so often.

If Melanie hadn't been a Hollister, Skylar would have been pleased they were friends. Thinking of which, a black Mercedes glided to a stop in front of the hamburger stand. It gleamed, without a speck of dirt daring to mar its perfection—a sharp contrast to her old pickup truck. She couldn't remember the last time it had been washed...probably before her husband's accident.

Skylar swallowed.

Actually, she knew exactly the last time it had been washed and waxed...the day Jimmie had died. He'd waxed both of their trucks that morning. The deep stab of loss was duller now, but it still hurt that he was gone. They were supposed to grow old together, and for months the sorrow and unfairness of it had kept her awake at night. The grief counselor had insisted it was anger at Jimmie for dying. Okay, maybe she was a little angry for a while, but it hadn't lasted. Mostly she was angry with the driver of that 18-wheeler for running a stop sign, not her husband for being in the wrong place at the wrong time.

"Uh-oh."

The gloomy voice broke into Skylar's dark thoughts. The girls were looking apprehensively at the Mercedes.

Aaron Andrew Hollister, or "Randy Andy" as he was sometimes called in high school, climbed out with a frown. "Melanie, I thought you were studying at the library this afternoon."

"We went already." She pointed to the pile of books next to her. "And Karin has some of mine in her bag 'cause there were more than I could carry. Don't worry. Mrs. Gibson is taking me home. It won't be long because we don't want to miss the baseball game."

"You already went to the library? School only let out an hour ago." His tone strongly suggested that she hadn't told the truth in the first place. "Your mother wants you to do better in your classes. She hopes your stay in California will make a difference, and you can catch up."

"Yeah. She always says stuff like that when she dumps me somewhere." The teen bit her lip, and Skylar could see the resentment in her eyes. The kid had been left with her half brother while her mother was off traveling the world with her second husband, or whatever it was the indolent rich did with their time.

"You weren't dumped here." Aaron's protest rang hollow. By all accounts, Melanie had lived with a dozen or more different relatives and friends of her mother, rarely finishing the year in the same school. That's how the Hollisters approached childrearing— as if it was someone else's responsibility. But leaving her with Aaron? Oh, *puleeze*. That was scraping the bottom of the barrel.

"I don't care what you call it," Melanie muttered. It hadn't taken long for her to transform into a sullen teenager with a chip on her shoulder. "You didn't want to come here, either."

His expression froze. "Our situations aren't the same."

Skylar perked up her ears. Aaron hadn't wanted to come back to Cooperton? That wouldn't surprise her; he used to be contemptuous of small towns and the people in them. Unfortunately for Aaron, his job at Cooper Industries was an inherited responsibility. He was the only Cooper grandchild—his mother, Celina Cooper Morgan, hadn't had more children after her divorce from S. S. Hollister, so Aaron was always expected to take over one day.

That was something Skylar didn't want for Karin. Granted, the Gibson Nibble Nook wasn't a huge company like Cooper Industries, but her daughter would have choices that didn't require slicing onions and flipping hamburgers. It wasn't a legacy; they could sell the place when the time came.

Melanie closed her geometry book with a snap. "I know you hate being here, Aaron. I heard you tell—"

"Melanie, we don't air our private business in front of strangers," he interrupted.

Strangers?

Skylar wanted to smack him. They were far from strangers. As much as she'd like to forget sleeping with Aaron over fourteen years ago, she couldn't. And if that wasn't enough, he'd bragged to his buddies about nailing her. After that, every guy in school thought she was an easy target. She'd already had a bad reputation, but it hit rock bottom when Aaron opened his big mouth.

Funny, she'd given Aaron little conscious thought in years, but now that Melanie was friends with Karin, she was getting daily reminders.

"They're just studying," Skylar said, trying to stay calm.

Fair was fair. Melanie was doing her geometry homework, not joyriding. Besides, the hamburger stand was only open for breakfast and lunch. The Nibble Nook intentionally closed at the same time the high school let out for the day; otherwise they could have a crowd of teenagers until late every afternoon. Still, she couldn't deny that a few farmworkers and other customers often arrived near closing and lingered over their meals.

She and Jimmie had discussed keeping the Nook open longer, but this way they'd had a better family life. It was the same decision his parents had made when they were running both the Nibble Nook and the Nibble Nook Too in Trident, where Skylar had gone to get a job when she'd learned she was pregnant. She sure couldn't have hung around Cooperton, where people knew her; it was hard enough returning as a married woman.

Aaron shot Skylar a cool look.

He'd been attractive in high school with his dark brown hair and eyes. Now he was downright gorgeous. Luckily she was immune—she knew his handsome exterior concealed a jackass of major proportions. And in the four months since he'd taken over as the managing CEO of Cooper Industries, his employees were discovering what she'd learned as a stupid, reckless seventeen-year-old.

The employees disliked Aaron intensely—he treated them as potential criminals, the company cafeteria prices had tripled and the shortened lunch break wasn't long enough to let them drive farther than the Nibble Nook for an inexpensive meal.

"Whether they're studying or not isn't the issue. And I'll handle my own problems, if you don't mind," he growled.

Then stop handling them badly, she wanted to add, except antagonizing him wouldn't be good for Melanie or Karin. She'd tried to remember that whenever he'd "visited" the Nibble Nook over the past several weeks.

A vision of Aaron's face the first day he'd shown up at the Nibble Nook rose in Skylar's mind, and she almost laughed; the Trident Hell Raisers had been there. They were a harmless group of retirees who'd formed a motorcycle club. Jimmie's uncle Fred belonged, and they came over once a week to talk, drink coffee and try to look like tough, seasoned road warriors in a defiant "FU" to lost youth.

So, in drove Aaron Hollister in his shiny black Mercedes and expensive suit, horrified to see his sister surrounded by a motorcycle gang. He hadn't asked questions, just rushed Melanie away so abruptly she'd forgotten her book bag. Skylar supposed she might have been concerned if their places were reversed, but really, the Trident Hell Raisers were retired accountants, doctors and firemen. Uncle Fred had irreverently nicknamed them the Bunion and Hemorrhoids Brigade.

Skylar could have reassured Aaron, but he was so damned obstinate and suspicious, he probably wouldn't have believed her, anyhow. And he'd just argue that *other* bikers ate at the Nibble Nook, too. It was true enough, but they'd never caused trouble.

"We *did* go to the library," Karin announced. "Mellie checked out a ton of books on President Lincoln for her history paper."

"I didn't ask you, young lady."

Skylar's temper flared at the stuffy censure in Aaron's voice. He had a lot of nerve.

"Thank you, Karin," she said, managing to keep her voice level. "Why don't you and Melanie go get milk and apples for another snack? I moved the organic fruit to the left side of the fridge in the back storeroom."

The teens exchanged glances.

"Uh, okay, Mom," Karin agreed, apparently deciding not to attempt her usual argument in favor of chips and soda.

Once her daughter and Melanie disappeared into the Nibble Nook, Skylar rounded on Aaron, throwing caution to the wind. "If you're upset that Melanie is coming here to study, then say so," she hissed. "Don't take it out on my kid. You implied that your sister lied about going to the library—Karin was just sticking up for her friend."

Aaron directed his intent gaze at her. "She was impertinent."

"Impertinent?" Skylar rolled her eyes. "La-di-dah, aren't we being high-and-mighty? Karin was only impertinent if you're a seventeenth-century land baron lording it over a peasant. Give me a break. This is the *twenty-first* century, and I own this property. If Karin had been rude, I'd be the first to chew her out."

He clenched his jaw. "I didn't accuse Melanie of lying, but she does have a history."

"Who told you that—other relatives who wanted an excuse to ship her back to her mother? You might check the facts before making assumptions." Skylar marched to the stack of books and opened one to the library's date stamp. "See? The return date is two weeks from today. That's the standard loan period for the Cooperton Public Library."

"You knew that because you already looked."

She slammed the book onto the table. "No, I didn't. Karin isn't an angel, but she's a good kid and usually tells the truth. I'm betting Melanie is the same. I'm also betting that I've spent more time with your sister than you have since she got to Cooperton."

"That's outrageous. She lives with me."

"Oh?" Skylar planted her hands on her hips. "You mean you eat dinner together every night? You check her homework? You go out to movies or take her for pizza? Do you even *know* what pizza she likes?"

A dull red flush crept up Aaron's neck. "I'm hoping to spend more time with Melanie, but things have been hectic at the office. It's critical to have a smooth transition from my grandfather's leadership at Cooper Industries to my own. I was returning from a meeting when I saw she was here. But if I hadn't seen her, I would have called to be sure she got home okay."

"Or your executive assistant would have called. Her name is Peggy, right? I've heard Melanie say her name when they're on the phone. That's child care by proxy."

She dunked her scrub brush into the bucket of sudsy water and slapped it on one of the tables. Aaron scowled and stepped back to avoid getting splashed. *Good*. His size didn't intimidate her, but she didn't enjoy being that close to an obnoxious jerk. Lord, he'd always had a gift for making her angry. Even on their few teenage dates they'd fought more than they kissed.

"I'm not delegating Melanie's care," he growled. "Peggy has experience from raising her own children and recommended a quick status check with Melanie after school, which she takes care of when I have other commitments. There's nothing wrong with accepting her help."

Skylar practically snorted. She finished scrubbing the brightly painted aluminum picnic table and hosed it down before starting on the next. Her workday didn't stop for spoiled rich guys wearing pricey suits and fine Italian shoes. At least she assumed they were

Italian; Aaron probably thought he was too good for regular American-made products.

She swept the remains of a French fry order into the trash. Cooper Industry employees weren't tidy customers; they ate on the run because their pay was docked double if they weren't back on time. That was another one of Aaron's unpopular new policies. Honestly, they could barely get out of the company's large parking lots in half an hour. Since he'd taken over management, the Nibble Nook's profits, while consistently respectable, had skyrocketed. They were located just outside the main gate, provided easy access to and from the road and could handle a feeding frenzy during the staggered factory meal breaks.

"Peggy must fill in a lot," she said after a moment. "I understand one of your commitments included a date with a former winner of the Miss California beauty pageant. In Sacramento. Did you get home at all that night?"

"Not that it's your business, but that was before Melanie arrived. And I didn't realize you were monitoring my social life."

Skylar rubbed unnecessarily hard on a smear of dried mustard. *If only it was Aaron's nose.*

"Don't flatter yourself, Hollister. Gossip in Cooperton is like ivy and blackberry briars, it's everywhere. You can't get away from it."

He crossed his arms. "Maybe you should try harder."

"Maybe you should remember how impressionable teenagers are."

"Oh, right, you're a fine one to talk, Skylar."

She stared, wondering how he had the gall to say any such thing. "As I recall, you're the one who did the talking."

He had the grace to look uncomfortable, or perhaps it was her imagination. She had to wonder…how much *did* he remember about the past? Was she just one of many girls who'd foolishly succumbed to his questionable charm and good looks? If so, she probably *was* a stranger. Who knew how many of them he'd discarded like yesterday's newspaper.

It was reassuring in a way; she didn't actually want him remembering too much.

MELANIE HID WITH Karin under the front counter of the hamburger stand, her eyes widening as the argument continued between Mrs. Gibson and Aaron. Eavesdropping wasn't nice, but she couldn't remember anyone defending her the way Karin's mom was doing. It was worth getting in trouble to hear it.

"Hey, I told you Mom was an honest-to-gosh redhead," Karin whispered. "Listen to her go."

"Uh-huh."

"You should have heard when she went off on the principal. The school didn't want me taking classes with sophomores and juniors 'cause I'm not fourteen yet, and boy, did she get hot. I was waiting in the secretary's office and wasn't supposed to hear, but they were talking real loud."

A stab of envy hit Melanie. She didn't think her

own mother would do something like that. Aaron had acted as if she was buying drugs instead of studying, and now Mrs. Gibson was sticking up for her. Aaron was just like the other family she'd stayed with, though what he'd said about hoping to spend more time together was nice—not that she wanted to hang around a brother she hardly knew.

"It must have been awesome."

Karin shrugged. "I guess. And I'm glad they gave me the classes I wanted. My…my dad used to calm Mom down when she got upset. He'd tease her, saying she had a hair-trigger temper and knew how to use it. That made her laugh, though I'm not sure why it was funny."

Her face was really sad, and Melanie didn't envy her any longer. Karin's dad was dead; he'd died in a car crash a year ago in August. *Her* father wasn't around much, but he was alive.

"I know what you mean. It's like when they say my mother has a credit card and knows how to use it," she said quickly. "That's totally lame. Everybody knows how to use a credit card."

"Maybe it's a gag from an old movie. Not a cool movie like *Star Trek,* but something else." Karin wrapped her apple core in a napkin and tucked it into her pocket. The argument outside had ended, or gotten quieter, and they couldn't hear it any longer. "Your brother won't keep you from coming here, will he?"

"I hope not." While Aaron hadn't forbidden her to

visit the Nibble Nook, Melanie knew he didn't like it. "But he's just my *half* brother. My mother is our father's sixth wife. Um...his sixth *ex*-wife. So we hardly know each other," she said hurriedly. Aaron was unpopular in Cooperton; she didn't want anyone thinking they were close.

Karin blinked. "Ohmigod, your dad's gotten married six times?"

Melanie cringed. People were curious about her father getting married and divorced so often. The newspapers called him "S. S. Hollister, the man with an ex-wife in every port."

"More than six now. He gets married a bunch."

"I'm never getting married," Karin announced. "I'm going to be a scientist and find the cure to everything. Like colds. I hate colds."

"Me, too," Melanie agreed, relieved at the change of subject. She liked that Karin didn't seem to know or care about the crap about her family.

It was strange to feel like an only child when she had four half brothers and three half sisters, all with the same father and different mothers. Well, except for April and Tamlyn, who were twins. You couldn't talk about "our" parents, just my mother, and their mother, and our father. And some of her ex-stepmothers had kids by other marriages, making it even more tangled.

Of course, since Aaron was the oldest, he probably had it the worst. She wasn't the youngest, though; Pierre was just seven and he was an obnoxious brat.

"We better get out of here." Crouching, Karin crept back to the rear storage room to keep from being seen through the windows. She straightened and opened the refrigerator. "Do you want milk or anything?"

"No, thanks," Melanie said absently. She was looking at a photograph on the wall over a small desk in the corner. It was Karin and Mrs. Gibson, a smiling man she knew was Karin's dad and two older people. She pointed to them. "Are they your grandparents?"

"Yup. My dad's mom and pop. They live a few miles away in Trident where they run the Nibble Nook Too. The Nibble Nook also used to be their hamburger stand, but they gave it to my dad when he married my mom." She sat on the desk and swung her legs as she drank a carton of milk.

"What about your grandparents on your mom's side?"

Karin shrugged. "She doesn't like talking about them."

That made Melanie feel better.

Maybe everybody had family who weren't so terrific. And most of her brothers and sisters weren't *too* embarrassing. There was Aaron, and after him, Jake and then Matthew. Jake and his mother were famous photographers, and Matt was a playboy, same as their father.

After Matt came the twins—April and Tamlyn were gorgeous like their Las Vegas showgirl mother, but didn't act bigheaded. It would be fantabulous to have *their* figures. Melanie had never met Oona, who was closest to her in age, but she'd had to watch Pierre once when they were both visiting their father. The little monster. She was personally in favor of putting him in a cage and feeding him through a hole.

"Melanie," called Aaron from outside the hamburger stand. "Get your books. I'm going home early."

"Coming," she called back, wrinkling her nose.

AARON TRIED TO make small talk with Melanie as he drove to the house, but her monosyllabic responses didn't help.

One of his biggest challenges was figuring out how much freedom his sister should be given. Her mother had mentioned a need for strong discipline, which struck him as ironic since Eliza only saw her daughter a few weeks out of the year. How would she know? Still, while he didn't want to treat Melanie the way *he'd* been treated as a kid, for her sake, he also didn't want to make the wrong choices.

He sighed as he pulled into the driveway. "Look, I'm sorry I didn't believe you about going to the library, but when I saw you at that hamburger joint I figured you'd…"

"Lied," she finished flatly.

"You know I don't approve of the Nibble Nook." He wasn't prepared to put the place off-limits, but he did want to discourage her from going there. He'd had a brief fling with Skylar in high school, and she was hardly the influence his sister should have in her turbulent world—it was tough enough being one of

S. S. Hollister's kids, a man who collected and discarded wives with casual speed. She certainly didn't need a smart-mouthed, troublemaking high-school dropout as a role model.

Melanie released her seat belt. "Why don't you approve?"

"Cooper Industry employees are the Nibble Nook's main customers, and some of them don't like the new rules I've had to make," he said. It was a valid concern, just not the whole truth.

"Yeah, right." She got out, slammed the car door as hard as possible and stomped toward the house, her heavy book bag slung over her shoulder and other books clutched in her arms.

"Leave the books. I'll bring them," he urged.

She didn't stop and Aaron grimaced.

There was a shred of truth in Skylar's accusations. Melanie needed more attention, but there just weren't enough hours in the days. Take the house for example...the lawn needed mowing and the gardener had quit. There weren't any other gardening service companies in town, and the local kids didn't seem interested in earning money by doing yard work.

For that matter, the house was another complication he hadn't anticipated. Originally he'd moved into an apartment over the company's business offices, which had been used only once by his grandparents when they were remodeling the kitchen and bathrooms in their house. But when his former stepmother had asked him to take Melanie for the school year, he'd found something more suitable for a teenager.

His cell phone rang and he pulled it out. "Yeah?"

"This is Jim Browning, down at the plant," said a vaguely familiar voice. "I got your number from Peggy in the main office. Mr. Cooper always wanted us to ring if there was a problem."

Aaron let out a breath. "What can I do for you, Mr. Browning?"

The employee droned on, detailing a minor issue with the processor for boxing up one of their products, a type of flavored tortilla chip. Cooper Industries produced a wide variety of items, and Aaron reminded himself that making snack foods might not be the same as creating life-saving drugs, but they were important to the company.

"I understand," Aaron finally broke in. "You've arranged for repairs and the boxes can be manually sealed in the meantime."

"Er...yes, sir. I'm sorry I bothered you, but Mr. Cooper *did* insist...." The foreman's words trailed off uncertainly.

Aaron drew a calming breath, realizing he'd probably been too abrupt. The people in Cooperton were chatty, while he wanted to get to the point and stop wasting time. "It's fine. Your instructions may be modified in the future, but in the meantime, you're following procedure. Thank you."

He turned off the phone with relief. He'd left a lucrative CEO position in the computer industry when his eightysomething grandfather finally decided to retire, but he never expected it to be so tough. George Cooper had been an old-school manager, with every decision, large and small, going across his desk. Basically, the place was still being run like a small mom-and-pop shop, rather than a major business producing dozens of different convenience-food items. Responsibility needed to be spread among divisions, with midlevel managers taking the lead on day-to-day operations—except the company couldn't afford that type of reorganization for a while.

Aaron dropped his keys in his pocket and walked into the house. His grandparents had halfheartedly offered to let him move in with them, but it wouldn't have been good for Melanie. His sister wasn't related to the Coopers except through their ex-son-in-law, and they weren't the warmest people in the first place. He knew; he'd grown up with them. And no matter what Skylar thought about him, he refused to inflict their idea of hospitality on his sister. Even if he didn't know what was best for a teenage girl, he wanted Melanie to be happy.

"Melanie?" he called. "What do you want for dinner?"

After a long minute she appeared at the top of the stairs and stared at him coolly. "You mean you're asking?"

Oh, God.

Pain throbbed in his temples. She was usually very sweet and accommodating—almost *too* accommodating—but apparently he couldn't say anything right at the moment. Not that Melanie didn't have cause to be touchy—he'd royally stuck his foot in his mouth—but if this was what it meant to be a parent, you could keep it.

"Yes, I'm asking," he said as calmly as possible.

"Whatever I want?"

Yeah, she could have whatever she wanted…as long as it came from a restaurant that delivered or had a take-out menu. He didn't cook. Toast, oatmeal and coffee in the morning were the extent of his culinary skills.

"Within reason."

Melanie lifted her chin. "I'll take a chicken sandwich and sweet-potato fries from the Nibble Nook."

"That isn't within reason. You know the Nibble Nook is closed for the day."

"Then I don't care. I have geometry problems and an English assignment to finish." She turned and disappeared.

The afternoon just kept getting better and better. Aaron arched his back, trying to release the tension. He really had to deal with the yard. The neighborhood association had written, complaining about the length of the grass. Why anybody minded, he didn't know. This wasn't the garden district of New Orleans, it was a little town that rolled up its sidewalks at night and on Sundays.

Despite his grandfather's expectations that he would eventually take over one day, Aaron had never wanted to live in Cooperton again…and yet here he was. Of course, coming back would have been easier if George Cooper had retired before the business had fallen apart. Once Aaron got it viable again he'd have to evaluate whether he was going to stay, or consider other options.

Putting on jeans and a work shirt, Aaron went out to the garage. The rented house hadn't come furnished, but he'd seen a lawn mower and had a couple of hours of daylight left to work.

Forty minutes later he was hot, sweaty, and his shoulders ached. He gazed perplexed at the mower that refused to start; he was a novice at cutting grass, but it shouldn't be tough to figure out. The mower had gas, and he didn't think it was terribly old. Yet the damn thing wouldn't go. Maybe the gardening service used to bring their own equipment because this one was broken.

Frustrated, Aaron shoved the mower back into the garage and headed into the house. The service had told him they were overextended with customers and regretted terminating him as a client, but their regrets didn't help him get the lawn mowed.

In the kitchen he leafed through a stack of menus. They hadn't ordered pizza in over a week, and Mama Gianni's also had a decent chicken Greek salad. Pizza from Vittorino's Italiano was better, but they didn't deliver except on weekends. He dialed Mama Gianni's and ordered the Meat Lover's special and a family-size salad. Yet as he hung up the phone, he heard Skylar's voice in his head.

Do you even know *what pizza she likes*?

Shut up, Skylar, he ordered silently.

She hadn't changed much since high school— she still had that gorgeous auburn hair and green eyes…and a mouth that wouldn't quit. She'd sassed the teachers, cussed out the principal, gotten suspended more than once for breaking every rule in the book, and finally dropped out before graduation. It was ironic that a girl who'd skated through classes by the skin of her teeth was now diligently overseeing her kid's homework. And she wondered why he questioned if she might be a bad influence.

Yet a part of him didn't blame Skylar for being antagonistic. She'd represented a challenge when they were kids—his pals had dared him to nail her and he wasn't proud of his teenage self for taking that dare, or for dropping her once he'd done it. No woman, young or old, appreciated being treated that way. It was also hypocritical to think her sexual activity in high school was any more questionable than his own.

When the food came, Aaron ran upstairs to tell Melanie. She was in front of the television, watching a baseball game. She didn't look up, just nodded and said she'd come down after a while.

"Don't you want to eat together?" The question had nothing to do with Skylar; he'd already thought they should share more meals. At the same time, he didn't want to force anything on Melanie—until recently they'd been little more than casual acquaintances.

"I don't care."

I don't care... How many times a day did he hear that from her? Good Lord, teenagers were impossible, and Aaron felt a fleeting sympathy for his grandparents. He wasn't close to them, though his grandfather had supposedly "groomed" him to take over the company...mostly with lectures about the value of hard work. Nonetheless, it couldn't have been easy to take on a resentful kid, tired of being shuffled between his divorced parents and other relatives. That was one of the reasons he'd agreed to have Melanie live with him for the year. He could have refused, but he knew what it was like to be a Ping-Pong ball in someone else's battle of wills.

CHAPTER TWO

SKYLAR PULLED A casserole from the freezer and put it in the oven to heat. She liked cooking; she just didn't enjoy it after spending hours over the Nibble Nook's fryers—the volume of French fries and onion rings they went through never failed to astonish her. As the owner, she filled in wherever necessary, and today the fry cook had phoned in with a child-care problem.

Tiredly she pressed a hand to the aching small of her back. The long, hard days used to be more fun. Jimmie had made everything fun, no matter what they were doing.

The cat walked into the kitchen and stared at his empty bowl in dismay. He meowed plaintively.

"Karin?" she called. "Bennie has to be fed and his litter box scooped."

"The first play-off game is on."

"Then you'd better hurry," Skylar said. "We've talked about this. You wanted a cat and he's your responsibility."

"But Mooommmm, I—"

"Now, Karin. He's hungry."

Karin stomped into the kitchen. "He isn't mine, not really. Bennie always ends up with you in the morning. He's supposed to sleep with me. It's like I'm kryptonite or something."

For an instant Skylar wished she could have a single evening free of teenage angst. "That's because he keeps getting kicked off the bed. You thrash around and when he's had enough, he goes someplace quieter."

"I do not."

"Trust me, I couldn't keep a blanket on you, even as a baby. A professional soccer team doesn't kick that much."

Muttering under her breath, Karin poured food into the cat bowl and petted Bennie, despite her sulk. It wasn't easy insisting she take care of her chores—she used to watch the baseball play-offs with her dad, and Skylar could see the weepy melancholy beneath her daughter's defiant surface. The previous autumn Karin had sobbed straight through her favored team's sweeping victory; hopefully this year wouldn't be as bad.

"Here," Skylar said. "I made a snack for you to eat during the game. And there's caffeine-free cola in the fridge. I'll bring dinner in when it's ready." Normally they ate meals at the table, but this wasn't a normal night.

Karin brightened and took the bowl of fluffy buttered popcorn. "Gee, thanks, Mom."

When Karin was back in the family room, Skylar sat at the kitchen table, feeling melancholy herself. She wasn't a baseball fan, and it used to drive her crazy during the play-offs and World Series to have Jimmie and Karin riveted to the television. More than once, a game had gone into extra innings or there'd been a rain delay, and he'd let her stay up to the bitter end, even on a school night. When she fell asleep at school the next day, there would be the inevitable phone call from her teacher, who was always mollified by Jimmie's abashed apology.

Skylar would give anything to have those days back.

Instead, she had Aaron Hollister and his sister and her temper getting her in trouble. She had to be more careful. Aaron hadn't seemed interested in Karin in their encounters, but she couldn't take any chances. She refused to think of him as Karin's father. *Jimmie* was Karin's dad. He'd soothed her as a teething baby, been scared stiff when she broke her collarbone in the fourth grade, saved for her education and welcomed each and every sticky child's kiss and homemade Father's Day card. Skylar ached at the memories— Jimmie romancing her as a new mother had been one of the biggest surprises of her life. They'd gotten married when Karin was four months old—he'd simply refused to see any reason they shouldn't be together.

She glanced around the kitchen, shivering though it was warm. She'd had such a good life with Jimmie, so much better than she had ever expected to have. He'd loved Karin without reservation, and his family had accepted them both. The Gibsons must have been worried for their son in light of her youth and disreputable upbringing, but they hadn't shown any hesitation. If Jimmie loved her, that was all they'd needed to know.

But Jimmie was gone now. If he were here, he would reassure her that Aaron or his family couldn't possibly hope to get custody of Karin after such a long time. It was a worry that Skylar had harbored over the years, pushed into the background of their lives together, yet still there.

Bennie rubbed against her leg, purring madly, and she reached down to stroke him.

"Hey, boy," she whispered. "You should go in with Karin. She needs you."

He wandered toward the door. She could swear that he'd understood, though being a cat, he had to show his independence. Anybody who said felines were just selfish little beasts was wrong. No matter how egomaniacal, Bennie *was* fond of his humans. He just had to act as if everything was his idea—dogs were far more direct with their affections.

She got up and gathered a basket of laundry. The problem with housework was that it was never done, especially with a teenager in the house. Why her daughter had to change clothes ten times a day was beyond her. When she was that age she had been lucky to have four or five outfits, much less an overflowing closet.

Skylar winced. Back then, clothes were the least of her problems. The police and her teachers had labeled her incorrigible, and she'd come close to self-destructing. Her mother and father hadn't noticed—they were too busy having public screaming matches and getting arrested for bashing in the windows of a neighbor's car or some other drunken behavior. Skylar had both envied and resented the other kids for having nice, ordinary parents who didn't knock them around, the way her parents did when they were tired of beating on each other.

Yet somehow, for reasons beyond understanding, she'd believed in the fairy-tale family, and Aaron's family had seemed oh-so-respectable from the outside. That could be why she'd finally gone out with him. She hadn't realized that being rich and publicly proper didn't mean a thing. You could still be a louse.

The phone rang, and Skylar hurriedly started the washing machine before answering.

"It's me, dear," said her mother-in-law. "Are you busy?"

"Hi, Mom. No more than usual." Skylar tucked the receiver under her chin as she folded clean towels. "What's up?"

"Nothing. But Joe has the baseball game on, and I was wondering how it's going over there."

Skylar pictured her daughter's stormy face. "The way you'd expect. Karin is watching, too."

"I figured she would be."

They were both silent for a long moment. Skylar wished she could tell Grace about her confrontation with Aaron, but she'd never discussed Karin's biological father with her in-laws. Jimmie was the only one who'd known it was Aaron Hollister. Well… almost the only one.

It was odd. She would have sworn that nobody had guessed she was pregnant when she dropped out of school, and she'd deliberately moved to Trident to keep anyone *from* guessing. Yet S. S. Hollister had tried to give her payoff money after Karin was born. Skylar figured Aaron must have put it together and told his father—but if she was wrong and he didn't know that Karin was his biological child, or had made himself forget, she'd rather keep it that way.

Payoff money…Skylar gritted her teeth. As if she'd gone to them for support or something else. She had ripped the check in half and told Sullivan Spencer "Spence" Hollister exactly what she thought of him and his son and where he could stuff his money. He'd simply laughed and walked away…forever, she hoped.

"Oh. Sorry, Grace, what was that? My mind was drifting," she apologized, realizing her mother-in-law had broken the silence with a question.

"I just asked how Karin is doing in school so far. She was obsessed with her studies last year."

"She's no longer obsessed," Skylar said drily. "This afternoon she informed me that her geometry problems are lame and aliens have replaced the principal with an android look-alike who drinks double espresso lattes all day and plots ways to kill students with boredom."

Grace chuckled. "Good Lord. Aliens?"

"Yes. She's now into *Star Trek*. Yesterday I found her practicing the Vulcan hand signal for 'live long and prosper.' At least I think that's what it was, not something rude."

"She wouldn't have to practice *that*."

Skylar instinctively looked at her fingers. No, you didn't have to practice rude gestures. She'd begun flipping birds at her teachers in junior high school…a piece of information she'd prefer her daughter didn't find out. Karin may have heard stories about her mother over the years, but since she hadn't asked any questions, she probably wasn't taking them seriously.

"When did this new interest in science fiction begin?" said Grace.

"That weekend she was sick and we couldn't come for dinner. One of her friends loaned her a set of the *Trek* movies. Two days and half a bottle of cough syrup later, she was a fan."

Grace chuckled again. "That's our Karin. When she embraces something, it's with all her heart."

They chatted another few minutes before saying goodbye.

Skylar put the clean linens away and went to check on Karin in the family room. Things had been awfully quiet—no yelling at the pitcher, no declarations that the umpire needed glasses, and no shouts of triumph or despair.

"Hey," she said. "What's the score?"

"Five–zip, Dodgers."

Skylar might not be a baseball fan, but she knew

Karin's three-word report meant the Los Angeles Dodgers were ahead. "Isn't that the team you're rooting for?"

Karin shrugged. She wasn't crying, but she wasn't happy, either. "It's only the bottom of the fourth inning. They'll probably blow it."

Skylar let out a discouraged breath. Karin was a bright, enthusiastic kid…except when she was thinking about her dad being gone. "And they might win," she reminded gently. "I'm sure Grandpa Joe would love to get on the phone with you."

Karin didn't respond, but she inched farther toward the end of the sectional couch. *Right.* She didn't want the phone; she wanted someone sitting next to her… she just didn't want to *ask* someone to sit next to her. Skylar thought of the dozen different tasks she should get done. It was a busy week, and she had a meeting on Thursday at City Hall that would take all evening.

She sat down. "Okay," she said. "It's time I learned more about baseball. Tell me what's going on. The ones in white are the good guys, right?"

A small giggle escaped from Karin. "You're really silly, Mom."

AARON DROVE PAST the Nibble Nook the following morning and scowled. He had a huge job in front of him getting Cooper Industries back in shape, and Skylar wasn't making it easier by befriending his sister. Well…her *daughter* had befriended Melanie, but it was essentially the same thing.

There were numerous cars at the hamburger stand, along with motorcycles and a couple of big rigs parked at the side of the road. They obviously served breakfast, and he had to admit, the scents wafting into his car were tempting. On the other hand, the presence of motorcycles and 18-wheelers was disturbing—the drivers of those vehicles weren't necessarily a bad element, but there were no guarantees.

Almost as if taunting him, a tattooed cyclist got up from a table and strolled to his Harley. He spat on the ground and adjusted himself in his grubby-looking jeans before roaring away.

Wonderful.

Exactly the element an impressionable teenage girl needed.

Peggy was at her desk when he walked in, and he gave her a brief nod. He wasn't thrilled with having Peggy as an assistant; she was efficient and responsible, but she was zealously loyal to his grandfather and likely calling him daily with reports on the company. *Someone* was informing George Cooper of the changes and new policies being made by his grandson, though he wasn't showing a great deal of interest other than to say, "What's good for Cooperton is good for Cooper Industries."

Any warmth George possessed had mostly been shown to his employees and the town. He could be a genial man-of-the-people in the flash of an eye, but inside his own home he was cold and uptight.

No wonder Aaron's mother had rebelled—she'd fled Cooperton and done nothing but play ever since.

The phone rang before he reached his desk. It was Peggy, saying his father was on line one.

"Yes?" he said, punching the button.

"That's a fine way to greet your old dad." Spence Hollister was only "your old dad" when he wanted something.

"I don't have time for games, *Dad*." Aaron tucked the receiver under his chin and sorted through a stack of phone messages Peggy had left on his desk. A new phone system with voice mail had been installed months before, but he hadn't decided whether his calls should continue to be screened by Peggy in a traditional executive style, or to take them himself.

"That's always been your problem—you don't enjoy life."

"Some of us have a job. Why didn't you call my cell phone?"

"I assumed you'd changed the number after moving to that Hicksville. You didn't have to take over the Cooper company, son. For God's sake, give it a decent burial and get out. Your mother never wanted to go back there—it's the only thing we ever agreed on the entire time we were married."

A headache stabbed Aaron's temples. Much as he regretted giving up his lucrative position as CEO of a computer company, he couldn't abandon Cooper Industries. He might *have* to give it a decent burial, but not until he'd done his best to keep it alive.

"What do you want, Dad?"

"I... Hang on. We're having a spot of trouble with a champagne cork."

A feminine laugh sounded in the background, and Aaron shook his head. His father was between wives, so his companion could be anyone from a London society deb to a belly dancer. Spence liked his ladies young, beautiful and endowed—and since he had an abundance of charm and wealth, they liked him, too.

"Sorry, son. I wanted to know if you'll join my crew in next year's America's Cup race."

"I haven't been on your yacht since I was nineteen and foolishly took a semester off from college to train and compete."

"Foolish? Nonsense. That was a damn good race— we won two of the heats, so I know you're the key to the *Sea Haven* finally getting the trophy. Will you do it?"

Aaron practically snorted. Spence wasn't into effort; he ran a yacht in the America's Cup because he loved the publicity and being seen as a sportsman. He'd particularly reveled in the media coverage the year his eldest son was a crew member. On the other hand, Aaron was still fighting the dilettante image he'd earned.

"Not a chance, Dad."

"But you can't save that place. What's the point of trying?"

"Thanks for the vote of confidence. By the way,

Melanie is fine. I'm sure she'll appreciate you asking," Aaron said, his voice laced with irony.

None of S. S. Hollister's kids had any illusions that he was especially concerned about them. You could be sure he didn't even remember your name, and five minutes later he could make you feel as if you were the most important person in the world. As a kid, Aaron had craved the moments when his father focused on him and would have done almost anything to get his attention. Now he was mostly wary. When S.S. called, he wanted something, and it usually wasn't to your benefit to give it to him.

"You would have let me know if Melanie had a problem," Spence said easily. "Are you sure you won't be a member of the *Sea Haven*'s crew? I'd make you skipper, but I've finally gotten Bill Driscoll to sign on and we have an ironclad contract. I do get to pick one crew member, and you're the one I want."

"Why don't you ask Matt? He doesn't have anything to do." Aaron's second brother was almost as much a playboy as their father, except he avoided serious relationships and was scrupulous about birth control. "Or Tamlyn or April or Oona?"

"Yachting isn't their thing."

Aaron snorted, suspecting his father had gone first to Matt and his three adult sisters before calling him. Spence wouldn't have asked Jake, though. Even *Spence* knew his second son couldn't be pried away from risking his neck in pursuit of the next great photograph—Jake's photography was stunning, but his pictures weren't taken in safe, convenient locales. It wasn't any wonder that some people speculated whether Jake had a death wish.

"Yachting isn't my thing, either, Dad. Give the choice back to Driscoll and let him win for you."

"Ah, well. Let me know if Melanie wants anything. I'll buy her a car as soon as she has her driver's license."

"No, you won't," Aaron insisted, a surge of adrenaline going through him. He did *not* want Melanie to have a car—he had good reason to know that teenagers did insane things when they were driving, and he had no desire to see his sister wrapped around a tree. She was going to have a top professional driving instructor and lots of practice before getting her own car was an option.

"Oh? I gave *you* a Mustang when you were sixteen. A sweet job. Just what a teenage boy needed to get girls."

"And you gave me another when I was seventeen. I totaled the first one, remember?" Aaron knew it was a miracle he hadn't killed himself when he'd spun out and slammed into a telephone pole—instead he'd gotten off with bruises and minor cuts. "Anyhow, Melanie is young for her age and I want her to have experience driving before she's handed her own set of keys."

"Fine, fine, just let me know when. Bye for now." Spence didn't sound upset—few things ruffled S. S. Hollister.

Aaron dropped the receiver in its cradle and looked around the office. He'd made a few modifications since returning to Cooperton, shifting the desk and adding file cabinets, but it remained furnished with his grandfather's ponderous mahogany furniture and deep red carpet. Redecorating was out for a while though; other things were needed more.

On a sturdy new worktable by the window was his proposal for updating and expanding the factory. To finance the project he would have to sell some of the land the Cooper family had held for generations throughout Northern California, but he was convinced the company wouldn't survive otherwise.

"Mr. Hollister?" Peggy said from the door. "The foreman in the tortilla chip division says there's still a problem with the repairs he phoned you about yesterday. It seems a part in the machine is no longer replaceable—the company that used to make the equipment is now manufacturing air conditioners."

"That's what happens when you're operating with antiques," Aaron muttered.

"What?"

"Nothing. Have them assign additional employees to tape the boxes, then get the records on the equipment and special parts needed. I'll research the matter."

Peggy left, and Aaron tried to unclench his jaw. His grandfather hadn't invested in significant capital improvements at Cooper Industries for almost three decades. The company needed so much, and here he was, spending time on an ancient machine that sealed boxes for shipping.

Perhaps if he got it taken care of quickly, he could get on with what he'd planned to do with his day. Three experts had reviewed the plans he'd worked up with an industrial engineer and now he needed to submit them to the Cooperton City Council for their approval—the town was so small they didn't have a planning department. Besides, there was a zoning issue.

It was frustrating that elected officials, rather than trained professionals, would have a hand in deciding the future of Cooper Industries, but it shouldn't be hard to get their support. After all, his company was the biggest employer in town.

"MELLIE, WASN'T THE game *awesome?*" Karin asked as they waited in line at the cafeteria to pay for their lunch. Her mom wasn't crazy about the food the school served, but didn't make her bring a sack lunch or anything. *Thank God.* Only the dorky kids ate sack lunches. It would be nice to eat at the Nibble Nook, but the school didn't allow them to leave the grounds except with a parent or written permission.

"Yeah, but I've never watched baseball before," Melanie confessed. She gave the cashier a fifty-dollar bill; the woman looked at it twice and glowered as she started counting out the change.

"How come?"

"I guess because I've moved around so much. A

long time ago, before my mother got married again, one of her boyfriends was a football player, but I never knew what was happening when we went to his games. Baseball is easier."

"I don't get football, either, though some of the players are okay." Karin nudged her friend, and they gazed longingly at Nick Jakowski as he talked to his friends across the room.

Nick was the *yummiest* guy in school and the captain of the football team. He was nice, too. He'd stopped the team from hazing a new boy who'd transferred from their biggest rival, Trident High, and he was friendly to freshmen, unlike most of the other seniors.

"Do you think he's really going steady with Tiffany Baldwin?" Melanie said wistfully.

Tiffany was a cheerleader and thought she was, like, the most beautiful girl who'd ever lived. Most of the time she wasn't too unbearable, except for an annoying, high-pitched laugh. And you couldn't deny that she was pretty, with light gold hair and green eyes.

Karin sighed. "I don't know. Susan Lightoller saw them kissing at the movies this summer, and Tory Wilson says they were holding hands at the Labor Day parade."

"Oh."

"But he wouldn't let her share his ice cream at the carnival afterward," Karin added, brightening at the recollection. "And Andrea Crane said that if they were French kissing a bunch he wouldn't mind if she licked his cone."

Melanie perked up as they took their trays to a table. "Your mom was great yesterday. She sure let Aaron have it."

"You don't like him, do you, Mellie?"

"Nobody does. Even so, I'm glad that I get to stay here this year."

"Me, too." Karin was still worried that Melanie's brother would say she couldn't come to the Nibble Nook. It was too weird being around her other friends now that her dad was dead; they wanted her to act as if everything was the same, and it wasn't. Melanie never tried to get her to act different.

Karin poked the cheese enchiladas on her plate, no longer hungry. Sometimes almost a whole week would go by without her getting that awful knot in her tummy, or the horrid cold chills that came when she remembered her dad's accident. Then she'd feel guilty, as if she was forgetting him.

"I wish we could eat lunch at the Nibble Nook," Melanie said, taking a bite of her Mexican rice. "But this is better than the stuff at my last school." She made a gagging gesture.

"Yeah, Mom makes awesome burgers." Karin determinedly began eating.

CHAPTER THREE

By MIDAFTERNOON Aaron had located a small company that specialized in replacement parts for equipment no longer used by most manufacturers. It was a niche business that probably got most of their profits from outdated places such as Cooper Industries.

"We'll send your order by overnight courier," the representative assured. "But I'm surprised we have these parts in stock. Did you know they stopped making this model way back in the nineteen—"

"I know," Aaron interrupted in a dour tone. "Thank you."

He hung up and called the tortilla-chip division, letting them know they'd soon be back to full working order. Hiring someone to handle this sort of problem was becoming a priority; it still boggled his mind that his grandfather had gotten involved with the nitty-gritty of daily operations. The company needed midlevel managers to take responsibility and make decisions.

They also needed a whole new factory.

An email message came in from Peggy, telling him the next city council meeting was in a couple of days. Surprisingly, Peggy was willing to use the computer system he'd put into the executive office. The only other area where she'd shown support was his attempt to watch after Melanie. Thinking of which....

He stepped to the outer office.

"Peggy, are there any known problems with drugs or anything at the Nibble Nook? Some of the customers I've seen there look questionable, and I've heard that in small towns, a local hamburger stand can be a center for drug pushers and gang activity."

Her perpetual frown deepened. "I've heard that, too, but the Gibson family built the Nibble Nook over thirty-five years ago, and their regular clientele largely come from Cooper Industries and other businesses. You wouldn't have known Jimmie Gibson when you were a boy here—he was four or five years older and living in Trident by then. He's gone now, killed in a car accident last year."

So, Skylar was a widow.

While Aaron had noticed she wore a wedding ring, he hadn't given it much thought. Mostly he had worried that being around Skylar and a busy, roadside hamburger stand were a bad idea for a shy, sheltered girl like Melanie. The issue of his employees eating there was valid, as well—they weren't happy about his new rules and could take it out on her.

"You seem to know something about the Gibsons."

"I should hope so. I've lived in Cooperton my whole life."

Somehow, Peggy's reply sounded critical, though Aaron didn't know why. Did she think he should have returned to the company after college and graduate school, working as second fiddle to his grandfather for the past seven or eight years? It would have made him crazy, and he wouldn't have learned anything about effective management.

"I... Yeah," he muttered. "Does Mrs. Gibson have any boyfriends who hang out at the Nibble Nook?"

The thought of tattooed bikers or knife-toting gang members had kept him awake more than once after discovering where Melanie was spending so much time. Honestly, it was hard to see Skylar Naples as a solid, upstanding member of the community.... Skylar *Gibson,* he reminded himself. She'd made so much trouble as a teenager, even his grandparents had been aware of her, partly because she'd get drunk and do insane things like balancing on the roof of a moving car and flashing her breasts at city hall as one of her hoodlum buddies sped past.

She'll end up dead. Or in prison, Sarah Cooper had grimly pronounced on more than one occasion. Then she'd shaken her finger at Aaron, *We're not letting it happen to you.*

Honestly, they had acted as if he was the devil's spawn. He understood they'd wanted him to turn out like them, rather than their flighty daughter, but why treat him as if he was one step away from reform school?

"Boyfriends?" Peggy sniffed, dragging Aaron's attention back to the present. "Skylar had *quite* a reputation once, but I wouldn't know about it now. I don't gossip about my neighbors."

"Of course." It wasn't the definitive answer Aaron would have preferred. "Your email said the city council is meeting on Thursday. Do you know how I get on their agenda?"

She shrugged. "Call city hall and ask, probably."

Plainly, she wasn't in a helpful mood. He hadn't confided in her—it might be different if he'd hired Peggy himself, but he hadn't; she had started in potato chips and moved up from there. Ironically, she could have been a valuable resource for him; instead she was a pain in the ass.

"Thank you," Aaron muttered, returning to his office.

He found the listing for city hall in the small Cooperton phone book and dialed it.

"Mayor's office," a woman answered. "Micki Jo speaking."

"This is Aaron Hollister, of Cooper Industries. I want to get on the agenda for the next city council meeting."

"Oh. Mr. Hollister." Micki Jo's youthful voice suddenly went ten degrees south of freezing. "What is this regarding?"

Aaron hesitated. He didn't want to discuss the matter with a secretary, especially since no one in Cooperton knew about his expansion plans yet. It would be best if he could speak to the council without them having any preconceptions.

"I'd like to make a presentation about Cooper Industries."

"With that and four bucks I can get a macchiato latte," she said drily. "The council has a full agenda this month, Mr. Hollister. I'll need more details before adjustments can be made to the schedule."

"I…uh, have some plans to discuss."

"What kind of plans?"

Aaron kept his temper with an effort. "For modifications at the company."

"What type of modifications?"

Great. He'd have to tell her—sounding too secretive would just make things worse. "Expansion plans. And there's a property-use rezoning issue that needs approval."

"Very well, I'll let the mayor know. You'll be notified if you've been added to the agenda."

If he'd been added?

"But I—"

The phone clicked off before Aaron could say anything else and he stared at the receiver in disbelief. What had changed in Cooperton in the past fourteen years? The town used to fall all over themselves to make his grandfather happy.

ON THURSDAY AFTERNOON Skylar pushed a large box of burgers and fries across the counter, followed by a half dozen milk shakes. "Here you go, Fernando."

"*Gracias,* Skylar. I promised my crew a meal and nothing would satisfy them except the Nibble Nook."

"That's a real compliment."

Fernando Rodriguez leased farmland that grew a variety of organic produce, and he'd brought a truckload of his workers over for a late lunch. Although Skylar had closed for the day by the time they'd driven up, she hadn't been able to turn him away.

She began counting out the cash registers while her remaining three employees cleared the counters.

"Greg, don't you need to go?" she asked the fry cook, who also managed the Nibble Nook every Saturday for her. Greg was a single father with chronic child-care issues and couldn't stay late as a rule, while his coworkers loved overtime.

"I'm okay for once. My sister doesn't work this afternoon, so she can watch the twins a while longer."

Skylar nodded, grateful she wouldn't have to empty the oil from the fryers herself. Delays always seemed to happen on the days she had something to do in the evening—not that she had a social life aside from Karin's school, church or city events.

Karin and Melanie arrived as she finished tallying the day's receipts. They sat at a table near the farmworkers, and Skylar hoped that Aaron wouldn't see them and stop. Fernando's employees were a great bunch of guys, but she was sure their rough appearance would appall Mr. Big Shot Hollister.

Skylar tucked the deposit into a bank envelope and

locked it in the sturdy safe they had installed several years before.

"Hey, girls," she said, stepping outside. "How was school?"

Melanie smiled shyly. "It was okay, Mrs. Gibson, but we have a bunch of homework."

"Every day they load it on," Karin muttered. "The teachers don't care about the baseball play-offs."

"Your team isn't playing tonight," Skylar reminded her. "It's a travel day for them."

Her daughter stuck her nose in her book. She was in one of her moods. Living with her would be a challenge until the World Series was over, along with the constant reminders that her dad wasn't there to share it with her.

Skylar went back to work, hurrying through her routine so she could get to her meeting on time. Melanie's presence troubled her. The teen had continued to show up every day, despite her brother's disapproval of the Nibble Nook, and the girls did their homework together. Of course, a fair amount of giggling and whispering accompanied the studying, but Skylar periodically checked their progress to be sure they were getting enough done. They also had plans for the weekend—something Aaron was certain to refuse to give his permission for.

Her employees left and she finished by scrubbing the picnic tables and watering the whiskey half barrels she used as planters. She and Jimmie had always taken pride in keeping the Nook clean, and she wasn't going to let it slide.

"Melanie, do you need a ride home?" she called as she stowed the hose in an outside storage cabinet.

"If you're not too busy, ma'am."

"No problem. Hop in the truck."

Skylar dropped Melanie off and got Karin settled at the house with dinner before racing to the bank, and then to City Hall. Jimmie had become a member of the city council years before and the mayor had "named" her as his replacement...without even asking. She'd wanted to strangle Chester, yet in a way it had been good for her. Still, she wouldn't mind if she didn't win the position in the next election.

"Did you hear?" twenty-four-year-old Micki Jo said as Skylar got a cup of coffee. It was hideous, but better than nothing at the end of a long day.

"Hear what?"

"Aaron Hollister is coming tonight to discuss expanding Cooper Industries."

"He'll probably increase mechanization so he can cut jobs," Chester chimed in before Skylar could say anything. "And he's going to stop buying local products. His purchasing agent told one of the farmers that Hollister claims it's more efficient to purchase from large producers. I know because Mr. Okishida told Doctor McWilliams's receptionist who told the pharmaceutical rep, and *she* mentioned it to our pastor."

Skylar tried to sort out who had been told what on

the rumor mill and decided it didn't matter. "Maybe somebody heard the story wrong."

"*Hah.* Do you know how many farmers it will affect? Not to mention their employees. Mr. Cooper would never do something like this, but Hollister is one of those big city CEOs who will do anything to turn a buck."

"At least the organic farmers won't be affected since Cooper Industries doesn't buy from them, anyhow," Micki Jo contributed.

The reminder didn't appear to encourage the mayor. Chester lacked real skills to lead a town, but he was honest and kept trying. Most of the council were second- or third-generation members—Chester "Chet" Vittorino's father had retired from the mayor's job when he turned seventy, and since a Vittorino had been mayor in Cooperton for the past forty years, Chet had practically gotten the position by default. His real talent was making Italian food at his restaurant; his chicken cacciatore and brick-oven-baked pizza were the best in Northern California.

"The whole thing is a disaster," Chet declared.

"That's our mayor," Hector Rodriguez murmured in Skylar's ear. "A real source of optimism."

Chet glared. His management skills sucked, but his hearing was excellent.

Doug Nakama rubbed the side of his face. "My wife works at Cooper. She used to love her job, and now she's looking for something else. It's not the pay—she says the whole atmosphere has changed."

"I've heard how unpopular Aaron's policies are," Skylar admitted. "My customers are always complaining."

The mayor perked up. "You call him Aaron? Then you know Mr. Hollister."

"We went to school together, that's all."

"Yeah, but my daughter told me that his sister pals around with your Karin."

Skylar tensed. She couldn't afford to have anyone start speculating about her and Aaron...or Karin. "That doesn't mean I'm friends with Melanie's brother. In fact, he—"

"But you know him," Hector interrupted. "That's a stroke of luck. I admit this news about the local farmers is a worry."

"I'm worried, too," Skylar agreed. "But surely the whole thing is a misunderstanding. Cooper Industries has always needed producers from outside our area, in addition to the local farmers, because they don't grow everything the factory needs."

"Misunderstanding?" Chet made a disgusted sound. "Want to bet?"

No, Skylar didn't want to bet. However hopeful she was trying to sound, it seemed exactly like Aaron to abandon the growers around Cooperton—he'd just call it good business.

The mayor called the meeting to order; his perpetually gloomy expression even gloomier than usual.

Aaron's presentation had been tacked on to the end of the meeting agenda, and he arrived during their midsession break wearing a crisp business suit and carrying two large cases.

"Er...Skylar," he said, looking startled. "What are you doing here?"

"I'm a member of the city council." She was pleased to see vague alarm in his brown eyes.

"They elected *you?*" He made it sound as if the town had elected a common prostitute.

"My husband was a member of the council. When he... Well, the mayor appointed me to fill his slot until the next regular election."

"I see." He looked around. "What's going on? I was told to arrive at seven since you had a full agenda and that I would come last. Surely the meeting didn't end early."

"Nope, we're on a break. Have some coffee. It's okay, it won't poison you—I didn't make it," she said innocently.

THERE WAS SOMETHING in Skylar's tone that made Aaron suspicious, and when he tasted the coffee, he knew why. It was god-awful. Dishwater would have tasted better. Nevertheless, he pretended to enjoy the evil brew; he wouldn't make friends by complaining about something so trivial.

The meeting was called to order again, and Aaron waited, surreptitiously looking around—the room was in good condition, but there were no signs of audio-visual equipment. Fortunately, he'd brought a computer and equipment of his own for the presentation. All he needed was an electrical outlet and a blank wall to project images onto.

The mayor droned on about various issues. Comments were invited and votes were taken. Over half the seats were filled with "interested" citizens, most of whom seemed bored by the business being handled. More drifted in until the room was full, though the chairs on either side of him remained empty.

Aaron mentally ran through his speech. He'd considered using a folksy approach, but had realized he would be lousy at it. Straightforward was best, though he didn't want to paint too bleak a picture of how Cooper Industries was doing. That wouldn't help the situation, either.

"Mr. Hollister is the final item on the agenda, Mr. Mayor," announced Micki Jo. Apparently she acted as secretary for the city council, as well as the mayor's office, though she didn't look old enough to be out of high school.

A rumble came from the assembly, and there was a general shifting of chairs as people sat forward. An ominous sensation went through Aaron.

All of these people had come for his presentation?

How had it gotten around Cooperton so quickly? Even though it was to everyone's benefit for Cooper Industries to expand, there were bound to be a few folks who didn't understand, or had environmental concerns, or another ax to grind. He'd hoped to convince the city council before the public heard much about it.

Aaron glanced about and saw an array of unfriendly expressions. *Not* an auspicious beginning. He stood up. "Mr. Mayor, I just need a moment to set up my equipment," he said. "I have graphics and other visuals to demonstrate what I want to accomplish."

The mayor held up a hand. "That won't be necessary, Mr. Hollister. During the break we decided that Mrs. Gibson is the best council member to determine whether your expansion plans should be approved."

Skylar jerked upright. "Mr. Mayor, I wasn't part of any such discussion."

"We had a sidebar while you were greeting Mr. Hollister."

"Chet, *I'm not*—"

"You'll have a chance to vote on the motion, Skylar."

"But—"

"I move that Mrs. Gibson handle the matter before us, regarding the approval or rejection of plans to expand Cooper Industries," interrupted one of the other men.

"I second the motion," another councilman said hastily.

"Being moved and seconded, all in favor say 'aye,'" announced the mayor.

A chorus of "ayes" followed, accompanied by an emphatic "no" from Skylar.

"The motion has passed. Mr. Hollister, Mrs. Gibson will be contacting you to discuss your proposal. All business now concluded, I adjourn this meeting."

The mayor rapidly gathered the papers in front of him and smiled genially at the assembled citizens. "Thank you to everyone for coming. It is important for the civic process to have the participation of its citizens."

A weak round of applause went through the room.

Skylar looked as if she was in shock, and Aaron wasn't far behind. This was even worse than having an elected council making the decision rather than a professional city planner—Skylar was that "wild Naples girl," a high-school dropout. She didn't have the education or background to make such a decision, and she was already pissed at him for telling Melanie he didn't approve of her going to the hamburger stand. Granted, Skylar was running a successful business now, but that didn't mean he wanted her having the say over his plans to restore Cooper Industries.

SKYLAR BOLTED FROM her chair and caught up with Chet and the other councilmen before they'd gotten to the exit.

"Oh, no. You're not going anywhere," she warned.

"It's late, Skylar," Hector protested. "My dog needs to be walked."

"And I have a kid at home. *Move,*" she ordered, pointing toward the back chamber, a windowless room that was mostly used for storing the building's holiday decorations.

Dragging their feet, they trudged through the door. She flipped the light switch and planted her hands on her hips, staring them down the way she'd stare down a troop of Girl Scouts who'd eaten too much sugar. "All right, I should have known something was up when you put your heads together during the break, but I never suspected this. I don't have time to deal with Hollister's expansion plans, or whatever they might be."

"Whatever they might be? Then you don't think expanding is what he really wants?" Doug asked uneasily.

"I have no idea, and I have no idea why you threw it in my lap," Skylar snapped.

"Come on, Skylar, don't be that way," Chet placated. "You know him. Besides, you're the only council member who doesn't care about getting reelected. You saw how many people showed up to hear Hollister's presentation—nobody attends our meetings, and look at tonight's turnout."

"That's because you had Micki Jo call around with the news that Aaron Hollister was coming and what he wanted. You were trying to see if it was a political hot potato."

Chet gave her a *duh* look he must have learned from his three children. "He's really unpopular. If we give him what he wants and the town is mad about it, we'll never get reelected."

"And if *I* do it, nobody will eat at the Nibble Nook any longer," Skylar said furiously. She didn't actually think it was true, though she might lose a few customers.

"Nobody will stop going to the Nook," Hector

assured. "Your business largely depends on Cooper Industries, so everyone will understand what you decide is based on keeping the company healthy. The town will respect that, but they'll think the rest of us are getting paid off, especially if jobs are lost. Come on, Skylar, everybody knows you're not a politician."

"Guys, surely you don't believe anyone else will run against you?" she asked as a last-ditch effort. Aside from everything else, she believed the town's big decisions should be made by more than one person. "Jimmie ran unopposed for his position in both elections. Nobody wants to be on the city council."

Doug looked at her, shocked. "That isn't true. Our families have always been on the council. It's a…a civic duty, but we want voter support. It was when the population increased and we needed another member under the town charter that we added a slot. You have to handle Hollister for us, Skylar. Things are getting tense with what he's been doing."

"Yeah, city hall gets daily calls," Chet muttered. "Everyone thinks he's violated labor laws or some other regulation with his new policies. They don't like it when we say another government office handles those questions or suggest they talk to the union."

A shiver ran up Skylar's spine. It wouldn't be so bad if she wasn't concerned about Karin. She might… Oh, who was she kidding? Anything to do with Aaron would be a pain. He'd gone from being a cocksure high-school jackass to an arrogant CEO jackass.

"Anyway, it's been voted on and passed," Chet

said. "Maybe we should have spoken to you before making the motion, but it's kind of… Well, it was something we all, that is…"

"You mean I would have been outnumbered, even if you'd talked to me ahead of time, so why talk to me?" Skylar said flatly. "The way you didn't ask when you appointed me to Jimmie's job?"

Chet at least had the decency to look embarrassed.

"You owe me a large Vittorino's Italian pizza with the works," she told him. "Bread sticks, garlic sauce, the whole thing. And that's just to start."

"Sure, sure. Absolutely. I'll even deliver it myself, whenever you want."

She eyed the rest of them. "And I'll be thinking of how each of you can make it up to me, as well."

With a chorus of agreement, they practically ran from the room. Skylar would have thought it was funny if she hadn't been so annoyed. She stepped into the main room and saw Aaron. Aside from the security guard who was probably in the lobby waiting to lock the front door, he must be the only one left in the building.

"I'll let you know when I can meet with you, Mr. Hollister," she said. It wouldn't hurt to be more formal with him.

"How about right now?"

"How about remembering it's after nine o'clock and we both have teenagers at home?"

Aaron looked startled. "Oh, yes, of course."

"I'll have to arrange a time when I can get an extra

employee to cover for me at the stand. Or we can meet after I close. Just not tomorrow."

"What's wrong with tomorrow?"

"It's Friday and I have plans." Those plans involved getting together with Grace Gibson and finalizing the arrangements for Karin's birthday party, but Skylar didn't want Aaron to start thinking about Karin's birthday. She especially didn't want him to start counting back and remember when Karin had been conceived.

"Fine," Aaron said. His teeth were gritted. "Let me know when and where."

"I will. But don't expect to show me a slick Power-Point program and get an instant approval. I'm sure we'll have several meetings."

If Aaron was dismayed, he hid it well. "My presentation is more than a slick PowerPoint—it has important information."

"Oh, I'll watch it, but even in Cooperton we've heard of computers—bells and whistles won't impress me." She smiled sweetly. "You're going to get lots of questions."

"Uh…yes. I'll be at your disposal."

Skylar found that doubtful, but she didn't have time to think about it. Ever since Jimmie's accident it had been emotionally challenging to leave her daughter alone for long periods. And it was worse now with Karin being so moody over the baseball play-offs.

"Fine. I'll contact your office in a few days with a date for our first meeting. Have a good weekend."

She had almost escaped through the door when Aaron cleared his throat.

"Cooperton used to try to accommodate my grandfather," he said. "But it seems as if everyone is opposed to the idea of Cooper Industries expanding, even though they haven't heard my ideas. It's the sort of thing that's good for a town, so why is it a problem?"

She hesitated, debating what to tell him, then chose cautious honesty. "Your grandfather was concerned about both his company *and* Cooperton. But no one knows what your priorities are...or what you'd do to protect them."

"That's absurd."

"Is it?"

AARON WAS ANNOYED as Skylar left; her reply hadn't made any sense. Maybe he didn't have George's commitment to Cooper Industries, but he didn't hate the company. And he didn't hate Cooperton. Sure, he didn't have the greatest childhood memories of the small town, but that didn't mean he was out to destroy it.

Belatedly he realized he should have walked Skylar to her car and hurried outside in time to see her drive away in the old truck he'd often seen at the Nibble Nook.

Frowning, he headed for home himself. Melanie was sixteen, not six, and leaving her alone wasn't irresponsible...yet somehow it *felt* irresponsible, having to be reminded that staying late for a business meeting wasn't necessarily the best idea.

By Skylar, no less.

Skylar.

Aaron shook his head. As a teenager she'd gotten under his skin with her curvaceous body and wild nature, and now she was still bothering him in other ways.

CHAPTER FOUR

KARIN LAY ON her bed looking at her geometry textbook. Algebra was all right, but this junk about points and lines and angles was so easy it was boring. Still, if she was going to be a great scientist and save lives someday, she'd better pay attention. She wasn't sure where geometry fit into being a scientist, but it must somehow. After geometry she had to take trigonometry and calculus, which sounded just as dull. She liked chemistry and other science courses the best.

Closing the book, she grabbed her smartphone and dialed Melanie's number. Honestly, how did anyone survive in the dark ages without cell phones? It must have been awfully primitive.

"Hi," Mellie answered. "Is your mom still gone?"

"Yeah, she said the meeting would go late."

"It might be over. Aaron just got home, and he doesn't look happy."

"Does he *ever* look happy?" Karin couldn't remember a single time when Mellie's brother wasn't acting pissed or disapproving.

"Sometimes he isn't so bad."

Karin heard the front door open and close. "Mom's

back, too," she said. "See you tomorrow." With a hurried "bye" she turned off the smartphone.

Her mother was in the kitchen putting the teakettle on to heat. "Sorry, it took longer than I expected."

Karin shrugged. "It's not like I need a babysitter or anything. Mellie told me that her brother was going to the meeting. What did Mr. Hollister want?"

"Just some city council business. You'll probably hear about it in a few days."

Uh-oh. Now her mom seemed uptight and not very happy, either. Darn it, anyhow. Karin was glad that Mellie had come to Cooperton and she wouldn't be here if her brother wasn't here, too, but why did he have to be so awful? The kids at school were always talking about Aaron because their parents worked at the factory and hated him. Jill Vittorino's dad was the mayor, and *she* said that her father was worried that Aaron Hollister might even move the company to another place where they didn't have to pay workers as much.

"Is everything okay?" she asked cautiously.

"It's fine. Did you get your homework done?"

"Define *done.*"

Her mother rolled her eyes. "Stop imitating that actor on *Psych* or I'm taking your television away until you're thirty. You know perfectly well what I meant."

Karin giggled. "It's done. Even geometry."

"Good. Parent–teacher conferences are coming up,

and I don't want to be asked why you aren't doing your assignments."

Karin laughed again, but an odd thought occurred to her. "What if I was flunking? What would you do?"

"*Are* you flunking?"

"No, I just wondered. Kids flunk, you know. Susan Lightoller is real smart, but she's blowing calculus, and everybody knows that Tiffany Baldwin got an F in English last year."

"From what you've said about Tiffany, I'm surprised she isn't failing *all* of her classes. It sounds as if she spends most of her time doing her hair and makeup and flirting with boys."

The kettle whistled and Karin fidgeted as her mom made a cup of tea. "So what *would* you do if I was getting F's? Like…ground me or something?"

"I would try to find out why you were failing. There's a difference between not trying to do the work, and having trouble with it. If you were having trouble, I'd get a tutor to help."

"And if I was just goofing off?"

"I'd ground you for life. We don't do things halfway in this family."

We don't do things halfway in this family.

Karin gulped. She hadn't heard that since her dad had died. It was something he used to say when they were having a special load of fun. He'd say something like, "You want a second ice cream cone, don't you?

We don't do things halfway in this family." Hearing it now made her feel both sad and good.

"Okay. I'm going to get ready for bed."

She practically ran to her bedroom, blinking to keep from crying and making her mom cry, too.

SKYLAR TRACED THE steaming rim of her mug, thinking about the past. At eighteen she'd been determined to raise Karin alone—scared, but determined. Then Jimmie had asked her to marry him, and she'd loved him so much she had finally agreed. Now she was back to doing it alone, with a grieving teenager to boot.

It was awful not knowing how to help Karin. They'd talked with a grief counselor, yet there were times when it seemed as if her daughter was hurting more now than in the first months after losing her father. Maybe it would get better after the pennant race and World Series was over.

And now Aaron was back in Cooperton, complicating matters.

Perhaps she should have explained to Karin why he'd been at the meeting. Her classmates might start talking about it, and they'd soon know her mother was responsible for deciding whether he did or didn't get approval.

It still astonished Skylar. She would never have guessed the city council was capable of such creative maneuvering; perhaps they were better politicians than she'd thought. Of course, since they couldn't know the history she shared with Aaron, they'd likely figured it was the best solution all around. Yet it was going to take a huge amount of work to do the thing right—the zoning question alone bothered her. She hated seeing farmland being covered by roads and buildings.

But Chet and the others *were* right about one thing—a big chunk of the Nibble Nook's customers were Cooper Industries employees. She might be able to stay in business if the company shut down, but what would the town do? You couldn't suddenly throw hundreds of people out of work without having a major impact on everyone. The town might not survive, which meant that no matter what she didn't like about Aaron's plans for expansion, she'd probably have to give her approval.

At least she hadn't been the only one blindsided by the city council. The look on Aaron's face had been priceless, both when he'd realized she was a member, and then when he learned he would have to deal with her to get what he wanted.

Skylar's tea had long cooled by the time she followed Karin to bed. She still hadn't decided how she was going to handle Aaron's proposal. It wouldn't be so bad if it was anyone else, but their personal history aside, she didn't have any faith in his concern for anyone except himself.

THE NEXT MORNING Aaron was driving Melanie to school when she cleared her throat.

"Uh…Aaron, Karin and I want to go to the movies tomorrow. There's a Matt Damon flick playing. The Saturday matinee starts at 12:20 and afterward we thought we'd go for pizza before the baseball game starts. Is that okay?"

Instant refusal hovered on his lips. Aside from Karin Gibson's mother, he didn't have anything against the teenager, but Skylar *was* the problem, along with the general undesirability of his sister hanging out at a place like the Nibble Nook. On the other hand, he didn't have any reason to think Skylar was still the outrageous troublemaker she used to be.

Aaron thought fast. "Actually, I'd like to spend more time with you and thought we could go to San Francisco tomorrow. It's close enough for a day trip if we leave early in the morning."

Melanie's hopeful smile vanished. "But you've been planning to work at the office. You know, I could have gone to the movies without telling you that Karin was going to be there, too. But I asked, just like Mother says I'm supposed to."

True enough. He ought to be grateful that his sister was being honest. And he *was* grateful. Taking her for the year had filled him with concern…. What if she got on drugs when she was in his care, or something equally bad, simply because he didn't know the right thing to say or do? He'd never considered having children, much less how to deal with a teenager, so it was uncharted territory for him.

"Wouldn't you like to see San Francisco instead?"

he urged. "It's a beautiful place and quite different from other cities you've visited like Paris and London. We could eat crab and fresh sourdough bread on Fisherman's Wharf and get ice cream at Ghirardelli Square. Maybe we would even go out to Alcatraz Island and take a tour of the old prison. They say it's haunted. You have all those DVDs of that *Ghost Hunters* television reality show, so I know you're interested in that sort of thing."

Melanie shook her head. "I'd rather see a movie with Karin. Please say yes, Aaron. I've never had a friend like her before. That's better than San Francisco."

Aaron glanced at his sister. Her eyes were wistful, and regret went through him. In one of their arguments Skylar had accused him of not caring about Melanie. He'd reacted angrily, maybe because he knew that it was partly true in the beginning—he had mostly looked out for his sister because it seemed the right thing to do. Now he was growing fond of her, and it was hard to think of her unstable childhood, being sent from one household to another. She had lived in a number of glamorous places, yet she'd never had a real friend.

"All right," he said slowly. "You can spend the afternoon with Karin."

Melanie's delighted smile made him sigh—he would have agreed to practically anything after seeing that sad look on her face. Hell, maybe he should even consider keeping her until she graduated.

He stopped in front of the high school. "Have a good day."

"You, too." She gave him an impulsive kiss on the cheek and got out.

Aaron watched her disappear inside the old building. The high school hadn't changed much since he was a kid. It was like everything in Cooperton, old-fashioned and tired. The whole town needed a face-lift...or a funeral.

He drove on and as he passed the Nibble Nook, decided to stop and see if Skylar was available. She'd claimed she would call in a few days to set up a time to meet, but he didn't want it turning into weeks or months.

At least two dozen customers were eating at the picnic tables, and more waited in line at the window. The scent of coffee and food wafted through the air and there was a babble of cheerful conversation. Yet as Aaron got out of the Mercedes and approached, the chatter faded into watchful silence. At a guess, a number of the customers were Cooper Industry employees—probably from the night shift, eating breakfast after getting off work. They must have recognized him.

Well, hell.

He didn't intend to justify his decisions, no matter how unpopular they might be. They were necessary to keep the company afloat and to preserve jobs, though he wasn't entirely sure *why* he cared if the business survived. At the same time, the hostile atmosphere heightened his concerns about Melanie being around people who so plainly disliked him. That was one of the problems with small towns: you couldn't get away from the people who knew you.

"Good morning," he said when he got to the front window. "Is Mrs. Gibson here?"

"No, sir. Skylar is picking up a load of produce, but she should be back soon." The tall young man smiled, a pleasant contrast to the sullen customers in the eating area. "Would you like to order something?"

"Sure." Aaron hadn't gone to a hamburger stand since he was a teenager, but he looked at the breakfast menu and ordered the spicy breakfast burrito and a cup of "special brew" coffee, whatever the hell that pretended to be. The prices seemed excellent, and the amount of food the server passed through the window was generous.

He went to the Mercedes to eat, and his first surprise was the coffee. He'd figured it would taste like pencil shavings, despite being billed as a "special brew." Instead it was rich and boldly flavored.

As for the burrito...Aaron took a bite and his eyes widened. It was stuffed with bacon, cheese, eggs, green chilies and potatoes and was absolutely delicious. The flavor reminded him of the breakfast burritos he'd eaten in Santa Fe where he and Matt had managed to meet up one weekend. Aaron liked Matt; he just wished his brother hadn't followed in their father's playboy footsteps.

When he finished eating, he phoned Peggy and

told her that something had come up and he would be later than expected. He settled back with his coffee, keeping an eye on the traffic from the road. Customers came and went, and it wasn't long before the old truck he'd seen Skylar driving the previous night arrived and pulled around to the rear of the building.

He followed and found Skylar putting down the tailgate of the truck. The cashier who'd helped Aaron earlier had come out and was talking to her.

"Here he is," said the young man.

She looked up and her expression turned chilly. "Did you need something, Mr. Hollister?"

Suddenly Aaron's plan to push for a meeting time to discuss Cooper Industries didn't seem like the best idea. Antagonizing her wouldn't help his cause, though he suspected he was already screwed after their clashes over his sister. Skylar wasn't likely to put her personal feelings aside to make a rational decision.

"Melanie mentioned she has plans to see a movie with your daughter tomorrow afternoon. Sharing a pizza was also discussed."

Skylar nodded. "They've been talking about it."

"I thought you should know that I told her she can go."

"You're okay with it?"

Aaron could tell that Skylar had expected him to refuse and felt like a fraud. He'd tried to talk Melanie into a trip to San Francisco instead of going with her friend—essentially a bribe. It spoke well of his sister that she'd chosen Karin, even if it wasn't what he had wanted.

"I'd prefer her spending less time at the Nibble Nook, but a movie sounded all right," he replied frankly. "And I could see how much it meant to her. I'll make sure she has cash for both the movie and food."

"Oh, that's something I've been meaning to bring up… Stop giving Melanie fifty-dollar bills to use. It makes her conspicuous. If she needs to carry so much money, give her tens or twenties and have her tuck most of them out of sight in different places in her wallet or purse so it isn't obvious how much she's got."

Aaron didn't appreciate the obvious being pointed out to him, but she was right. Somebody might get tempted by the idea of easy cash.

"I should have thought it through better," he admitted grudgingly. "I've just been giving her whatever's in my wallet, and I know my father sends her cash in large bills. I'll tell Melanie to have me change it into smaller denominations."

Skylar lifted a crate of lettuce and handed it to her employee. "Thanks, Peter. You should get back inside. I heard more cars arrive out front."

When they were alone, she dusted her hands. "Why didn't you just call and leave a message about okaying the girls' plans? Aren't you too busy for this kind of personal contact?"

Was that a subtle criticism, or was he just being overly sensitive?

"I was driving past on my way to the office and decided to stop. I'm not familiar with the appropriate protocols for dealing with a teenager."

"Whatever." She hopped back into the truck bed and shoved a stack of boxes closer to the tailgate, a healthy flush of color in her cheeks.

One thing Aaron had to say for Skylar, she worked hard. He just wasn't sure of anything else when it came to her—while she may have changed since her disreputable high-school days, he had a hard time trusting people in general, and women in particular. Ironically, his father seemed to be the opposite. S. S. Hollister was an eternal optimist, always on the lookout for romance.

It was his children who'd learned to be wary of marriage and relationships.

"Don't you have employees to handle the heavy lifting?" Aaron asked, resisting an impulse to help. She must do this sort of thing every day; she didn't need him.

"They're busy. When things are quieter midmorning, I'll have them slice the onions and tomatoes and wash lettuce for the lunch crowd. We want our ingredients to be fresh."

"We?"

Her expression went blank. "Saying *we* is a habit. I ran this business with my husband for more than a decade, and he's only been gone a year."

Aaron wasn't sure how to respond. He'd been noticing how well Skylar filled out her jeans and T-shirt—slim, yet sweetly curved in all the right places—only to be reminded she was a widow.

"I see," he said awkwardly. "Well, I'll go, since you're obviously busy. You'll call when we can get together to talk about my expansion plans?"

Her eyes narrowed. "As I said last night, I'll contact you in a few days."

"Good. *Great*. We'll speak then."

Aaron made his way back to his Mercedes. He still didn't have anything settled, but it couldn't be helped. Diplomacy took time, and he was already at odds with Skylar. And it wasn't as if they'd ever gotten along in the first place.

THE FOLLOWING Wednesday Skylar drove to city hall shortly before the time she'd set for her meeting with Aaron. He'd suggested they meet at Cooper Industries, but she was too smart to agree. She refused to be treated like a flunky on his payroll—city hall was her territory, and he was the one asking for something from the community, not the other way around.

Cooperton City Hall was one of those grand old buildings built in a confident era when they'd believed the town would soon need a large home for its government. Money and love had gone into planning and constructing the place. The offices beyond the public facade were nice, but the rotunda was the town's pride and joy—with an ornate dome overhead and a beautiful mosaic wood floor that had been covered by carpet for several decades. When the restoration committee had pulled the carpet up three years ago, expecting the original surface to be ruined, they'd discovered it simply needed a good cleaning and basic repairs for carpet-tack damage.

It was a soothing atmosphere, but Skylar didn't have time to appreciate the rich glow of wood, brass and polished granite. She trotted up the stairs and through the swinging doors of the mayor's reception area.

Micki Jo looked up from the computer on her desk. "Hey, Skylar, ready for your big meeting with Aaron Hollister?"

"I suppose. Do you have those reports?

"Yup." Micki Jo pointed to a box on the corner of her desk. "Copies for you, and copies for the big shot. And here are the keys for the council offices—keep them. I had duplicates made. You should have your own set. Everyone else on the council does."

"Is that an executive decision, or a Micki Jo ruling?"

"Micki Jo, all the way. The mayor is too busy wringing his hands over what Mr. Hollister is doing with Cooper Industries to be bothered with minutiae. Small-town government requires secretaries who are willing to make decisions in the temporary absence of leadership."

Skylar pocketed the keys. "Would your college professors approve of that theory?"

"Probably not. Secretaries aren't appreciated enough."

It was true, in more ways than one. Micki Jo had started working for city hall two years before, and despite her youth and inexperience, now practically ran the place behind the scenes. Chet was only in his office a few hours a day; the rest of the time he managed his restaurant. Micki Jo, on the other hand, worked full-time and eagerly jumped into every aspect of Cooperton's government. She was taking night classes toward a bachelor's degree in political science.

"How are your studies going?" Skylar asked.

The other woman flashed a smile. "I got A-pluses on my last two tests, and I'm writing a paper about Thursday night's council meeting for my poli-sci course. The guys sure did a fast duck and cover with Aaron Hollister's expansion proposal."

"Tell me about it. Mr. Hollister wants a swift approval, but it isn't going to be that easy. You may hear some yelling before we're done."

"My money's on you, but if you come to blows, try not to get blood on the floor," Micki Jo advised. "Our preservation chairperson will have hysterics if that hardwood gets damaged. You know how excitable she is."

Skylar laughed and headed for the city council's offices with the box of reports tucked under one arm. Three rooms in city hall were allotted to the council—including one for small meetings. She'd never expected to need the offices, so having a key hadn't occurred to her. Come to think of it though, Jimmie may have had a set. If so, it would still be with his key ring in the dresser drawer, in the envelope....

Her lingering humor faded as she recalled being handed a large yellow envelope by the coroner's office after Jimmie's accident. "His valuables," they'd said gruffly. She'd barely looked in it, tucking the thing under a pile of his T-shirts. Grace had helped her pack up most of Jimmie's clothes and personal items, but Skylar had left that drawer alone. Somehow it seemed symbolic, a small goodbye yet to be said.

The council office was stuffy, and Skylar pushed thoughts of her husband's accident from her mind as she opened a window. She'd gone over the Nibble Nook's schedule, trying to find the best time to meet with Aaron, finally deciding morning would be best. Several of her employees were eager for extra hours, and she could get them to cover for her when she was gone.

Precisely at 9:00 a.m., Aaron came through the open door carrying a soft-sided briefcase. "Good morning," he said with a formal smile. "You agreed to look at the PowerPoint program on expansion plans, so I brought my computer."

"That's probably the best way to start." Skylar wanted to ask how Melanie was feeling, since Karin had mentioned her friend had been out of school sick both Monday and Tuesday, but it was best to keep the meeting on a purely professional level.

Aaron set up his laptop, and she realized they'd have to sit side by side while he changed the slides and talked.

Damn.

He moved his chair next to hers, and his elbow came perilously close to her breast as he started the program. Grimly she focused on the information. It was concise and to the point...and a big problem as far as she was concerned. Keeping her expression neutral became a challenge, and when the final slide had been clicked off, she had trouble unclenching her jaw.

"You want to expand east of the factory," she said finally.

"It's the best location."

"That property has been leased to organic farmers for years."

"But is still owned by Cooper Industries. The lease is coming up for renewal, so it's an opportune time to move forward with updating and expanding the factory complex. The land just needs to be rezoned."

Skylar thought of the farmers who'd worked so hard to grow pesticide-free produce, going through the trouble and expense of being certified organic. She wanted to scream. Granted, the land *didn't* belong to those farmers, but she knew old Mr. Cooper had promised they'd be able to stay. What's more, the Cooperton Organic Farmer's Market lured shoppers from as far away as Sacramento and San Francisco— shoppers who spent much-needed dollars in their town instead of somewhere else.

"What about the area south of the existing complex?" she asked, deciding not to bring up the organic issue unless it became necessary. "It's more marginal farmland owned by Cooper Industries and isn't currently in use. Rezoning would be much more palatable there for everyone."

Aaron looked taken aback, and she could swear he hadn't considered an alternate site. "I believe services are better in the other location."

She would have to look at the city and county maps to determine if that was actually true, or just an excuse. On the other hand, she knew the roads around Cooperton and enough about other town projects to ask a few questions.

"Maybe, but are you aware the proposed site for a new waste-sewage treatment plant is south of the factory complex, as well? By expanding that direction, you would likely reduce your sewage costs and possibly limit any retrofitting to meet new regulations."

Aaron's forehead creased in thought. "Does Cooperton *have* the money to build a new treatment plant? This town is so old and tired, I'm surprised they're even talking about it."

"Cooperton is old—that doesn't mean it's tired."

"Really? How about the high school? Or city hall for that matter? This place is ancient. Most towns have abandoned these aged buildings for something modern."

Skylar's blood started a slow simmer. "Modern isn't always better. Have you taken a good look at this place? City hall was restored three years ago with a private grant and placed on the national registry for historic buildings. And believe it or not, Cooperton High students test quite competitively with other students in California."

Aaron gave her a narrow look. "This is a switch. You didn't have a good opinion of Cooperton when we were kids, either—you thought the people who lived here were nothing but tongue-wagging, judgmental hypocrites."

"I've grown up since then and discovered most people are basically nice if you give them a chance. And it isn't as if my parents were pillars of the community—I don't blame anyone for being glad when they left."

Skylar stuck out her chin with a hint of her old defiance. She wasn't even sure where her mother and father were living; they'd left Cooperton shortly before she'd married Jimmie and she'd never tried to find them. As far as she was concerned, the Gibsons were the only grandparents her daughter needed. But then, it was Jimmie and his parents who'd changed Skylar's mind about Cooperton, helping her see it was more than a place which had made a teenage girl angry and rebellious.

"Regardless, my opinions are not your concern," she added, realizing the conversation had gone far out-of-bounds.

"Anything that influences your decision is my concern. After our clashes over Melanie…well, the situation is awkward enough."

Skylar's nerves tightened. "I'm not biased, I just want to make the right choice for Cooperton. Now, do you have a written proposal to leave with me? I'll study it so I can have a better idea of what questions to ask at our next meeting."

"Yes, I have it with me." Aaron opened his briefcase and took out a thick book with a spiral binding. "This is the basic plan."

She took the book and wondered if he'd hoped to impress people with the volume of paper in his "basic" plan. How would she know, anyhow? She ran a hamburger stand—a highly successful stand—but a far cry from a business like Cooper Industries.

"I'm sure that at some point our building inspector will need to see full-size copies of the blueprints," she murmured. "And any approval I give would still be contingent on subsequent building permits and inspections and the like."

"Of course. I'll bring copies to the Nibble Nook."

A surge of adrenaline hit Skylar. She didn't want Aaron conducting business at the Nibble Nook. Besides, her customers had already complained about his visit the previous Friday—they acknowledged it was a free country, but still resented him giving them a sour stomach.

"No, leave them with Micki Jo," she said.

"But the hamburger stand is so close."

Skylar squared her shoulders. "I realize the Nibble

Nook doesn't compare to Cooper Industries, but it's my livelihood. I'm entitled to keep city council business from intruding any more than needed."

A variety of emotions crossed Aaron face until he finally nodded. "All right. Micki Jo will have them by noon."

"Okay. Let's meet again next week, same time, same place."

"A week?" He sounded as if she was suggesting a century, instead of a few days, and Skylar could have kicked him. It was typical of Aaron to think she should drop everything to study his proposal. In a lot of ways he hadn't changed that much—he was still convinced the world revolved around him and his needs.

"Yes, a week. In the meantime, I have material for *you* to read." She gestured to the stack of reports that Micki Jo had copied for her, including the public works study on the new wastewater treatment plant.

Her stack topped his proposal by several inches. Whether any of the reports were applicable was another question, and he might have seen them already, but at least they were a start. And she hoped that getting them would show she was trying to give his proposal a valid hearing.

Skylar knew it was vanity on her part—Aaron obviously believed she was going to let personal feelings get in the way of her decision, and she wanted to prove him wrong.

CHAPTER FIVE

SKYLAR WAS GLAD to return to the Nibble Nook and tried to keep from thinking about Aaron. It was harder than she expected.

Each time they'd talked or argued she was conscious of the secret that she wanted to keep him from learning...or remembering. It was as if she had a sword hanging over her, dangling by a thread—she didn't know if it was going to fall, and what damage it would do if it did. It was exhausting.

She didn't see how Aaron couldn't know about Karin, but anything was possible. Or maybe he'd never believed Karin was his child in the first place, and his family just tried to give her money to be sure that trouble wouldn't crop up later.

"Skylar, are you okay?" asked Greg at one point during a lull between customers.

She shook herself, realizing she'd been staring into space. "Sorry, I have a city council matter on my mind. It was partly true—her nominal responsibilities as a city council member had become a huge headache.

"I heard about the meeting last week. Is that why you took off this morning?"

It wasn't a surprise that he knew—the whole county probably knew about what had happened, gossip being the lifeblood of a small town. "Yeah. I'll be seeing Mr. Hollister several times to discuss his plans before making a decision."

Greg made a face. "I'm glad it's not me—I'd blow up and ask why he thinks everyone who works for him is a thief. My sister says working there sucks now. She wants to get another job, but it isn't easy in this area."

Skylar thought of the stack of job applications she'd gotten in the past few months and nodded wryly.

"It isn't just the short lunches and stuff—it's the way he acted about people taking factory seconds home with them. They weren't stealing," Greg said indignantly. "Mr. Cooper encouraged folks to take stuff that couldn't be sold. I guess some employees took advantage, but not that many of them."

"I know." Skylar often sent food home from the Nibble Nook that would get thrown out otherwise, and the Nook was a much smaller operation than Cooper Industries. It might be different if Aaron had opened a store for selling factory seconds, but he hadn't. "I'll keep an ear out for any job openings."

Greg gave her a grateful smile. "Thanks."

A new group of customers arrived and they jumped to work. Determined to stop thinking about Aaron, Skylar thought about everything she needed to do for

Karin's birthday party. Her daughter wanted a picnic in the park and even with Joe and Grace's help there was a lot to get done.

"I FEEL BETTER. I'm going back to school," Melanie announced to Aaron on Thursday morning. She'd stayed home with a cold all week and was tired of it.

He frowned, looking up from some papers he was reading at the kitchen table. "You're still coughing."

She shrugged. Her cold was mostly gone except the yucky parts—a cough and drippy nose. Aaron had acted kind of cute about it, telling her to stay in bed and buying a bunch of new DVDs for her to watch. He'd filled the refrigerator with orange juice and had gotten gazoodles of chicken soup from one of the delicatessens in town, though she was sneaking other junk to eat because the soup was gross.

Heck, he'd even come back from work a couple of times a day to check on her. *That* was weird. Not that he wasn't always weird, it was just weirder than usual. It was also nice. He hadn't acted like it was inconvenient or anything, but as if he was worried and just wanted her to feel better.

"I don't want to miss too much and have to catch up again," she said.

"All right, but call me if you start feeling worse."

She hastily finished dressing while Aaron drank his coffee, and raced out to the car. She coughed as she put on her seat belt and Aaron frowned again.

"Maybe it's too soon to go back to school. Your mother was adamant that you weren't to stress your lungs."

Disappointment shot through Melanie. She should have guessed he wasn't *really* concerned about her. Every time Eliza wanted one of the relatives to take her, she fed them a line about her daughter needing a stable environment because of her "delicate" lungs. It was just an excuse. Melanie's mom and her step-father traveled constantly, living in fancy hotels and stuff. Her stepfather wasn't a bad guy, but he didn't understand kids and didn't want to change his life to make room for one.

"There's nothing wrong with my lungs," Melanie muttered.

She got out at the school and hurried inside without looking back. Having Aaron give her a ride every day was awkward—there was always somebody hanging around to see her arrive. She'd mostly gone to big schools where hardly anybody knew who you were, but *everyone* in Cooperton knew she was Aaron Hollister's half sister.

She didn't have a chance to talk to Karin before lunch, and at noon went straight to the cafeteria to look for her.

"Hey, how do you feel?" asked Karin from behind.

Relieved, Melanie turned around. They hadn't talked much when she was home sick, and she'd worried that her friend was mad for some reason. "Not so great, but it's better than being stuck in my room with horrid chicken soup from the deli. I hope you *do* cure colds when you're a scientist."

Karin made a face. "I have to pass geometry first."

"You will," Melanie said stoutly. Karin was in the accelerated program for almost every subject. "You'll get an A-plus, just wait and see."

"Maybe. It isn't hard, it's just Dullsville."

They got their lunch and went outside where it was quieter. All at once the food didn't smell so great to Melanie and she pushed it around her plate with her fork. Normally she liked the chicken potpie they served in the cafeteria.

"Don't forget my birthday party is on Saturday," Karin announced. "It's going to be in the park in the first picnic area by the river. That way if it rains, we'll have cover. You're coming, aren't you?"

"Aaron said he'd think about it when I asked."

"It should be okay, shouldn't it? He let you go to the movies last weekend."

"I hope so." Melanie pushed her tray back. She'd already gotten Karin's birthday present—a set of all the *Star Trek* movies on both DVD and Blu-ray— and could hardly wait to give them to her. "Will your grandparents be there?"

"Natch. Grandma Grace is making her toffee fudge trifle cake, and Grandpa Joe is barbecuing." Karin smacked her lips. "His barbecued ribs and chicken are the *best*. And we're also having Mom's potato salad and baked beans and a bunch of other stuff, including her homemade custard ice cream. It'll be just like the picnic we throw for the Nibble Nook and Nibble Nook Too employees every summer. You'll love it, even if it's old-fashioned."

It didn't sound old-fashioned to Melanie. It sounded like more fun than she'd ever had.

"Are any kids from school coming?"

Karin shrugged. "A few, along with their parents. We've been going to each other's birthday parties since we were little. Well, not last year. I told you about that."

Melanie nodded. Karin hadn't wanted a birthday party so soon after her dad's accident, so her mom and grandparents had taken her to San Francisco to see a Broadway show on tour from New York. Melanie's own birthday usually got lost in the shuffle from one household to another. It came at the end of August, and her mother and stepfather would give her a check, but that wasn't the same as having someone throw you a party the way Mrs. Gibson was doing for Karin.

"I love your mom," she murmured. "I know she gets uptight sometimes, but she's terrific. My mother doesn't cook, much less throw birthday parties."

"Thanks." Karin looked embarrassed. And pleased.

It was a really warm day for October, yet Melanie shivered and zipped her jacket up the front.

"Are you okay?" Karin asked.

"My chest is tight and hurts a little, but it's probably just from coughing."

Maybe she should have waited an extra day before

going back to school, but she'd felt okay when she woke up. And it wasn't even that she felt bad, mostly wobbly.

Karin stood up determinedly. "Come on. Let's go see the school nurse. The worst they can do is have your brother come get you."

That was the problem. Melanie didn't want someone to call Aaron—it would be the same as saying he was right about her staying home longer.

AARON SAT IN the doctor's office reception area, waiting as his sister was examined. The school nurse had said not to worry, that the cold going around Cooperton was causing a few mild secondary infections, but he wondered if he ought to call Eliza, anyway. Could he even reach her? She and her husband were in Zimbabwe, and he didn't know if there were cell phone towers on a game preserve.

For the brief time Eliza had been his stepmother, she'd been nice enough—bright but flighty, like a number of his father's ex-wives and girlfriends. Aaron figured she'd asked him to be Melanie's godfather in an attempt to build family unity, except Eliza's marriage to S. S. Hollister hadn't lasted much beyond Melanie's christening, so any attempts at unity were futile as usual.

Aaron had mostly gotten acquainted with his siblings as an adult, though some of them were easier to see than others. Jake and Matt were chronically difficult because they never stayed long in one place.

Tamlyn and April lived back East and he'd visited them on business trips. Oona was in Italy, but she'd flown to Chicago periodically when he was based there. Pierre was in Paris, but his mother harbored so much resentment against her ex-husband, she didn't welcome visits from the rest of his progeny.

Then there was Melanie.

A worried frown tightened Aaron's mouth. He'd wanted to insist that she stay home another day, but had thought it was best to let her make the decision for herself.

"You can come in now, Mr. Hollister," said the medical assistant finally.

He was led to an office and saw Melanie slumped morosely in one of the chairs. The doctor walked in and shook Aaron's hand.

"It's nothing serious," the physician assured him. "Just a touch of bronchitis. A round of antibiotics should clear it quickly. Keep your sister at home, drinking lots of fluids, until her temperature is normal for a couple of days. After that she can return to class—I should say Monday or Tuesday."

Melanie shot to her feet. "*No.* I'm going to a birthday picnic on Saturday. I can't miss Karin's party."

"We have to follow the doctor's orders," Aaron said. He didn't remind her that she didn't have *permission* yet to attend the party. It was one thing to say she could go to the movies with Karin, another to let her go to a picnic with people he didn't know anything about. Lord, he remembered the park where the party was being held—when he was a teenager it was where kids had gone to drink and make out.

"You just don't want me seeing Karin."

"We'll discuss this later, Melanie."

"I'm afraid Saturday is out of the question," Dr. Jenkins advised. "Mr. Hollister, would you like us to call the prescription in to the pharmacy? Calder Drugs will deliver for an extra fee."

"That would be great," Aaron said. Melanie was going to be angry about the party, and the sooner he got her back to the house, the better. She could pout in peace and quiet—hopefully without making him crazy. He was going to drive himself crazy enough without any help, knowing he should have taken Melanie's temperature that morning before letting her out the door.

After he'd gotten additional instructions and paid the bill, his sister stomped to the Mercedes ahead of him. "You don't like anything in this town," she accused as he fastened his seat belt. "What's wrong with the Nibble Nook and Mrs. Gibson and Karin?"

"I'm not the one who said you couldn't go to the party—it was Dr. Jenkins," Aaron replied. Granted, he found the doctor's orders convenient, but admitting it would just make things worse.

"You made him say that. I hate you."

She hunched her shoulder away from him, and Aaron sighed. He knew she felt lousy and was saying things she normally wouldn't, but life would be much easier if she wasn't friends with Skylar Gibson's daughter.

Skylar *had* changed—the question was, how much?

A picture went through Aaron's mind of the vibrant, in-your-face teenager he'd once known. She'd hung out with the toughest, most foul-mouthed, joy-riding kids in town, several of whom had ended up in prison. From the top of her flame-colored head to the tip of her brightly painted toenails, she'd exuded rebellion. He couldn't think of a rule she hadn't broken, or someone in authority she hadn't flouted, but what was exciting to a seventeen-year-old boy was a huge problem to a big brother.

At the house Melanie went upstairs. He didn't want to return to work while she was this upset, so he notified his office and settled down to read another one of the reports Skylar had given him. In normal circumstances he would have reviewed them as part of the planning process, but he'd been trying to work on his expansion proposal without anyone in the local community learning about it too early.

Skylar had made a valid point concerning the new wastewater treatment plant. You never knew if there were going to be regulatory changes, and retrofitting could be expensive. On the other hand, he still preferred his original site.

Aaron sat back, having trouble concentrating. Skylar surprised him—she was more beautiful than ever, and though he'd expected her to give a cursory look at his PowerPoint program and reject his plan out of hand, she'd asked for more information and scheduled another meeting.

She was also an experienced mother of a teenager, and part of him wished he could get her opinion on the best way to handle Melanie. Pushing the ironic thought away, he took out his smartphone and calculated the time in Zimbabwe to be sure he wouldn't be calling in the middle of the night. He dialed and waited before hearing a static-filled "hello."

"Hi, Eliza, it's Aaron."

"Aaron, it's so nice you called," Eliza said, making it sound as if hearing from him was the most delightful thing that had ever happened to her. "Is everything all right with Melanie?"

"Yes, except she had a cold, and now has a mild case of bronchitis. It isn't serious. I just wanted you to know."

"She does? How odd."

"Odd? I thought you were worried about her lungs."

"Well…uh, yes. But you said it wasn't serious."

"The doctor isn't concerned. She'll be on antibiotics and can return to school when her temperature is normal."

"It sounds as if everything is under control, but you're a dear to call. We're having a wonderful time, going about everywhere…places like South Africa and Tanzania—do you know that most people in Tan-

zania speak at least two languages? And Mount Kili-
manjaro is simply gorgeous. I never want to leave."

"Weren't you just going to Madagascar and Zimbabwe?"

"We were, but it's such a waste having those travel
vaccinations and not seeing more of Africa, don't you
think? You really must— What's that, dear?"

Aaron heard a low male voice murmur in the background, followed by one of Eliza's charming laughs.

"Aaron?" she said after a moment. "My darling
husband tells me that Madagascar isn't in Africa, but
it's really quite close. We're going to Kenya next."

Aaron let out a breath. If he didn't jump in, Eliza
was capable of reciting an hour-long travel mono-
logue. "That's great, but don't you want to speak with
Melanie?"

"Let her rest. Tell her I love her and to call when
she feels better, so we can have a nice chat. Bye-bye
for now."

SKYLAR RACED UP the city hall steps the following
Tuesday. It was Aaron's fault she was late, though
he probably wouldn't see it that way.

She found him leaning against the wall near the
council offices, one eyebrow raised.

"Running behind?" he asked.

"Yes, thanks to you." Skylar unlocked the door and
gestured for him to go ahead. Aaron brushed past and
she sucked in a breath at the sheer sexual awareness
that went through her. It was an unwelcome reminder

that her body was fully functional, even though her husband was gone.

He put his briefcase on the table. "What do I have to do with it?"

"Every farmer I buy from has something to say about you, that's what. The news has gotten around that I'm making the decision on your expansion plans, so they all have an opinion about what I should or shouldn't do."

"For or against?"

"Do you really care?" Skylar muttered as she shut the door.

As usual, Aaron was wearing a suit and tie—the kind that probably cost a fortune. *She,* on the other hand, had come directly to city hall after picking up produce and dropping if off at the Nibble Nook. There hadn't been time to change from jeans into something more professional.

"Of course I care. The support of the local community is always important."

"You're just spouting public relations rhetoric, but it *should* be important. You have so much potential at Cooper Industries to make a difference, even more than your grandfather, because you must have a more contemporary point of view."

"What has that got to do with anything?"

"Well, how about an in-house child-care facility? And I'm sure you've heard of job sharing. It's not practical for assembly-line work, I suppose, but there are other positions at Cooper Industries where it could be implemented."

Aaron didn't look excited by the idea. "I'll put it on my list of things to consider, but I've always doubted it works well in practice. It's the kind of situation where people just take advantage."

Skylar gritted her teeth, yet it was the sort of cynical comment she should have expected from him; even as a teenager he'd thought the worst of people.

He pulled a chair out for her and she hesitated before sitting down. She didn't want the small courtesies from Aaron, particularly if they put her in closer physical contact with him. It was painful to realize she could still respond as a woman, especially to a man like Aaron Hollister.

She opened the folder she'd brought with her and skimmed the notes she'd made.

"I told you I'd have a lot to ask."

Aaron took out his copy of the plan. "Fire away."

She began posing her questions, and as she carefully wrote down his replies, the surprise on his face grew.

"You've really given this some thought," he said finally.

Skylar tried not to be insulted. *Of course* she'd given his proposal some thought. She had stayed up almost every night the past week comparing information on the local area and region to his plans, along with gathering every other piece of data she could get.

"Everybody knows Cooper Industries is important

to the town," she responded carefully. "The decisions you make will affect the whole area. For instance, there's a rumor that you've decided to stop buying from local farmers."

She'd hoped it was an unfounded story, but the expression on Aaron's face told her it wasn't.

"It's better for Cooper Industries," he explained. "Once our local contracts are satisfied at the end of the next growing season, we'll only be purchasing from large producers. The ones we're already dealing with are eager for us to diversify and increase our orders."

"They're all outside the area."

"Yes, none of the large corporate farms are nearby. But even taking the increased transport costs into account, it will make our operations smoother. They can be relied upon to provide as much as we want, when we want it, or pay a penalty."

Aaron sounded sincere, yet the tip of Skylar's pen dug into her notebook. She'd gotten an earful from the farmers lately. It would hurt them to lose their contracts, but they also had valid reasons to think the advantages of working with them were outweighed by the disadvantages.

"And it may reduce quality," she said carefully. "The local farms harvest and deliver their produce to the factory at the peak processing point. Corporate farms will harvest earlier to take shipping delays into account. Some of it could sit in cold storage for days or longer."

Aaron waved his hand, dismissing the concern. "I'm sure the difference will be negligible. And this way we can process larger quantities than before and increase our sales. You must understand that sales are the key to our survival and growth."

"Oh, I understand. But while I don't have a degree in business administration like you, I know *repeat* sales are key to your growth. Mine, too. Do you think anyone who gets a lousy burger at the Nibble Nook will ever come back?"

Frustrated, Skylar pulled out two individual serving fruit snack-pack cups she bought in case they were needed—one was from Cooper Industries and one was from another convenience food manufacturer. She peeled the plastic top from both and handed Aaron a spoon. "See if *you* think the difference is negligible."

"This is ridiculous," he protested.

"Think of it as market research."

Clearly seeing it as a waste of his time, Aaron ate a bite from the first fruit cup, followed by a spoonful from the one processed by Cooper Industries. His eyes widened.

"Yeah," she said when he remained silent. "The one from Cooper is much better. They fly off the grocery shelves, even though the price is higher than what other companies charge. If nothing else, you should continue to manufacture these using local fruit and label it a 'special reserve' product."

Aaron still wasn't saying anything, and she figured

he was probably annoyed that she was talking about things that had less to do with expansion, and more with how he did business.

"For that matter," she continued, determined to say her piece, "I can speak with the farmers and suggest they form an agricultural cooperative. That way you could deal with the cooperative rather than each of them individually."

AARON STARED AT the plastic containers in front of him, shocked that he'd left *quality* out of his equations. All he'd seen was the issue of reducing costs and increasing output.

Yet he was equally shocked that it was *Skylar* who'd seen the flaw in his plans.

"I know it's just convenience food, but this is what parents are feeding their children when they're too busy to cook," she continued. "People are proud that Cooper Industries manufactures products that are tastier and healthier than a lot of stuff on the market. Take away that pride, and you're going to have bigger personnel problems than the ones you have now."

"I don't have personnel problems," he said quickly, though it wasn't true.

There *were* problems, which he was resolving. He'd implemented policies to ensure employees would take their lunch breaks within appropriate time frames. He'd also stopped the flow of Cooper Industry products he had seen going into employee car trunks, along with several other behavioral issues. Surely, once the employees adjusted, morale and absentee-ism would improve, though he doubted he'd ever be popular.

"That's a matter of opinion. Maybe if you didn't distrust your workers, things might get better. The families you employ have been loyal to Cooper Industries for generations, and you have no idea how big a difference you can make in someone's life by treating them with respect."

Aaron fixed Skylar with a sharp gaze. "I realize my employees are upset with me, but it's because they're getting used to the new rules. Why do you think I've discouraged Melanie going to the Nibble Nook? Most of your customers work for Cooper Industries, and I don't want her around people with a chip on their shoulder."

"That's only *one* of the reasons you don't want Melanie at the Nibble Nook, but that isn't what we're here to discuss."

Getting up, she went to a credenza and took out two bottles of water. She handed him one and sat down again.

"About your plans, I'd really like you to rethink part of it, especially the location. Building on the land to the south will have less environmental impact."

"Except it's closer to…" His voice trailed when Skylar glared.

"Closer to the 'poor' part of town?" she demanded. "Heaven forbid the factory should be closer to some of the people it employs."

"That isn't what I meant. But crime is probably higher in that part of Cooperton."

"Not really. Besides, what is anyone going to steal from you? Fruits and vegetables and a forklift?"

"Vandalism is also an issue."

"Have you driven through that section of Cooperton lately?" Skylar asked. "The people who live there are hardworking and keep their homes very nicely. I don't think the police have gotten a single drunk and disorderly call since my… That is, they probably haven't gotten one for years. We really don't have a bad part of town any longer. Talk to the police department and find out for yourself."

Aaron wondered what she'd started to say, then realized she must have been referring to her parents.

"I'll take your comments into consideration."

"Fine. And here's something else to consider— what about incorporating an organic division for certain products? It's hard to find things like organic potato snacks or veggie chips. I think it's an underdeveloped niche market and could be very profitable with the growing concern for eating pesticide-free."

With that, she pulled out a stack of statistics she'd put together, and Aaron had to admit they were impressive. He was also aware that she was probably making a sideways pitch for him to continue to lease Cooper Industries land to the organic farmers who were already using it.

For someone who didn't have a business degree or even a high-school diploma, Skylar seemed to have a good grasp of market trends and needs. Though being the mother of a teenager, she probably had a built-in barometer for what kids were eating.

All at once she glanced at her watch. "I didn't realize it was so late. I have to get back to the Nibble Nook before the lunch rush. We can continue this tomorrow if you like."

"Sure."

Aaron walked her down to her truck and as she got in, cleared his throat. "By the way, thanks for the food you dropped off on Saturday after the picnic. Melanie was upset she couldn't go to the party. Seeing Karin and getting to eat homemade ice cream made her feel better. But you should have come in while they were visiting."

"I thought it was better to wait in the truck. And bringing the food was Karin's idea. They're friends."

"She's a nice kid. Tell her I appreciate it."

"Uh…sure. I'll see you tomorrow, same time as this morning."

She drove away, and Aaron stood for a while, looking around him. City hall was shaded by tall elms that had been there since before he was a boy and was surrounded on three sides by a small city park with neatly mowed grass and a tidy bandstand from the 1890s. A bust of the town's founder, Nelson Cooper, was on a pedestal to the left of the granite steps, and a life-sized bronze figure of a grizzly bear rested on the lawn opposite.

Except for the cars circling the square, it probably didn't look that different from the days of horse-drawn carriages and ladies in long, elegant dresses. Perhaps he'd been too hasty, dismissing city hall as a useless relic…. It was a reminder of a bygone era when life was simpler and people were still convinced the world's problems could be solved.

One point to Skylar, he mused.

What Cooperton City Hall lacked in modern conveniences, it probably made up for in charm. The place might be better off as a museum, but he could see why the town clung to its small piece of the past.

As Aaron drove past the Nibble Nook a few minutes later, the parking lot was full as usual, and he saw Skylar at the one of the three cashier's windows, handing out an order. She was smiling in a way he hadn't seen since his return to Cooperton, and his gut tightened. There was a brief time in high school when Skylar had smiled at him that way, her green eyes shining with merriment…and devilry.

God, she had fascinated him.

And she was just as compelling now in a different way. He was impressed by her careful appraisal of his plans for Cooper Industries and she had presented some interesting ideas he would have to evaluate. He couldn't imagine the rebellious girl he'd once known caring about organic snack foods or creating job-sharing opportunities *or* being concerned for the people who worked for Cooper Industries.

Aaron frowned, recalling what Skylar had said about him distrusting the people who worked at the factory. He hadn't thought of it quite that way, but it was accurate. Trust didn't come easily to him, and abuses were rife amongst his grandfather's employees; he was trying to fix the behavior without having to fire a load of them.

The families you employ have been loyal to Cooper Industries for generations....

The words echoed in Aaron's ears and his frown deepened. Skylar had looked so passionate when she was talking about the loyalty of the factory employees and making a difference in their lives. He was convinced there was hidden meaning to what she'd said; he just didn't know what it might be.

But one thing *was* clear...he was thinking far too much about Skylar. In view of how much she'd intrigued him when they were kids, it had to stop for his own peace of mind.

CHAPTER SIX

SKYLAR THOUGHT HER meeting with Aaron the next morning was going well…as well as it could with a man who'd already made up his mind about what he wanted to do and how he wanted to do it. Yet he seemed odd, looking at her with a question in his eyes that made her nervous.

"Unless more issues come up, we don't need to schedule another meeting right away," she said. "Research is mostly what's needed now. Also, I've sent the information to various county offices for comment and I'm waiting for their responses. Then there are the things I've asked you to reconsider in your plan."

"I'm working on that." He shifted in his chair, his leg brushing her knee, and it was as if an electric current shot through her veins and settled low in her abdomen. If he'd just keep his distance, she'd be a whole lot happier.

"So…uh, what does your grandfather think of all this?"

A shutter closed over Aaron's face. "We don't discuss Cooper Industries any more than necessary."

"Oh."

Skylar didn't know what else to say, though she'd already guessed his relationship with George Cooper wasn't the best. He certainly didn't seem to feel any special fondness for his grandparents, and he'd lived with them ten months out of the year for better than half his childhood.

Despite Aaron's closed expression, she saw a hint of the old pain in his eyes...a sadness beneath the arrogance. She'd forgotten it, and the way it had once made her think they might have something in common. Not that she believed it was real, not any longer. As a teenager he'd probably cultivated a trace of false vulnerability to get girls into bed. He could even have a bunch of kids, the same as his dad—according to the headlines in the scandal rags, S. S. Hollister had ex-wives and lovers and children spread across more than one continent.

"Of course, we'll need to review any changes you make," she murmured. "And *if* your plans are approved, you wouldn't be able to alter anything without checking with us first."

"You don't trust me, do you?"

"Probably no more than you trust anyone."

The remains of his smile vanished, and the haunting, sad look in his eyes returned. "That's an interesting thing to say. Have you ever trusted someone completely?"

"My husband and his parents," she replied without hesitation.

"Has anyone ever betrayed your trust?"

"Once or twice," Skylar said, swallowing. *Aaron* had betrayed her trust, but reminding him of the few weeks they'd dated would be stupid. He stared at her, and she wondered what else he wanted to know.

The intense moment was broken when his cell phone rang and he pulled it out with a murmured apology. She sank back in her chair and let out a breath.

Despite his faults, Aaron was handsome enough to have seduced a thousand women. Even knowing what she did about him, she still felt the tug. It was proof you didn't have to actually *like* a man to find him physically compelling.

She'd even dreamed about Aaron the other night, though it was more of a nightmare. He'd kissed her, threading his fingers through her hair and easing his knee between her legs…only to draw back and say that he didn't make love to immoral women.

Was fear the reason for her nightmare, fear that he would try to take Karin away, believing she was something she wasn't?

Or maybe it was guilt. People kept telling her it was all right to find someone else, but part of her still *felt* married to Jimmie…and that being attracted to another man was like being unfaithful. It was hard being alone, and physical closeness was something she missed along with the laughter and love she'd shared with her husband. Guilt was a powerful motivator, and it could have caused her subconscious to pair her with someone she despised. And she *did* despise Aaron—he might be educated, wealthy and successful, but he was still an angry, suspicious man.

God, she *had* to keep Karin away from him.

His cool cynicism was even worse than when they were kids, and she didn't want her daughter to become anything like him or the rest of the Hollisters. Or the Coopers, for that matter. They were civic-minded, but their family relationships seemed to be a mess, as well.

Karin was a great kid, excited about the future when she wasn't thinking about losing her father. She didn't need such dysfunctional people and screwed-up values in her life.

Aaron disconnected the call and apologized, saying he had to go. He hurried out, and Skylar waited until she was sure he was gone before getting up herself.

She was grateful their difficult conversation had gotten interrupted. They were being forced to work together, but the dark currents beneath their superficial cordiality were unchanged. And she didn't doubt that he still saw her as a woman whose background was too unsavory to ever be truly respectable.

KARIN WALKED WITH Melanie across the football field and through the opening in the fence to the Nibble Nook. The schools were lined up in a row, and by the road it was over half a mile to get from them to the hamburger stand, but it wasn't far on foot if you knew the shortcut. That is, if you were *allowed* to take the shortcut. Her mom hadn't let her do it by herself until this year and still acted nervous about it sometimes.

"Hi, girls. How was school?" called her mother.

"It was fine, Mrs. Gibson," Mellie answered.

Karin would have said differently, but she guessed it hadn't been *that* bad.

They put their backpacks on one of the tables and settled down to do their homework.

A few minutes later her mom came out with snacks and two extra-large cups. Karin's mouth watered—after-school snacks had included the yummiest smoothies since Mellie had come back to school.

"Thanks, Mom."

"Let me know if you want more."

Karin looked in her cup, delighted to see it had ice cream swirled into the smoothie, which smelled like a mix of strawberry, pineapple and peach. Her absolute *favorite*.

Melanie scooped a big mouthful from her cup. "Ohmigod," she said when she'd swallowed. "This is so good. I'm awful tired of orange juice. And that chicken soup Aaron gets from the deli…." She shuddered. "I guess he's trying to take care of me, but it's gross."

"Mom always makes smoothies when I'm sick and her chicken soup is yummy. And she bakes home-made pretzel rolls to eat with the soup. It's almost worth having a cold. Not really, but you know what I mean."

Melanie giggled. "I know. I wish I could live with you."

Karin froze, her brain working furiously.

Well, why not?

It wasn't as if Mellie's family cared that much about her. Or at all. She put down her cup. "Do you mean that?"

"Mean what?"

"That you want to live with us."

"Well, *yeah*. It would be like I belonged someplace, instead of being dropped on whoever will take me. Besides, you'd be there, and your mom is great."

"She can get cranky when she's tired," Karin said, determined to be honest. "And we don't get to eat burgers and French fries and ice cream that much, even though we own the Nibble Nook."

Melanie put her smoothie down, too. "I don't care if she's cranky; she's a real mom. She helped me with my history paper, and even though I'm not her kid, she makes sure I do my homework, too. I never had anybody who cared that much. Well, Aaron asks sometimes, but he knows I do it here."

"Okay." Karin leaned forward and dropped her voice. "Then tell your brother that you want to come live with us. I'm sure it'd be all right with Mom, and that way we could be the same as sisters."

Mellie looked excited, then her face fell. "I don't know…Aaron might not like it. He hasn't said much about the Nibble Nook lately, but I know he doesn't want me coming here."

"At least you could ask."

"All right. I'll try to find a good time."

Karin grinned happily. She'd always wanted a sister, and it would be awesome to have Mellie live with them.

MELANIE TIPTOED DOWN to the kitchen early on Saturday morning so she could fix Aaron breakfast. She couldn't really cook, but she'd gotten frozen breakfast food at the grocery store and had hidden it behind the ice-cream cartons in the freezer. There were waffles you put in the toaster, and eggs and bacon and potatoes that had microwave instructions. It shouldn't be too hard.

She scooped coffee grounds into the filter. Keeping her fingers crossed, she put water in and flipped the switch. After a few seconds there was a pop and sizzle and Melanie jumped backward, appalled. Had she broken it? Was it going to start a fire?

Then she realized it was steam, not smoke, coming out and laughed nervously. *Silly.* She'd never paid much attention to coffeemakers and should have remembered they made noises like that when the water touched hot metal.

She was supposed to be at the school at 9:00 a.m. to help set up for a carnival they were having to raise money, and Aaron was probably going to the office. He almost *always* worked on Saturday mornings.

She was trying to get her nerve up to ask him about moving in with the Gibsons and hoped fixing breakfast would show she was responsible and able to take care of herself. April and Tamlyn had gone to college when they were sixteen, and *they'd* lived in their own apartment; all *she* wanted to do was live with a different family.

Aaron wandered in at seven-thirty, yawning, and opened his eyes wide at the table she'd set. "What's this?"

"Breakfast. I'll get you a cup of coffee."

Melanie's finger hurt where she'd burned it on the toaster, but she had six waffles toasted. She piled three on a plate and put it in front of Aaron, along with a large cup of coffee, then started the microwave now that he was awake.

"Is it okay?" she asked anxiously when he took a drink. The expression on his face was kind of odd.

"Sure, it's fine. Thanks." He put syrup on the waffles and she rushed over to refill his cup. "Oh, I've got plenty."

"But you always drink a *bunch* before going to work."

The microwave dinged before he replied, and Melanie ran to get it. Using pot holders, she carried it to the table.

"Aren't you eating?" Aaron asked. "You need food with those antibiotics you're taking."

"I took it with a glass of milk. The teachers are bringing doughnuts for everyone setting up for the carnival. Karin says the apple fritters from the Bing Bing Donut Shop are awesome. You haven't forgotten I'm going to the school to help, have you?"

"Of course not. I'll give you a ride on the way to the office. I remember the Bing Bing Donut Shop. Karin is right—their apple fritters were delicious." All at once he smiled at her. "Fixing breakfast was very thoughtful, Melanie. Thank you."

"Uh…sure." She sat down and nibbled a waffle as she watched Aaron eat. He steadily drank the pot of coffee, though at one point he started coughing.

"Thanks, crumb went down the wrong way," he said after she'd thumped his back.

"That happens to me, too." Melanie sat down again. It was so comfy and pleasant, she didn't want to say anything about living with Karin and Mrs. Gibson.

She'd have to ask him later.

AARON HAD PURCHASED a new lawn mower after getting another letter from the neighborhood association about his grass, but he hadn't used it yet. So early that afternoon, he dressed in jeans and a long-sleeved shirt and rolled it out of the garage.

He walked around the machine, regarding it suspiciously. The safety manual suggested wearing protective clothing and goggles, and warned against practically everything except getting bitten by a tsetse fly.

Hmm.

He put on his sunglasses. They would have to do as safety goggles. And he wasn't barefoot, he was wearing sturdy athletic shoes. It seemed a reasonable middle-of-the-road option since he'd seen people running mowers in nothing but flip-flops and a bathing suit.

He paced through the long grass, searching. It didn't appear to have anything in it that could represent a hazard.

Next he looked about.

There were no small children nearby who could be injured by flying objects, and Melanie was still at the high school, helping out. One of the parents was bringing her home, and he was taking her to the carnival later that evening himself.

A grin spread on Aaron's face as he recalled the breakfast she'd made that morning. The eggs had been cold in the middle and the waffles slightly burned, but he'd eaten them anyway, as well as drinking the coffee…so strong it had almost dissolved the enamel on his teeth.

The truth was, though he hadn't been eager for Melanie to live with him while he was taking over Cooper Industries, he enjoyed having her. Well, except when she was in a blue funk. He just wished she'd spend more time at home, instead of at the Nibble Nook with Karin.

Sighing, he bent over, hooked his fingers on the handle of the lawn mower starter cord, and yanked.

Once.

Twice.

Three times. But the blasted thing didn't turn over or whatever it was supposed to do, and Aaron cursed under his breath. The hardware store had claimed this was their most popular model, reliable and easy starting with just one or two pulls on the cord, but it wasn't any better than the broken one it replaced. Damn it. He'd hoped to get an electric mower, but they'd said his yard was way too big and overgrown. Gritting his teeth, he began yanking the cord over and over, only to hear someone laughing.

It was Skylar and he glared.

"What the hell is so amusing?"

"*You*. Didn't you ever mow a lawn when you were a boy?"

Aaron stiffened.

While his grandfather had believed in old-fashioned chores for children, he'd hired a man to mow the vast lawns around the house twice a week—probably to be sure every blade of grass was cut to a precise length. The Cooper's twenty-four room Victorian was the only mansion in town, and it was meticulously maintained.

Nothing ever changed there.

He had eaten a Sunday dinner with his grandparents shortly after his return to Cooperton, and it had been like going back to his childhood—every stick of furniture was the same, along with the few pieces of expensive bric-a-brac. No personal photos for the Coopers on shelves or the top of the grand piano—the closest thing to a display of sentiment were the white roses his grandmother kept in a crystal vase beneath a portrait of Nelson Cooper, the town's founder.

"No, Skylar, I've never used a mower," he said shortly. "What are you doing here?"

"I gave Melanie a ride. The girls are in the house getting a glass of water."

"Oh." He should have guessed the parent who brought his sister home would be Skylar.

"That looks new," she observed, looking at the mower. "A nice model, too. Mind if I have a go?" she asked.

"Don't bother. There's something is wrong with it."

Skylar grinned and bent over the machine, first checking the gas tank. He would have told her it was full if she'd bothered asking. She shifted a U-shaped bar and fit it to the upper handle. Holding it there, she put a foot on the surface of the mower and gave a quick tug on the cord. The motor roared into life.

Damnation. Aaron clenched his teeth, wishing he'd read more of the manufacturer's handbook.

Skylar continued grasping the handle as she looked at him. "This is a safety feature," she called above the noise, gesturing to the U-shaped bar. "If you trip and let go, it either kills the motor or stops the blades from turning. See?"

She let go and the thing went silent.

He thought about the lawn mower he'd assumed was broken. It was probably fine; he just hadn't known how to get it running. Hell, he wasn't an engineer and had never claimed to be. And apparently it was something he'd missed in the safety manual, or hadn't read yet.

"You'll have to do it in narrow strips. The grass is so thick and long it will choke the blades otherwise," Skylar advised. She attached the grass catcher to the mower and started it again, running across a thin line at the edge of the lawn before turning it off. "I wouldn't go any wider than that."

Aaron fought a battle with his pride and decided it was pointless. "I suppose the grass catcher has to be emptied frequently."

"With this much overgrown lawn, yes. I'm surprised you don't have Joaquin's Gardening Service out here taking care of things."

"They quit a few weeks ago—claimed they'd taken on too many clients. I offered to pay a premium, but it didn't do any good. And there don't seem to be any kids in the neighborhood who are interested in earning a few extra bucks."

The amused expression in Skylar's eyes sobered. "Oh. Well, I'm sure you'll discover that gardening is satisfying. And it's autumn, so the growing season is nearly over. Fortunately the leaves haven't started turning on the trees since it's been such a warm October. However, I'd get the lawn mowed shortly before they do drop—it's easier to rake or use a leaf blower that way."

The trees…

Aaron looked up at the tall elms around the house.

He'd been eight when he had come to live in Cooperton, and one of his first chores was raking leaves. Lord, his arms had ached. His grandparents' property had numerous trees in addition to the spreading lawns, and he'd thought those leaves would never stop falling. Only sheer stubbornness had gotten him through the endless hours of raking and stuffing leaf bags, his arms feeling as if they were going to fall off.

No way would he have given his grim-faced grandfather the satisfaction of saying it was too much for him.

Pulling weeds in his grandmother's kitchen garden was assigned the next spring, and when he got tall enough, washing the three cars was added—twice a week, whether they'd been used or not—and waxing them once a week, along with any other task his grandfather found to give him. It had never been wise to be caught goofing off. "Idle hands are the devil's playground," George would thunder with the fervor of an old-time preacher before telling him to go sweep the long brick driveway.

Aaron had sworn to himself that once he got away from Cooperton, he would spend all of his time having fun and to *hell* with being responsible. That was probably why his father had been able to convince him to take a semester off from college to join the team competing for the America's Cup. But he'd quickly learned the playboy life wasn't for him, so George Cooper's values about hard work must have rubbed off.

"Is something wrong?" Skylar asked, breaking into his thoughts.

Aaron forced a smile. "No, of course not."

All at once, Karin and Melanie came barreling out of the house, breathless and giggling.

"Are we going now, Mom?" Karin asked brightly.

Skylar looked surprised. "Sure. Get in the truck."

The girls whispered something to each other, and Melanie waved as the truck backed down the driveway.

"Okay, what's up?" Aaron asked.

His sister gave him an innocent smile. "Nothing."

"I haven't been a kid for a while, but I know when something is going on."

"Okay. See, I've been thinking. You had to rent this house because of me and it's a pain having a kid to take care of, anyhow."

Aaron was appalled. He knew how it felt to be taken out of duty and treated as an inconvenience and had never intended to make his sister feel that way.

"*It's not a pain*. I'm very fond of you, Melanie."

"Yeah, but I'm sure you'd prefer working longer hours at the company and stuff, and when that new part of the factory is being built, you'll be busier than ever."

"You don't need to worry about that—we'll work it out. I'm just sorry I'm not much of a cook. I bet you're tired of take-out food."

"That's okay," Melanie said earnestly. "But since you're getting along better with Mrs. Gibson, Karin and I have been talking. The way we see it, Mrs. Gibson already *has* Karin to take care of, and having one more kid shouldn't be a big deal. Besides, they have an extra bedroom."

Aaron's eyes widened as he realized what she was getting at, but before he could head her off, Melanie finished.

"So I'd like to move in with them. It's all right with Mrs. Gibson, so you just have say yes and get Mother and Father to agree. I mean, not that I've ask—"

"No." His refusal came out sharper than he'd intended and he took a breath. "I'm sorry, that isn't possible. They aren't your family. We can make another arrangement if you aren't happy staying with me, but you aren't moving in with the Gibsons."

"I don't want to leave Cooperton," his sister said hastily. "I just want to live with Karin and her mother. Mrs. Gibson is a great mom, just like I always wanted…." Her voice trailed and she blushed.

"There's nothing to discuss. It's out of the question."

"But you *must* know how it feels not have a home."

"You've got a home, right here. And I'm going to do more to make it comfortable. You'll see."

Melanie bit her lip. "It's not the same. You've been nice, but next year I'll have to go somewhere else. You got to stay with your grandmother and grandfather when you were growing up. You didn't have to keep going to new schools and being with people you didn't know and not being able to make real friends."

Aaron couldn't explain that living with the Coopers hadn't been any picnic, either. *Home* implied a place that was warm and inviting, but living with the Coopers was akin to living in a refrigerated museum, though it was more the way they'd acted than the place.

"I *do* understand how you feel, Melanie. But you can't move in with strangers."

"They aren't strangers. Karin is my best friend, and Mrs. Gibson makes sure I do my homework, same as she does with Karin. And she helped with my history paper—you were real happy I got an A on it, remember? She does mom stuff all the time. The parents are raising money for the school, so she's doing a hamburger stand at the carnival. And she makes yummy fruit smoothies for me because I was sick."

"Melanie, I—"

"You were great, too," his sister said hastily. "But you're not a mom."

No, Aaron didn't have the equipment, though perhaps motherhood was more a state of mind than whether you were a man or woman. It was a curious thought for him. His own mother had always seemed like a lovely butterfly, flitting from flower to flower. And while a few of his stepmothers weren't bad women, his father never stayed married to them long enough to have a noticeable impact on his children's lives.

Actually, Aaron had always wondered what would have happened if Jake's mother, Josie Chambers, had been willing to marry Spence. Spence still carried her picture in his wallet…the only ex-lover whose picture he'd ever kept. Aaron could see the appeal. Josie was stunning. She was also an independent nonconformist who'd decided that being a wife would interfere with her life as a globe-trotting photographer. But motherhood hadn't. She'd given birth to Jake while on a photo assignment in Iceland, and had taken him everywhere with her.

When it got down to it, Jake was probably the only one of Spence's kids who'd enjoyed childhood. He'd seen more of the world by the time he was ten than Aaron expected to see in a lifetime. And the constant travel and periodic dangers must suit him since he'd become a photographer himself.

"I know things have been tough for you, Melanie," Aaron murmured. He cared about his sister and hated to see her unhappy. "But you can't join a family the way you'd join the Marines. Now go inside. I want to get the lawn done before we leave for the carnival."

Melanie looked utterly crushed, and Aaron wished there'd been an easier way of letting her down.

Damn it all. What did Skylar hope to accomplish by giving Melanie permission to move in with them? And was Melanie just looking for attention? She knew he didn't approve of the Nibble Nook and was defying him by continuing to go there. Yet in a way, the defiance was reassuring. He didn't want to deal with an out-of-control teenager, but she had been so quiet and anxious to please when she'd arrived in

July that it bothered him. Her moments of rebellion since then were probably a good sign.

As for Karin, he was enjoying her, too. It was even possible that she was a healthy role model for Melanie.

He started the lawn mower—it was absurdly easy now that he knew the trick—and directed it along the edge of the grass that Skylar had already cut. Back and forth, taking only a few inches of the overgrown section at a time, and emptying the catcher every five or six passes.

Hell, Skylar must have loved seeing him yank on that cord when there wasn't a prayer of it going. He didn't appreciate being the butt of a joke, even by accident.

I want to live with Karin and her mother.

The words echoed in his head, inescapable however hard he tried, and he wondered how Melanie had ever gotten the notion that he'd approve of her living with virtual strangers.

And yet it was just as disconcerting to know that she'd rather live with those strangers than with him.

KARIN SAT WITH Melanie on a bench at the edge of the midway, munching a corn dog. The carnival was raising money for a new computer lab, and everybody was donating the money they made on food and stuff. Her mom and grandparents were running a booth for hamburgers and fries and it had the longest line of all.

"Aaron wouldn't even consider me living with you,

'cause you aren't family." Mellie kicked a clod of dirt. "I was so nervous, I said it was okay with your mother even though we haven't asked yet. But I guess it doesn't matter since he refused."

Karin made a face. "It'll be okay with Mom. Tell your brother we *are* family, we just aren't related." It was what she'd heard her grandparents say to their employees and it sounded nice.

"I don't think he'll buy that. He's awfully stubborn."

"Maybe we can think of something else to do." Karin had put a ton of mustard on her corn dog and kept having to turn it back and forth to keep the mustard from dripping. Grandpa Joe always teased her for using so much, but she loved how the sour mustard tasted with the sweet, crispy cornbread around the hot dog.

In some ways Karin felt older than Mellie, instead of younger. Mellie's father wasn't dead like hers; he just wasn't around much. And her mom and stepdad traveled all the time, leaving her with relatives she hardly knew...this year with a half brother that nobody in town liked. Karin's own mother had to work a lot, but she was always *there*. And she came to school events and stuff, no matter how busy it was at the Nibble Nook.

Mellie tossed her own corn-dog stick into the trash can. "It must be legal stuff. You know, because he's my temporary guardian while my mother and father are gone. Maybe I should have asked them before talking to Aaron. They usually don't mind what I do, but now he'll tell them that he said 'no,' and they might think they have to go along."

"Legal stuff…" Karin repeated absently as she took another bite of mustard and corn dog.

On one of her weekends with Grandma Grace and Grandpa Joe they'd watched the three *Back to the Future* movies, all in one night. In the second movie, the inventor guy said justice moved swiftly in the future because they had outlawed lawyers. Grandpa Joe had laughed and laughed and said he was sure it would happen someday.

"What if we talk to a lawyer?" she murmured.

"How would that help?"

"Well, if moms and dads can get divorced, then kids should be able to divorce their parents and live where they want."

Mellie's eyes widened. "I never heard of someone doing that."

"Me, either, but it can't hurt to try. The problem is, it probably costs a bunch. I wasn't supposed to hear about it, but after my dad…that is, Grandpa Joe and Grandma Grace went to a lawyer a few months ago and had a will made. Mom started crying and told them they shouldn't have spent so much money, but they wanted to be sure we'd be okay. I'm not sure why it was such a big deal."

"I've got money," Mellie said. "My mother and father are always sending me checks or cash, and Aaron gives me more than I need. I put most of it in a bank account, so I bet there's enough."

Karin's brain worked furiously. "Okay, we'll start calling on Monday during lunch. I'll look in the phone book and get the names and numbers of the lawyers in town."

Mellie began to look excited, too. "My stepfather says that an attorney can get people to do practically anything you want."

"And your mom and dad can come visit you at our place, same as at your brother's house."

"They don't visit much, anyhow. My mother and stepfather take me someplace every summer, but if I'm staying with you, my mother won't have to talk anybody else into keeping me for the school year. She'll like that."

Karin didn't understand the way Mellie's family did things. Mellie had said that some of her half brothers and sisters had ended up in boarding schools when they were growing up and she was really glad she hadn't gotten sent to one so far. But apparently it had been touch-and-go this year until Aaron agreed to take her.

It was weird. Karin had never been away from her mom for more than a week, and that was just for science conservation camp and other school trips, or hanging out in Trident with Grandpa Joe and Grandma Grace.

"Where *is* your brother, anyhow?" she asked, glancing around for fear that their talk about lawyers might have been overheard. "You said he brought you to-night."

"I don't know. When we got here the principal was trying to talk him into selling tickets or something. He said Aaron would be great for the dunk tank, 'cause they'd make a bunch of money, but somebody *else* said that his employees would be afraid to dunk him because he was their boss. Aaron didn't seem too happy about that, but I didn't hear what happened because he handed me a bunch of money and told me to go enjoy the carnival."

"You don't think he'd fire someone who dunked him, do you?" Karin nibbled the last crusty bit of dough from her corn-dog stick and threw it away.

"I don't know. He got awful mad when he caught an employee putting six boxes of beef jerky in their car without paying for it, but that was different."

Karin blinked. "Six whole boxes?"

"Uh-huh. He didn't say who it was, but he was hopping mad when he came home that day. Say, let's see if the line is shorter at your mom's hamburger booth. I'm still hungry."

"Me, too."

She followed Melanie and even though the line was still huge, they decided to wait…mostly because Nick Jakowski had gotten there just ahead of them.

"Oh, hi," he said when he turned around. "You're Karin, right? The coach was talking about you the other day. He said you played soccer in junior high and was wondering why you didn't try out for the high-school team."

Karin shrugged, tongue-tied.

They went to a small school where you knew practically everyone's name, but it was dazzling to think that Nick remembered anything else about her. After all, he was the captain of the football team and absolutely *gorgeous* with his athletic jacket and crooked smile.

"The team could use another good player. I like soccer better than football," Nick admitted when she still didn't say anything. "But I'm hoping to get a scholarship and thought it would be easier playing football." He kept sending quick looks at Melanie and Karin nudged her friend forward.

"Uh…this is Melanie. She saw the World Cup a couple of years ago."

"Wow, that must have been *awesome*. What was it like?"

Mellie's cheeks got pink. "My dad took me. We were—"

"I wondered where you'd gone to, Nick," interrupted a voice, and Karin could have screamed. It was Tiffany Baldwin. Tiffany checked the line of people waiting behind them and pouted. "Would you mind *awfully* letting me cut in with you, Nick?"

He seemed embarrassed. "Well, uh, that wouldn't be fair to everyone else."

"I guess you're right." But she didn't step away. Instead, she hugged his elbow and focused on Melanie.

"Did you hear Nick is being scouted by the biggest schools? I'm so proud—he's going to get a fabulous football scholarship."

"Cool it, Tiff," Nick growled. "That isn't for sure."

"It's what my dad says, and he should know."

Tiffany enjoyed reminding people she was the coach's daughter, and it was doubly annoying to have her butt in when they were talking to Nick.

Well, he'd mostly been talking to Mellie.

Karin wrinkled her nose. Her chest still hadn't developed, so guys didn't check her out the way they checked out girls like Tiffany and Melanie. But Mellie wasn't smug about being pretty, and Tiffany was full of herself.

They moved closer to the front of the line—her mom and grandparents knew how to feed a bunch of people fast—and Karin saw Grandpa Joe wink at her as he took money from a customer.

"You'd better go get a place in line," Nick told Tiffany.

"Whatever you say, Nick." She'd obviously hoped he would forget and let her stay with him. "Maybe we could take a ride on the Ferris wheel later."

"Maybe." When he got to the counter, Nick took out his wallet. "We'll take three burgers and three fries," he said to Grandpa Joe. "Is that okay with both of you?" he asked, looking back at them.

Both Karin and Mellie nodded, dumbfounded.

Mellie started to open her purse, but Nick shook his head. "Naw. My treat."

The pink in her cheeks got brighter and Karin had a hollow feeling in her stomach. If Mellie got a boyfriend, would she still care about moving in with them?

CHAPTER SEVEN

"MOM, DAD, THANKS for the help," Skylar said as they were finishing the cleanup following the carnival.

Her father-in-law grinned. "It was fun."

"Right. Fun. Five hours of hard labor."

"It was fun doing it together. You need to tell us when you've volunteered for these things," Grace scolded. "We wouldn't have even known about it if those two employees hadn't gotten sick at the last minute."

"Besides, you were going to give them overtime, and we work cheap. Now pay up." Joe held out his arms and Skylar walked into his hug. As long as she'd known the Gibsons, she'd never stopped marveling at what decent people they were.

"I love you, Dad," she whispered. Never in her life could she remember saying that to her own parents and meaning it the way she cared for Grace and Joe.

"You're our girl," he said gruffly. "Don't you ever forget that. You and Karin."

"I won't."

They went back to work, sorting out the few remaining bits of food and putting the equipment in the back of her pickup. She'd park it in the garage for the night and deal with getting everything back to the Nibble Nook early in the morning. They counted up the proceeds and Skylar was pleased to see the total. She had sold out the way she'd hoped, but you could never tell what teenagers would decide to eat.

"How did you do?" asked Mrs. Torval a few minutes later. She was the chairperson of the event and was going from booth to booth, collecting preliminary totals.

Skylar showed her the figures, minus the cash she'd brought to make change, and Mrs. Torval beamed in delight. "That's amazing. Do you have any idea how much it will be once your expenses are taken out?"

"There aren't any expenses," Joe Gibson declared. "The Trident Nibble Nook Too is donating the supplies."

"*Dad,* you can't do that. You worked, that's more than enough," Skylar said, spinning around. She hadn't told them she planned to donate the cost of her supplies in case they tried to do it instead. It was also one of the reasons she hadn't told them she was doing a booth at the carnival in the first place...knowing they'd go overboard. They always went overboard; it was their favorite thing.

"We can, too," Grace Gibson asserted. "Our granddaughter attends school here, so we have to support it, as well."

"At the very least we're splitting it."

"Nope." Grace had the stubborn look she got whenever her family was involved.

Mrs. Torval didn't care who was donating what, she simply looked ecstatic and added the preliminary figure Skylar had given her to the clipboard she carried. Each vendor at the carnival had a special bag to leave in the night depository at the bank, and Skylar methodically counted the money again, with Grace cross-checking the amounts and completing a deposit slip.

"Looks good."

They each signed the slip and sealed it in the bag. Since Skylar closed out a cash register every day and wasn't subtracting anything, she was reasonably certain her figures would stand firm. Some of the others—the service organizations and churches and school clubs—would probably take a while to come up with final amounts. There were always the stragglers, the folks who hadn't yet provided the receipts of what they'd spent for supplies and would take days to discover the pocket or jar or car glove compartment where they'd left the slip of paper.

She peeked into the cab of her truck, parked at the back of the booth and saw Karin was sound asleep, her head pillowed on her backpack. It wasn't any wonder she was exhausted. She'd overeaten, mostly junk food, ridden every ride on the midway, played every game…and could be on the way to getting her heart broken.

Skylar sighed as she remembered the fearful, happy look on Karin's face when the tall football player had bought her and Melanie a burger. From the little she'd seen, he seemed like a nice enough kid. Stories about him were common in the *Cooperton Chronicle*—all about his talent on the field and how he was going to help them win the state championships. The newspaper saw him as a town hero.

Yet Skylar doubted a seventeen-year-old football star was romantically interested in a fourteen-year-old freshman—no matter how sweet and terrific that fourteen-year-old might be. Three years was a lot when you were a teenager. Melanie, on the other hand, was a different case—she was sixteen and becoming a beauty. And Nick's expression when he looked at her was decidedly different than when he looked at Karin.

Skylar herself hadn't developed until she was a year older than Karin, possibly the only thing saving her from becoming a mother at a younger age, considering how wild she'd been. She *had* drawn the line at indiscriminate sex, but that was practically the only line she hadn't crossed. And as it turned out, Aaron hadn't been interested in her in the first place—he'd just made a bet with his toadying buddies that he could get inside her jeans.

A shiver went through Skylar.

She'd smoked in the girls' restroom, cut classes, gotten arrested for joyriding, nearly flunked out, partied hard…and generally done her best to live down to her parents' low reputations. Getting pregnant had been a wakeup call. Except it didn't matter that she'd turned her life around; Aaron could use her past against her and Karin would think she was a hypocrite.

"Are you okay?" Grace asked as she put a box in the bed of the truck. "You got quiet all at once."

"I'm fine, just concerned about that football player and…" Skylar gestured toward her sleeping daughter inside the truck. It was partly true—the only part she could discuss with her mother-in-law. "If she has a crush on that boy, and her friend Melanie does, as well…."

"I know. Try not to worry."

Both Grace and Joe had commented on Nick Jakowski buying fries and burgers for Melanie and Karin. They'd looked pleased and concerned at the same time, probably mirroring Skylar's expression. Their little girl was growing up enough to notice the opposite sex, though Skylar wasn't foolish enough to think it had just happened; it was simply the first time they'd been confronted with it. For that matter, it probably would have come up earlier if Karin hadn't been preoccupied with her father's death.

"They say broken hearts are part of growing up, but it's a lousy lesson to learn. Especially when your best friend is involved," Skylar said, wiping down the counter of the booth so it could be disassembled by the volunteer fire department in the morning. Community fund-raisers were common in Cooperton, and the town kept the booths stored in one of the maintenance sheds.

"And almost as hard for a parent to watch," Grace

murmured, "because you can't do anything about it. Fortunately, Jimmie never really broke his heart... except over a milk shake."

Skylar remembered Jimmie telling her about his first love...a cute little number whose affection for him was largely driven by her passion for the Nibble Nook's strawberry malts. They'd been eleven. Jimmie had been philosophical about it—after all, the Nook really *did* serve great milk shakes—but he'd added he was happy that Skylar didn't care for strawberry malts.

She smiled and touched her wedding band, remembering her husband's teasing wink.

"Of course, that young man is blind if he doesn't prefer our Karin," Grace announced, sounding very much the biased grandmother. "Karin is much lovelier."

"And three years younger. At any rate, I'm not ready to be the mother of a dating teenager. As a matter of fact, I want to lock her in a closet until she's forty."

"Oh...I hadn't thought of that. All right, if that boy is looking for a blonde, blue-eyed girl, he's better off with Melanie. Let her brother keep tabs on the situation."

Skylar's face went stiff. Melanie and Karin bore an uncomfortable resemblance to each other with the same dark blond hair, blue eyes and wide grins. Actually, Aaron and his father *both* had the same smile as the girls, but since Aaron wasn't prone to good humor these days, maybe no one else would spot the similarity.

"I'm not sure Aaron Hollister is the right person to keep tabs on a teenage girl who's starting to date."

The only thing Aaron seemed to care about was whether Melanie was at the Nibble Nook, and that was because he thought Skylar might be a bad influence and didn't want her around his unhappy employees or the rest of the people who ate there.

"Oh. Maybe you can slip a word in with Melanie."

"I'll try."

She gave her in-laws another hug. They were dropping the receipts at the night depository and she was grateful to avoid the stop on the way home.

Karin wiggled upright and yawned when Skylar started the truck. "What time is it?"

"Almost midnight. We've been cleaning up. Put on your seat belt."

But her daughter just yawned again and rested her head against the window.

"Seat belt," Skylar prompted. "Now."

"Mmm." Karin wiggled and pulled the belt across her body, snapping it into place. "Do you know that Melanie never had a corn dog before?" she mumbled. "How weird is that? Can we have them for snacks on Monday?"

"I'll think about it." Skylar smiled and headed for the house. It was a quiet moment, perhaps the calm before the storm, but it was nice. Karin *hadn't* broken her heart and maybe wouldn't; her friend was still her friend, and they had tomorrow to relax.

MELANIE GULPED HER lunch on Monday and hurried outside with Karin to a far corner of the school's front parking lot.

"Are you sure you still want to live with us?" Karin asked. "I don't want to push or anything."

"More than ever. Aaron is pretty nice, but I'm only supposed to be here until next June, and if I'm not there, he could move into that apartment over the factory offices. Then he could work, like, twenty-four hours a day."

"*Awesome.* I got a list of names and numbers. We have to keep phoning until we find someone who will help, even if we have to hire someone as far away as Sacramento or San Francisco."

The first call didn't last longer than Melanie's first few words. "We do *not* represent children. Don't waste our time," said the woman who'd answered, sounding annoyed. "If you really require an attorney, have your parents call someone."

Melanie was mortified, but Karin just rolled her eyes. "Let me talk to the next one, I'll put it on speakerphone." She read over the list she'd brought and picked out a name that had something scribbled next to it. "Hello, I want to speak to Mr. Newman," she said when a man answered. "My friend needs a lawyer and I'm helping her."

"You don't sound old enough to need a lawyer."

"I'm old enough to read Mr. Newman's advertisement in the phone book. It says, 'free one-hour initial consultation.'"

"Yes, the secretary takes information from a caller, and we decide whether or not there's a reasonable basis to offer a consultation."

Karin's chin rose. "That's *not* what the ad says. Are you telling me you're guilty of false advertising? I thought there were laws in California against that kind of thing. Besides, your ad was much smaller than everyone else's, so you can't be too good at lawyering. I should think you'd be glad to get our business."

The man on the other end of the phone began to laugh. "That's an interesting argument. As a matter of fact, *I'm* Jeremy Newman. My secretary went home sick and I've been answering the phone between appointments. I set up my law practice a few months ago and decided not to spend money on a bigger ad immediately."

Karin let out a heavy sigh. "Then how do we know you have enough experience to handle our business? Especially if you aren't even willing to listen and find out if we have a case."

Ohmigod.

Melanie clapped a palm over her mouth in both shock and admiration. She couldn't imagine talking to anyone the way Karin was talking to that lawyer. And the lawyer thought it was funny.... He was laughing again.

"All right, young lady, you get your free hour. Tell me about this problem of yours."

"It's for my friend—she wants to divorce her mother and father so she can live with me and my mom. See, her parents are divorced, too, and her mom keeps dumping her with family she doesn't know so she can go off and travel. Mellie spends a few months here and there, and it's really hard keeping up with her classes. She knows all about my mom being strict and stuff, and she doesn't mind, so if she—"

"Whoa. Hold on there," Mr. Newman ordered. "Let's start over. Is your friend—Mellie—there?"

"We're on speakerphone."

"Uh...hello," Melanie said awkwardly when Karin put the phone closer. "I'd really like your help, Mr. Newman."

"Hello, Mellie. How old are you?"

"Sixteen."

"Have you ever been in trouble with the police or at school?"

"No, sir," she replied. "My mother *promises* I won't get in trouble when she leaves me with someone. My grades aren't great, but I'm really trying and Karin helps. So does her mom. I'm just...I'm just so tired of moving around and not belonging to anyone," she burst out, horrified to find she was almost crying. People seemed to think she had it made because her parents were rich and she had seen a bunch of famous places, but it wasn't great at all.

"I understand," the lawyer said, sounding as if he

really did know how she felt. "Maybe we just need to send a letter to change things."

"You'll have to send it to my half brother. My mother and stepfather are in Africa, and my father is…well, I don't know. He goes all over."

"Does your brother have legal custody?"

"He has some papers from a lawyer. My mother wants to be sure I can see doctors and things."

"How do you expect to support yourself?"

"I have a trust fund."

Mr. Newman asked more questions and finally said to call again the next day. Melanie didn't know whether to be hopeful or worried when they got off, but there wasn't time to think about it.… They had to hurry or be late for class.

Something else kept bothering her, though, as the afternoon went by… How would Aaron and her parents react? She felt funny about the idea of divorcing her mother and father—it was the same as saying, "I don't love you anymore." She *did* love them, but they didn't have time for her, so why should they care if she lived with the Gibsons? Surely it would be easier than convincing different relatives to take her for six months or a year.

If only her mother was more like Skylar. Mrs. Gibson was really strict and like Karin said, she could be cranky sometimes…but she was a *mom* from top to bottom.

"Miss Hollister, are you listening?" asked Mrs.

Ramirez, their science teacher. "I asked if you knew the periodic table symbol for neon."

"Oh, yes." Melanie's ears burned as the other kids giggled. "It's Ne."

"Thank you, that's correct." Mrs. Ramirez gave her a kind smile. She was Karin's favorite teacher and Melanie liked her, too, but she didn't let the kids goof off.

She went on talking about neon being a gas, and Melanie tried to listen, but she kept wondering if they *should* have asked Mrs. Gibson if it was okay for her to move in with them. *First.* Before calling a lawyer. Karin seemed sure it was all right, but what if it wasn't?

"What's up?" Karin asked as they packed their general science textbooks in their backpacks.

Melanie shrugged. It was probably too late now to worry about it, and she didn't want to jinx anything.

On Friday, Aaron hurried to the post office shortly after lunch. He had gotten a notice at the house the previous evening saying a registered letter was waiting, but he'd had meetings that morning with sales reps from two of the large corporate farms which supplied raw materials to Cooper Industries.

They weren't thrilled that he was considering extending his contracts with the local growers, but Skylar had made a valid point about quality. Cooper Industries might be in trouble because they were antiquated and needed more efficient management, but their products sold well—keeping up with demand was a chronic issue. The trick was updating without destroying the reason they'd survived this long.

He'd called Skylar a few days before to see what the local farmers thought of her idea to form an agricultural cooperative. It *would* be a big improvement over the current situation and make it easier to continue doing business with them. Apparently the suggestion was generating interest, and she'd promised to update him once they met as a group.

There was a long line at the post office, and as he waited, Aaron wondered what he could do to encourage a growers' association. At the minimum they'd need office space and other facilities—perhaps he could donate a building to support the effort. Yet as the thought formed, he could practically hear Skylar's voice asking, "With how many strings attached?"

Aaron made a face.

He was cynical about people with good reason, but Skylar had a skeptical attitude *herself* when it came to him and his family. While he wouldn't impose any conditions if he supported a growers' association, he was honest enough to hope it would improve his relations with Cooperton in general.

At the counter he showed his identification to the postal clerk and signed for the registered letter; the return address was from a local attorney. That seemed odd. Any issues with the company or the employees should be coming to Cooper Industries, not his home address. Frowning, he opened the envelope and read the letter inside, his face darkening with each sentence.

Couched in cautious legal language, the lawyer stated that his client, Melanie Elizabeth Hollister, had consulted with him, asking about a parent–child divorce. The attorney went on to say that as her temporary guardian, Aaron might avert a court request for emancipation by seeking parental approval for Melanie to live in the household of her choice. The letter further pointed out that since she had a trust fund to provide monthly support payments once she was legally responsible for herself, there were no financial barriers to emancipation.

The household of her choice? Aaron knew exactly which household his sister wanted to live in; the same one she'd asked about last Saturday.

Hell and damnation.

A parent–child divorce? Was Melanie out of her mind? The lawyer, too, for that matter. His sister wasn't abused *or* neglected; there was no basis for emancipating her, despite her trust fund being available for support.

Skylar *had* to be behind this nonsense. After all, she'd already given permission for Melanie to move in with her, and it just didn't seem appropriate for her to do that without talking to him first. She'd also made it clear she didn't approve of the way he was handling his sister. It was ironic considering Skylar's early history as the wildest troublemaker in Cooperton.

Aaron pressed a finger to his temple.

He didn't have much faith in women. His own mother was spoiled and demanding and cared more for herself than anyone else. In his experience the opposite sex was inordinately interested in money. The one time he'd flirted with the idea of marriage was as a dumb twenty-three-year-old graduate student, only to discover his prospective bride was a compulsive spender with a lover on the side. His ego had gotten more damaged than his heart, but it reinforced his opinion about relationships. *They weren't worth the trouble.*

Aaron jumped into the Mercedes and swung into the flow of traffic around the city hall square, still too angry to wonder if he was being unreasonable about Skylar. He had to stop this idiocy. Five minutes later, he slammed the car door and stomped up to the Nibble Nook.

"I need to talk to you," he growled when Skylar appeared at the ordering window. "In private."

"In case you haven't noticed, Melanie isn't here right now," she said. "You have nothing to complain about."

"In private."

A curious expression flickered in her eyes and was gone so fast he couldn't read it. "Unlike some people, I don't have a private office."

"We can talk in my car."

"Yeah, right."

"Your truck, then."

The employees inside the hamburger stand had

ducked their heads and were casting them sideways glances. But one, a lanky young man with shoulders that seemed too big for the rest of his body, stepped closer.

"Is there a problem, Skylar?"

"Everything's fine, but will you take over for a while, Greg? I'm going to step into my truck to speak with Mr. Hollister." She gave Aaron a sweetly false smile that turned into a glare as they climbed inside the cab of the old pickup in the rear of the hamburger stand. "This better not be about city council business, Aaron," she hissed after she slammed the door. "I warned you about that."

"It's about this damned letter you put Melanie up to having sent to me." He waved it in her face. "Are you insane?"

"I have no idea what you're talking about. I didn't put Melanie up to anything."

"Don't expect me to believe she came up with this nonsensical notion on her own. She's around you and your daughter every day, even though you *know* I don't approve of her being at the Nibble Nook. She rarely goes anyplace else. It must be your idea."

"What idea? And watch what you say about me. *I* don't have to worry about my daughter being around my employees the way you worry about Melanie being around yours."

"Not funny." Aaron thrust the letter from Jeremy Newman into Skylar's hands and clenched his fists as she read it.

PARENT—CHILD DIVORCE?

Skylar blinked as she read the phrase. Was that possible outside of a Hollywood movie? Yet she had a sinking feeling she knew who'd come up with the idea…her own daughter.

"This is the first I've heard about it," she said.

"The same way you know nothing about Melanie asking if she can move in with you and Karin, I suppose? I know you've already given your permission. Hell, I didn't think even *you* would try to alienate a child's affections from her family. But you're not getting anything, Skylar. Just forget whatever extortion scheme you've got in mind. What is it? A kickback for approving my expansion plans, or maybe a generous monthly check from Melanie's trust fund for taking care of her?"

"Extortion? Alienating her affections?" Skylar said in disbelief. "You are really out there, Aaron. Do you know that? You've completely lost touch with reality."

If she had wanted anything from the Cooper *or* Hollister families, she would have taken the money his father tried to give her to keep quiet about having Aaron's baby. Of course, maybe Aaron didn't know about the money. Maybe he didn't know about Karin. But it didn't matter, because he was a complete and utter frigging *jackass*.

"And for your information, I couldn't have given permission to Melanie, because I was never asked," she added.

Aaron snatched back the letter from the lawyer and crumpled it into a tight ball. "My sister—"

"Your sister is a lonely teenager," Skylar interrupted. *Loudly.* "Alienation of a child's affections? Hah. Her mother and father and the rest of your so-called 'family' have done an excellent job of that already. I'd say sixteen years of alienation and making her feel as if she's less important than a trip to Paris or Bali or wherever the idle rich spend their time."

"You don't know anything about my family."

"I know they think child rearing is someone else's responsibility. Melanie deserves better. And if she wants to live with us, she's welcome any time she pleases, no strings attached," Skylar announced impulsively. "At least that way she'll be with people who notice whether she walks in the door at night."

"*Damn it, Skylar.* Don't you dare suggest I'm neglecting my sister."

"That's right—you're always willing to stop by the Nibble Nook and complain because she's here doing her homework and eating nutritious after-school snacks."

"I haven't complained about her snacks."

"It's a good thing, because I'd have to remind you that pizza and salad don't make a balanced diet for anyone, much less a child her age."

They were both breathing hard, and for some unfathomable reason, Skylar was reminded of the last time they were in a car together. It had been…what… February, nearly fifteen years ago? They were both still seventeen at the time, and Aaron's father had given him a bright red Mustang for Christmas to replace the bright yellow one he'd totaled the month before.

Having sex in a Mustang was a challenge, but they'd managed it. Aaron's experience in that area had greatly outstripped her own, though he obviously hadn't noticed—randy boys didn't have a reputation for being overly observant. And considering the contorted positions required to connect in a sports car, it wasn't any wonder that the condoms he'd used had either failed or been worn incorrectly.

An unwelcome twinge went through Skylar's abdomen. Their last time together he'd handed her the condom and she had unrolled it over him, fascinated by his reaction to her touch. All that pulsing heat, and soon it would be inside her... What a stupid idiot she'd been to think she meant more to him than his other girlfriends.

Sex with Aaron had been the greatest mistake she'd ever made, yet how could she regret having Karin—the smart, funny, terrific kid who was the light of her life?

"I'm trying to do better with her food," Aaron muttered. "I don't cook. And I have to be better for her than a stranger."

He gave Skylar an annoyed look that said he still thought she'd influenced Melanie out of some unknown, underhanded motives. That was Aaron. He didn't trust anyone and thought the whole world was out to get him.

Yet a chill went through her. If he got upset enough, would he try to get custody of Karin?

Surely not.

It was hard to imagine him caring after so long—he hadn't even mentioned Karin except in connection to Melanie. Besides, Skylar had kept the proof that S. S. Hollister had tried to pay her off, and it was damning evidence that Aaron and his family had neglected Karin for fourteen years. The awful part would be Karin learning everything in such rotten circumstances. She may have heard rumors about her mother's behavior in high school, but she believed Jimmie was her biological father and had adored him. They ought to have told Karin the truth, but time had slipped by, and then Jimmie was gone.

"We don't have anything more to discuss," she told Aaron, ice in her voice. "Frankly, I don't care if you believe I'm behind that letter from the attorney. And I had nothing to do with my daughter becoming friends with your sister. That was entirely her own doing."

"You didn't discourage her from coming to the Nibble Nook or stop them from spending time together." Though Aaron still seemed annoyed, he didn't sound as belligerent.

"Yeah. Unlike you, I don't see the Nibble Nook as a den of iniquity. My daughter lost her father a year ago this past August and misses him desperately. Having Melanie as a friend makes her happy, even though they mostly just study together. And as for the studying, you ought to be pleased your sister's grades are improving."

Aaron's mouth opened and closed, then opened again. "Of course I'm pleased."

"Think about that the next time you gripe about Melanie doing her homework here a couple of hours a day. Now, if you don't mind, I have a business to run."

Stomach churning, Skylar got out of the truck and walked back to the hamburger stand. Years ago she had stopped hating Aaron for what he'd done, the feeling swept away by the love Jimmie and his parents had showered on her and Karin. Unfortunately, now Aaron was giving her whole new reasons to hate him.

CHAPTER EIGHT

AARON PARKED AND stormed to his office, ignoring Peggy's raised eyebrows. He kicked the corner of his desk, mostly by accident, and spent five minutes cursing as his foot throbbed and his temper cooled.

One of his faults was jumping to conclusions, and he didn't actually *know* that Skylar had encouraged Melanie to see a lawyer, though he was convinced she was hiding something.

But what?

And did it even matter?

Skylar couldn't take Melanie away from her parents. What's more, he had probably blown any chance she would approve his plans to expand the factory. When it came to business he always kept a level head—it was critical to be dispassionate, particularly when hard decisions had to be made. Now Skylar had turned him into a raving lunatic.

What was it about her that triggered such irrational behavior? Despite having dated her on a bet, he'd liked Skylar when they were teens, and her defiant bravado had fascinated him. She'd broken the rules and damned the consequences. But she hadn't been the kind of girl he could have taken to meet his grandparents. Their impossible standards had driven him crazy, yet he'd bought into them at the same time.

Dragging a deep breath into his lungs, Aaron began counting to a hundred in French. It was a method he'd employed when his grandfather was lecturing him about some damn thing or other. Losing his temper with George was as pointless as arguing with a granite boulder.

Perhaps his real issue was being back in Cooperton, making him lose all sense of proportion. He'd hated his childhood here, being shuffled off to live with people he hardly knew...people who didn't approve of energetic small boys. As the years had passed and he'd gotten older, he had spent as little time as possible with the Coopers, hanging out with his friends and doing after-school sports—anything to put off walking into that formal, unfriendly house.

The funny thing was, as much as he'd resented his grandparents as a kid, he'd also craved their approval.

But Melanie's situation wasn't the same as his. Perhaps he'd seemed unreasonable about the Nibble Nook, but she'd kept going there, anyhow. What's more, he didn't assign chores, he gave her money for whatever she wanted and he was trying to get involved in things like the school carnival, though he wasn't a parent and never planned to be.

Oh, God.

The carnival.

Aaron grimaced as he recalled the debate between the principal and president of the Parent–Teacher's

Association over whether he should take a turn at the carnival's fund-raising dunk tank. He'd finally pointed out that he hadn't brought a change of clothing, which put an end to the discussion. Instead he'd given a donation to the cause and wandered around, trying not to pay attention to how inseparable Melanie and Skylar's daughter appeared to be.

Yet with so many people there, he should have been glad the girls were using the buddy system. Besides, Karin was a nice kid—funny and smart and mature beyond her years. And she didn't take guff from anyone…a trait she obviously inherited from her mom.

Aaron stood by his window and gazed at the land beyond. The administrative offices were at the extreme edge of the factory complex. While the view wasn't particularly beautiful, it was better than looking out on a sea of buildings. If he adjusted his plans to suit one of Skylar's suggestions, all the new buildings would be constructed in that direction and the vista would change to a vast expanse of concrete.

Of course, if she didn't approve his plans, he might have to move the company to another county— Cooper Industries owned a good deal of land north of Sacramento, and properties in the state capitol and San Francisco, as well. He planned to sell some of the holdings to obtain financing, but he could also *build* elsewhere.

Yet as Aaron thought about the alternate sites, he recalled Skylar's accusations the night of the city council meeting…that nobody knew what he'd do to protect his priorities. If she found out that he was considering building a whole new facility away from Cooperton, she'd probably stick a knife in his chest, because ultimately it would ring a death knell for the local plant.

A tap on the door jolted him from his darker thoughts, and he turned around. "Yes?"

Peggy stepped inside. She was an iron-ramrod sort of woman, with short, no-nonsense gray hair and a mouth perpetually drawn in an expression of disapproval. Not unlike his grandfather, Aaron mused.

"Mr. Hollister, I've prepared a file of messages Mr. Cooper issued to the employees, along with other paperwork pertinent to the company," she said, extending a folder.

Aaron raised an eyebrow as he took it. "I didn't ask to see these."

"*I* felt it was a good idea."

A muscle tightened in his jaw.

Peggy's biggest fault was trying to get him to return to his grandfather's way of doing things. This must be her latest salvo in the battle. What she didn't understand—or anyone else apparently—was that the company couldn't survive if it kept doing things "George Cooper's way." Sure, they could go on for another decade, their place in the market slowly diminishing. Yet sooner or later the costs of outdated manufacturing equipment and facilities would become greater than their profits.

"I'll read it if I get a chance," he told Peggy, flipping through the file, noting dates that went back to when he was a boy.

"Mr. Cooper *always*—"

"Mr. Cooper isn't running this business any longer," Aaron reminded her impatiently. "It's time for modernization."

She drew herself up and practically sniffed. "Modern isn't always better."

"It's necessary if you want your neighbors to have jobs in ten years." His tone was unnecessarily sharp, but he was tired of her attitude. It felt like a lifetime since he'd returned to Cooperton—five nonstop months of trying to fix problems before they became critical and having his methods questioned. If it wasn't Peggy, it was somebody else.

"Fine. If you want modern, you can have my resignation. It will be on your desk by the end of the day."

"That isn't what I said, but I would appreciate your support, rather than attempts to stuff my grandfather's methods down my throat," he returned bluntly, gesturing with the thick file she'd given him. "You have a wealth of knowledge about Cooper Industries and could be a valuable asset to me, but you need to accept that I'm in charge now, not George Cooper."

Peggy turned on her heel and slammed the door. He didn't know if it was to write a letter of resignation or return to work, and at the moment he didn't care.

The company belonged to him now; his grandfather had signed it over when he retired…not that it was worth much any longer aside from the property it owned. What puzzled Aaron was where the company profits had gone for the past thirty years. *Nothing* had been reinvested in the business—there was a modest account for emergency repairs and that was all. Grandfather had subsidized the company cafeteria for a decade, yet that wasn't enough to explain things, either.

Granted, the company profits represented the only compensation Aaron himself would receive. It had been the same for his grandfather, but his grandparents' personal needs weren't extravagant. They could have afforded to keep the factory updated and still have plenty. Of course, his grandparents might have saved the money or given it to various causes, such as the restoration of Cooperton City Hall…though in the end it would have been kinder to keep the business viable.

Pain pulsing in his temples, Aaron sat down at his computer.

He needed to let his father and Eliza know about the attorney's letter, but how did you tell someone their daughter no longer wanted to be their daughter? Even Spence might get a momentary ripple in his peace of mind over that.

Still, it was just a letter; no legal action had been filed. He could put off telling Spence and Eliza until he'd spoken to Melanie. And Eliza was probably out of touch, anyhow. She'd sent an email about trekking to a remote game preserve where there wouldn't be a signal for her cell, though she'd provided a satellite phone number for "absolute emergencies."

He didn't think she'd consider something like this an emergency. Very little bothered Eliza, and she'd probably dismiss it as a bid for attention …the way *he* had when Melanie asked to move in with her friend.

Aaron fished the crumpled note from the attorney out of his pocket and smoothed the paper. Yet as he reviewed the careful legal language, his ire began to rise again—if Skylar didn't have anything to do with this scheme, how *had* Melanie come up with it?

SKYLAR HURRIED HER employees through cleanup and sent them on their way so she could get a private moment with Karin and Melanie when they arrived.

The girls were settled at their favorite table by the time Greg and the others had gone. Skylar took a tray out and set it down. "Karin, please go inside for a few minutes. I need to talk with Melanie."

Karin set her mouth stubbornly.

"Please let her stay," Melanie pleaded. Her eyes were terrified.

Skylar sat down. "All right. I had a visit from your brother earlier. He was upset about a letter he received from a lawyer this afternoon."

"H-how upset?"

Livid.

Yet Skylar suspected Aaron had mostly been angry with *her,* rather than his sister.

"He's concerned," she said carefully.

"Why did he talk to *you,* Mom?" Karin asked. "Mr. Newman didn't say where Melanie wanted to live in his letter. I mean, it's with us, of course, and I guess we should have asked first, but I was sure you'd want Mellie."

"Is it okay?" Melanie's eyes were big and anxious, and Skylar saw the fear that she wasn't really wanted...*again.*

Damn.

"I told Aaron that you were welcome to move in with us."

The sixteen-year-old's shoulders sagged in sudden relief, and her eyes were bright with tears. "Thank you, Mrs. Gibson. I'll be good, I promise."

Skylar squeezed her hand. "I'm not worried about that, but it isn't that simple."

"It should be," Karin asserted.

"Karin, Melanie is underage and she *has* parents and other family who care about her," Skylar said slowly. "And, Melanie, I don't understand why you didn't talk to your brother before contacting a lawyer."

"I did. Last Saturday before the carnival. I asked him if I could live with you and Karin, but he wouldn't even think about it."

Skylar hid her dismay. She sympathized with the lonely teenager, yet all of this was stressing an already-difficult situation. It was a miracle Aaron hadn't confronted her before, especially after getting his nose out of joint over the lawn-mower incident.

Honestly, why did men refuse to read directions?

Skylar had laughed when she saw Aaron yanking on that lawn mower cord, but he hadn't looked ridiculous, he'd looked sexy. When he ditched his suit and wore jeans and a shirt like a mere mortal instead of a CEO, he was so attractive he made a woman think irrational things. She pushed the image away; Aaron Hollister's sex appeal was the last thing she ought to be thinking about.

"Did you tell Aaron I'd already given permission for you to move in with us?"

"Uh…" Melanie looked scared again. "I kind of did. I didn't mean it the way it came out and tried to say that I hadn't asked yet, but it got mixed up when he said no, and then I didn't think it would matter. I'm really sorry. I'll tell him right away."

"All right." Skylar couldn't bring herself to scold the teen. "Is your lawyer willing to talk to your brother?" Somebody needed to check the attorney out and make sure everything was aboveboard. Aaron was the logical person as his sister's temporary guardian.

"I don't want Aaron talking to Mr. Newman," Melanie answered, flustered. "But you can. Mr. Newman asked who he could speak to, and I told him you and nobody else."

"They just talk on the phone," Karin volunteered. "His office is on Main Street. He's new."

That made Skylar feel better, but she still thought

someone should meet the man face-to-face and make sure he wasn't taking advantage of a kid.

And…well, if he *was* legit, it wouldn't hurt to have someone to call in case Aaron tried to get custody of Karin.

She told the girls to eat their snacks and went inside to call the attorney. His secretary said he was available at four o'clock, so she bundled Melanie and Karin into the truck to run them home.

Mr. Newman's office was upstairs in one of the 1910-era buildings on city hall square, with twelve-foot-high ceilings covered by decorative pressed tin. The ice-cream-and-sandwich parlor on the first floor was a favorite with young and old, yet the cheerful din below couldn't be heard as Skylar stepped into the front office and introduced herself.

"Hello, Mrs. Gibson. Go right in," his secretary invited her with a smile.

The lawyer stood as Skylar walked inside and stuck out his hand. "Hello, I'm Jeremy Newman. I've wanted to meet Karin's mother—your daughter is a very determined young lady."

"Unfortunately I can't return the compliment. Today is the first I've heard of their scheme, Mr. Newman."

He chuckled. "I suspected they were acting on their own. Please have a seat. And call me Jeremy."

Skylar sat down and studied the lawyer. He was blond, tanned, and had an easygoing smile and boyish eagerness that make him look more like a Southern California surfer than an attorney. On his third finger he wore a broad wedding band that looked shiny and new, the way her husband's ring had looked in the first months of their marriage.

"In the first place," Jeremy said, "let me assure you that I have not, and will not, meet with Melanie alone. If it becomes necessary to see her in person, my secretary will be present. Or you, if Melanie agrees."

"I'll make sure she understands that," Skylar murmured.

"Excellent. Now, I take client/attorney confidentiality very seriously, but she's given permission for us to speak."

"In that case, I want to know what you hoped to accomplish with that letter."

The lawyer leaned forward in his chair. "A change. Melanie is two years older than your daughter, has traveled extensively, comes from very affluent circumstances, and yet she's far less self-assured. She desperately wants a place to call home and people who show how much they care about her. It's enough to question if her mother and father are blind, or truly aren't concerned for their child's emotional welfare."

"Be careful," Skylar warned. "S. S. Hollister is one of the wealthiest men in the country, and his ex-wife is the daughter of a prominent New York senator who could be our next president."

Jeremy shrugged. "Correspondence from me isn't going to intimidate either one of them, but it could push them into trying harder."

Knowing what she did about S. S. Hollister, Skylar

doubted the aging playboy would change his ways. Melanie's mother could be another matter. From the teenager's stories it sounded as if Eliza Tremont had been more involved with her daughter's life before she remarried. If she woke up and made the choice to *be* a mother, it would be best for Melanie, though it might mean she would have to live elsewhere.

A twinge of worry went through Skylar.

The two girls had become such fast friends, who knew what the "best" thing was? They were both dealing with serious issues and felt alienated from other kids. If they hadn't met at the preschool term mixer the principal hosted every August, they probably would have still gravitated together in a school as small as Cooperton High.

"What about the parent–child divorce?" Skylar asked.

The lawyer grinned engagingly. "Got your attention, didn't it? I think it was your daughter's idea. My specialty isn't family law, but I'll help Melanie file to be an emancipated minor if she insists. However, I'll tell you what I told her—I don't believe she has the maturity and confidence yet to make adult decisions, and a judge is likely to recognize it, as well."

"And pursuing emancipation could alienate her further from her family," Skylar said.

"Precisely. Besides, a judge may look at it this way—Melanie's physical needs are generously met, she is always left in the care of responsible adults, her trust fund ensures a future of her choosing and she sees her parents nearly as often as a child in boarding school. What's more, Melanie acknowledges they love her. And to be honest, I'm personally not partial to legal action between a child and parent except when there's abuse."

"Maybe you should have studied family counseling instead of becoming an attorney."

"You could be right, except I like having the law in my pocket when everything else fails. And sometimes the *threat* of legal action is just as effective as anything you could do in court. An attorney's letterhead can be impressive."

Skylar recalled Aaron's angry face. "You didn't impress Aaron Hollister—you pissed him off. He raced over with a full head of steam, blaming me."

"My letter didn't mention you or your daughter."

"Aaron and I don't get along well—he doesn't approve of my hamburger stand as a hangout for his sister, though we're closed by the time they arrive and all they do is study together. The girls know how he feels, but apparently Melanie still asked if she could live with us. When he refused, they called you."

Jeremy Newman's eyes narrowed, and Skylar got the feeling he was a lot tougher than his laid-back appearance suggested. "Interesting. In light of what I've heard about Mr. Hollister's relationship with his employees, he may not be the best guardian for a sensitive adolescent."

Curiously, Skylar felt a fleeting impulse to defend Aaron. He was making questionable personnel decisions at Cooper Industries, and she herself had criticized his efforts with Melanie, but parenting was tough, and he'd gotten thrown into the deep end without any preparation.

"According to Melanie, she almost ended up in boarding school this year before Aaron agreed to take her. She hates the idea, so it's hard to say what's best," Skylar said noncommittally. "Anyhow, it's getting late and I need to get dinner ready. I may need to… That is…thank you for meeting with me."

"You're welcome."

They shook hands again and Skylar hurried out. At least the lawyer appeared straightforward and concerned. She'd been on the verge of telling him that Aaron was Karin's biological father, only to change her mind. It wasn't the right time, and she could always call him later if she needed legal advice.

Karin *would* have to be told someday, but with Jimmie gone, Skylar wanted to wait until she was old enough to handle it.

AARON CAME TO an inescapable conclusion over a sleepless night—he owed Skylar an apology. She had good reason to think he was a maniac the way he'd accused her of every crime under the sun.

She still got to him.

And as much as he wanted to keep seeing her as the rebel who'd broken every rule in the book, the image of a hardworking, outspoken Skylar kept intruding. She was a far cry from the women he'd dated over the years, but that was a good thing…. He couldn't see them working so hard and still being the kind of mother that Melanie envied her friend for having.

Hell, Skylar was a member of the city council. She ran a business. She had a fresh-faced kid who was far more likely to ask for an ice cream than to sneak a shot of whiskey. And Melanie had made a point of saying she'd gotten an A on her history paper because of Skylar's help.

Aaron dropped Melanie at the library and drove to the address that he'd found in the phone book for the Gibsons. It was a comfortable-looking place, possibly an old farmhouse, located on a larger lot than most of the surrounding homes. Nobody answered when he rang the bell and he glanced around, noting the yard-waste recycle barrel on the driveway and Skylar's truck parked on the street.

She *had* to be there.

He followed a flagstone path on the north side of the house and peered through the open gate. Skylar's back was to him as she knelt, spreading dark wood mulch around a cluster of ferns. The snug fit of her denims made Aaron's mouth go dry.

Living with a teenager had put a serious crimp in his social life, yet he suspected Skylar would affect him, regardless. If anything, her figure had improved since they were teenagers, and back then every boy at Cooperton High had been hot to get into her jeans.

"Uh…hello," he called.

Skylar turned her head and regarded him without smiling. "Here to throw more accusations at me?"

"I came to apologize. I'm sorry for the way I acted."

"Yeah, right."

Obviously, she wasn't going to make it easy. Aaron stepped past the corner of the house and looked around in surprise. The landscaping in front was nice, but this was a masterpiece—private, artfully simple, with a water feature that flowed over native rock slabs into a natural-looking pool. It was as if he'd stumbled across a mountain stream in a forest clearing. Even the deck was largely concealed by native bushes and ferns.

A flash of silver came from the large, shaded pool and Aaron walked over, expecting to see brightly colored koi in the water. Instead there were long, brownish fish, occasionally flipping their iridescent bellies to the sky.

"Those are rainbow trout," he exclaimed, kneeling to look closer. "This yard is extraordinary—you should be a landscape architect."

"Why? Because flipping hamburgers is too common?" Skylar got to her feet and lifted a bucket with hand tools sticking from it. "By the way, this is private property, not a public park."

"Are you going to have me arrested for trespassing?"

"No, but only because it would upset Melanie."

She walked to an opposite gate and he followed. Between the house and the detached garage was a vegetable plot, with tomatoes still turning red in the lingering summerlike autumn weather.

"I had no idea you were such a gardener. This must take hours every day to keep up," he mused.

"Not really, it's low maintenance wherever possible. I need to get out here a couple of times a week during the summer, but I don't mind. Gardening helps clear your head."

"Maybe, but I hated yard work when I was kid. Raking, weeding, watering—it was endless around my grandparents' house, and they were fanatics about everything being exactly so."

"You mean the Coopers didn't hire people to do that?"

"Nope. The only thing I didn't do was the mowing. My grandparents felt children should be seen and not heard, and had to be taught the value of hard work by doing chores. Lots of them. I can't tell you how many times I heard my grandfather declare that idle hands were the devil's playground, but I didn't see *him* out there raking leaves."

Skylar lifted an eyebrow. "Are you suggesting you were abused?"

The question took Aaron aback. "Of course not. But they went overboard sometimes, and were distant and authoritarian."

"Weren't they almost sixty when you came here? It couldn't have been easy at their age, taking in a young child."

"Maybe, but nothing I could do was good enough

for them. It doesn't surprise me that my mother hates coming back to Cooperton and has my stepfather hire someone to do everything for her. She must have gotten just as tired of their nitpicking as I did."

"Sorry to disagree, but from what I've heard, your mother didn't *do* chores."

"She must have. It's the Cooper philosophy of child rearing."

"Not according to the people who knew her growing up." Skylar knelt and began picking bell peppers into a basket. "According to the stories, Celina Cooper was adored and indulged like a princess. It's the same story from everyone. A retired teacher who attends our church says Celina wasn't even expected to do her schoolwork."

"That's just small town gossip," Aaron muttered. He was already regretting telling Skylar about his life with the Coopers—it wasn't a secret, but his grandparents kept their personal affairs private and he tried to respect that. "It doesn't mean anything."

Still, his mother *did* act like a princess who couldn't be troubled by unpleasant realities. The biggest trauma in her life was divorcing her first husband—Spence was far too egocentric and self-indulgent to stay married to anyone for long. So when she remarried it was to a New York businessman whose chief pleasure in life was indulging her.

Aaron frowned.

He'd always known his grandparents hoped he'd turn out different from his mother, but he hadn't realized their treatment of him was so disparate. Not that he'd wanted to be indulged, and the chores hadn't actually been that bad if he was honest, but surely it wouldn't have killed them to pat his back occasionally. Or how about a word of praise every now and then?

Mostly it would have been nice if they'd cared about him as their grandson, and not a responsibility they'd accepted out of their damned sense of duty.

CHAPTER NINE

SKYLAR TRIED NOT to look at Aaron as she continued picking peppers from her garden. The sad, isolated expression was back in his eyes, the one that had gotten to her as a girl. It made her want to comfort him, which unsettled her the same way her fleeting impulse to defend him to Jeremy Newman had disturbed her.

Aaron was not a vulnerable boy who needed her defense. He was a grown man, more than capable of taking care of himself.

Still, it must have been strange growing up in a town named after his mother's family, a place where everyone knew his business because he was George Cooper's grandson. People enjoyed gossiping in Cooperton, and they particularly enjoyed gossiping about their founding family. It had been one of the challenges of moving back here with Jimmie—she couldn't get away from idle chitchat about the Coopers. Her husband had left the decision to her, but she hadn't wanted Karin attending school in Trident, with them working in Cooperton. So they'd bought their house and she'd dealt with the reminders of her connection to Aaron.

Skylar moved to a row of green beans, and to her surprise, Aaron crouched beside her and began picking them, as well. The silence was curiously tranquil.

"You seem interested in organic products," he said at length. "Is this all pesticide-free?"

"Yes. The area used to be farmland, so I can't be sure what chemicals were used in the past, but my vegetable garden is on the site of three chicken coops and was never under commercial cultivation."

Aaron scrunched up his nose. "Chickens?"

"Yeah. Chicken manure is great fertilizer. The soil is quite fertile, though usually by this time in October I'm just getting remnants from the summer crop or it's done altogether."

Together with Jimmie, she'd planted a variety of fruit trees when they bought the house. At the end of the growing season she had the freezer filled, in addition to the jars of jams and jellies and applesauce she put up—her mother-in-law was an enthusiastic home canner and had taught Skylar the art.

Skylar supposed it wasn't necessary to have a large home garden when she could get organic fruits and vegetables for relatively low prices from the farmers, but it was satisfying to grow your own food. The neighbors had expressed their surprise when she had kept it up after Jimmie's accident, thinking it would be too much for her, but she'd needed the solitude and sense of renewal.

"By the way, where is Karin?" Aaron asked.

It was the first real inquiry Skylar remembered

him making about Karin that wasn't connected to Melanie, and her nerves went on alert.

"Er…down at the church. The youth group painted the social hall and restrooms in the basement several months ago, but the colors they chose were appalling. Chartreuse for the men's room, fluorescent pink for the women's and yellow for the public areas."

"The yellow doesn't sound too bad. The rest must be hideous."

"They're all bad. We just have small, high windows in the basement, but you need sunglasses to go down there. It's like being inside a psychedelic lemon. As for the women's restroom, our eldest member practically had a heart attack the first time she walked in and turned on the light."

Aaron chuckled. "Why take so long to repaint?"

Skylar tossed a last bean into the basket and straightened. "At first the trustees were trying to find a gracious way of telling the youth leaders that they'd completely lost their minds letting teenagers pick out the colors without any guidance."

"Why not be blunt? I wouldn't put up with such poor judgment from an employee."

"Because they're not employees, Aaron, they're *volunteers,*" Skylar explained, exasperated. "And even if they weren't, it's a big job to lead a youth group. You want the kids to have fun and at the same time be service-oriented, so mistakes get made, like giving them too much freedom at the home-improvement store. They've made other decisions that were fine. Besides, the kid's intentions were good—they wanted to brighten things up."

"How did it get resolved if everybody was trying to be diplomatic?"

"The youth decided on their own to go out and raise money for more primer and paint. They asked the treasurer's wife to pick the new colors—she works in Sacramento as an interior decorator—and then had the trustees approve her choices."

According to Karin, the decision to paint again came when they overheard someone say they'd rather pee their pants than go into one of *those* restrooms.

"How did they raise the money?"

Skylar shrugged. "Car washes and bake sales, that kind of thing." She knew they had done yard work as well, but didn't want to tell Aaron. Though a number of teenagers in Cooperton had an active business in door-to-door lawn mowing, it wasn't surprising that they'd avoided his house, especially if their parents worked for Cooper Industries. She doubted Aaron truly understood how unhappy his employees were with him. There probably *were* stinkers in the bunch who'd gotten away with murder, but most people were hardworking and meant well.

"Mind if I try them?" Aaron asked, gesturing to her cherry-tomato vines. "I've never seen ones like that."

"Go ahead."

He picked several of the small round tomatoes and popped them in his mouth. Pleasure spread across his face. "Delicious. What variety are they?"

"Sweet 100s. I don't think they're very commercial because of the size, but home gardeners like them, and some of the truck farmers sell containers at roadside stands."

A second basket was overflowing with tomatoes and squash when Skylar had finally had enough. Her gardening was done for the day, and she didn't intend to invite Aaron into the house. She dropped her clippers into her tool bucket and faced him.

"Aaron, you've apologized. Why are you still here?"

AARON DIDN'T HAVE an answer, mostly because he didn't know why he was hanging around.

"I thought…that is, as part of my apology, I want to invite you to dinner."

Skylar's eyes narrowed in suspicion. "Dinner?"

"Yeah, dinner. Someplace nice. We can drive into Sacramento. There's a great French Creole restaurant on a restored riverboat in Old Sacramento called the Dixie Damsel—they make a fabulous jambalaya. And their traditional red-beans-and-rice dish could be right out of a restaurant in New Orleans's French Quarter. Or we could go somewhere else. How about it?"

Now that he'd proposed the idea, it seemed a perfect way to make peace between them.

"I…well, maybe."

The fact she hadn't instantly refused was encouraging.

"How about tonight? I can arrange a sitter for Karin if you think it's needed."

"She's too old to need a sitter for an evening, but I don't like leaving her alone late."

"In that case, I'll buy a couple of movies and a pizza from Vittorino's and bring Melanie over here. I'm sure they'd love it." It was bizarre that he was proposing any such thing in light of his sister's wish to live with the Gibsons, but it was also possible that if he stopped trying to end the friendship, Melanie wouldn't care as much about moving in with them.

Skylar shuffled her feet, indecision on her face. "There's no need for us to have dinner. It won't have any impact on my decision about your expansion proposal."

"I didn't think it would. Come on, wouldn't it be nice to have an adult night out?"

"I suppose."

"See, that didn't hurt too much to admit. When do you think Karin will be done with her painting project?"

"It shouldn't be later than three or four. It's a two-step process. The colors are so intense they have to cover them with primer and let it dry. They won't actually put the top coat of semigloss on until next Saturday." She glanced at her watch. "Come to think of it, I have to leave in a few minutes. The parents are providing lunch for the group, and I'm supposed to pick up an order of deli sandwiches from the supermarket."

"Then I'll bring a pizza for Melanie and Karin

when I come, and we can decide where to eat while driving to Sacramento."

Skylar didn't respond for a minute, and he wondered if she was trying to find a way to refuse. "Okay, but Karin likes her pizza with everything except anchovies and bell peppers, and Melanie's favorite is Hawaiian, so make it half-and-half. Better yet, *ask* your sister what she wants."

Hawaiian?

Aaron winced, recalling all the meat-lover's pizzas he'd ordered over the past few months. Skylar had been right when they'd argued a few weeks ago—he *hadn't* asked Melanie what pizza she preferred; he'd just assumed.

"Uh, sure. How about a salad? I can get something from Mama Gianni's."

"No, I'll make one."

He glanced down at the variety of fresh-picked vegetables in the two baskets. Skylar would probably concoct something healthy and delicious out of them, but it didn't seem right. "You shouldn't have to cook."

She shrugged. "I prefer making it myself."

Aaron didn't want to annoy her again, so he didn't argue. Once they'd agreed on five o'clock, he left quickly. Sudden doubts were assailing him about the evening out, since his married acquaintances claimed two kids could get into four times as much trouble as one. He was new to all of this and didn't want to make a mistake, though it was becoming obvious that Eliza had exaggerated her daughter's health issues, along with her supposed habit of lying. Melanie *had* lied about Skylar giving her permission to move in and shown a few other behavioral problems, but nothing serious.

He pushed the thought from his head.

Parenting Melanie for a year was probably going to give him gray hair and take ten years off his life, yet he was really enjoying having her.

SKYLAR SPENT THE afternoon kicking herself for agreeing to Aaron's plan.

Never in her life had she expected to eat dinner with him again. Not that they were going out on a date. He'd said the invitation was an apology, and it *was* possible he regretted acting like an idiot. What he probably didn't understand was that letting Melanie spend the evening with Karin was more of an apology than having dinner at a dozen expensive restaurants.

One of the other parents dropped Karin off shortly before three. Her clothes, hair and skin were generously streaked with primer, and she wore a happy grin.

"It's gonna be great having Mellie over," she exclaimed when she heard the news. "And I can show her the spare bedroom."

"Don't get your hopes up about her moving in," Skylar warned. "That isn't what tonight is about."

"It *could* happen," Karin said earnestly. "Her mom and dad don't care where she lives."

"You don't know that. Anyhow, go into the bathroom and get those clothes off so I can put them in the washing machine. And take a shower. You must have more paint on you than on the walls."

"Naw. You should have seen some of the other kids."

Her daughter cheerfully tossed out her T-shirt and shorts, and Skylar dumped them into the washer to soak. She doubted much of the primer would come out, but it didn't matter. They were the clothes Karin had used in the original painting project and already bore liberal dabs of pink, chartreuse and yellow. The only reason Skylar hadn't thrown them away before was because she'd suspected the youth group would be *re*painting the restrooms and social hall.

Karin's skin was red from scrubbing—and still not free of paint—when she emerged from her bedroom.

"I did my best, Mom," she said, exasperated when Skylar tried to scrape bits of primer from her hair.

"It looks as if you painted with your head, instead of a brush."

Karin rolled her eyes. "The guys got silly, that's all. But Mr. Calderas stopped them when it was too bad."

"I should hope so."

"Honest, I didn't get nearly as much on me as the others. Well, *some* of the others," her daughter modified, her cheeks turning an even-brighter crimson.

Skylar didn't question her further—she imagined Karin had been in the thick of the fun, but if Alonzo Calderas or Mrs. Hashima hadn't called to say she needed to go home, it was probably all right.

"Fine. I want you to feed Bennie and take care of his litter box before Melanie gets here. And you didn't make your bed this morning or pick up your room, so that needs to be done, as well."

Karin kept her good humor as she set to work, but Skylar remembered what Aaron had said about his chores as a boy. She believed children should have age-appropriate responsibilities, but they should still get to be kids. *Had* his grandparents gone overboard, the way he claimed, or was it just a spoiled boy's view of things?

She didn't have time to think about it, though—it was nearly five and she needed to get ready. Racing in and out of the shower, she grabbed a dress from the closet and pulled it on with barely a look in the mirror. She'd just finished brushing her hair and was walking down the hallway when the doorbell rang. Karin ran ahead of her to answer.

"Hello, Mrs. Gibson," Melanie said as she stepped inside, Aaron behind her. "Thank you for having me."

Her polite words made Skylar's heart ache—so formal and anxious, even though she'd been coming to the Nibble Nook to study with Karin for over a month.

"You're welcome. *Anytime.*"

Skylar was conscious that Aaron's jaw had tightened, but it seemed more important to reassure Melanie than to keep peace. If he wanted to keep believing she was trying to sway his sister's affections, that was *his* problem.

"Come on, Mellie, I'll show you my room." Karin half dragged her friend to the back of the house.

"This way," Skylar said to Aaron, taking the pizza box and carrying it into the kitchen. He set two groceries bags on the counter.

"I hope it's all right. I also brought sodas, ice cream and chips and dip," he said. "Melanie has the DVDs— she thought Karin would like to start watching the *Star Trek: The Next Generation* television series, so that's what we got instead of movies."

"Sounds good."

He was wearing a suit, and she cast a quick look down at her dress. It was a dark green jersey knit, which wasn't especially dressy, and she couldn't recall the last time she'd worn it. Well, tough. If it wasn't good enough, that was *also* his problem.

Aaron took out two cartons of ice cream and handed them to her. It was an expensive brand, and she shrugged as she put them in the freezer. Karin wouldn't get spoiled in one evening, and Melanie probably didn't know there was any other kind of ice cream. The soda was an all-natural brand, and she put it in the refrigerator as well, along with the dip.

"I didn't make reservations since we hadn't decided where to eat," Aaron said. "But we're early enough, so it shouldn't be a problem."

"The Dixie Damsel sounds fine if I'm dressed okay."

"You look terrific." He sounded sincere, and Skylar fought a faint flash of satisfaction. She hadn't intended to say anything about her clothing, but her ego had momentarily taken control of her mouth.

"It's my 'mom dress,' at least that's what Karin calls it."

"Mom dress?"

"Dull, in other words." She didn't add anything else, and didn't know why she said it in the first place. "I'll check on the girls and let them know we're going." Skylar hurried to Karin's bedroom and found the teens sitting on the floor, petting Bennie and chattering away.

They looked so much like sisters that Skylar's breath caught in her throat. She was insane to have Aaron anywhere around Karin. What if he saw the resemblance?

"Karin, the pizza is on the counter by the stove," she said hoarsely. "There's also a garden salad in the fridge. And, uh, Melanie's brother brought ice cream and chips and soda."

"Thanks, Mom."

"Yes, thank you, Mrs. Gibson." Melanie smiled shyly.

"You're welcome. Have a good time. Call my cell phone if there's a problem and keep—"

"The doors locked," Karin finished for her. "I know, 'cept I want to show Mellie the backyard first."

"All right, lock up after that."

Skylar grabbed her purse and a shawl and practically ran back to the kitchen. Aaron looked mildly startled as she bolted in, and she tried to smile naturally.

"Shall we go?"

"Sure."

He was a perfect gentleman, helping her into the Mercedes and closing the door for her…old-fashioned courtesies he'd obviously learned since they were teenagers. Or else he hadn't thought it was necessary to be a gentleman toward a girl with her reputation.

Not that she'd really *expected* those courtesies, either.

Skylar frowned at the thought.

It was an unpleasant pill to swallow, but maybe, deep down, she'd believed she deserved Aaron's treatment. After all, how could a girl with her background expect better? The same way everyone in town had known about his parents and grandparents, they'd known about her folks—the shabby house with the weeds and broken-down cars, the foul-mouthed exchanges with the neighbors and police…the drunken, violent fights. Her mother and father were probably in jail or had killed each other by now.

Maybe her cocky teenage defiance had covered even more insecurity than she'd realized.

But there was one thing Skylar was certain of…she wouldn't let anyone make her feel worthless again.

MELANIE THOUGHT THERE couldn't be anything better than lying on the big, comfy couch in the Gibsons' family room, eating pizza and watching *Star Trek*.

"I'm stuffed," Karin said, dropping a pizza crust on her plate.

"Me, too. But I want to have some more of your mom's salad. Did she really grow it all herself?"

"Uh-huh."

Melanie had seen the vegetable garden, along with the pond in the backyard, but it still seemed like magic that you could grow something yourself and eat it. Most of the places she'd lived didn't have gardens. Maybe they had grass or something, and flowers in window boxes, but nothing like the Gibsons' house. The place Aaron was renting had an awfully big yard, only it was just grass and trees, too. Living with Karin would be awesome. Of course, she'd thought so *before* she'd seen their house, but it was even better now.

She'd expected Aaron to be pissed when he found out about the lawyer, but he'd been pretty nice about it and had tried to listen when she explained. Not that he'd understood. He just kept telling her it wasn't possible, and that he was sure things would get better if she talked to her mother. She noticed he didn't bother saying she should talk to their father.

"Don't you think it's weird that my mom and your brother are going out to dinner?" Karin asked.

Melanie ate another bite of pizza. Aaron had gotten half Hawaiian with extra pineapple, the way she liked it best. Nobody ever got extra pineapple for her, and she *loooved* it that way.

"I bet they're talking about Aaron's company," she said. "He's been having meetings with her, and according to my uncle Jackson who's a stockbroker, more gets done over dinner than in regular meetings. He says cocktails grease a lot of deals."

"It won't work with Mom—she doesn't drink. She didn't mind if my dad had a beer, only she wouldn't have any herself."

"When we were in Paris this summer my mother gave me a glass of wine. Yuck."

"But Paris sounds great."

Melanie shrugged. "Much better than the trip two years ago. We went to an ashram in India." She made a face.

"What's *that?*"

"Kind of a monastery, I think. They were nice and all, but all they do is yoga and meditating. You have to be quiet and they tell you to clear your mind and focus and stuff. *For hours.* They wouldn't even let me have my MP3 player."

"Borrrring."

"Yeah. I wanted to see the Taj Mahal, only there wasn't time."

"We go camping for vacation. You should have seen Grandpa Joe when a raccoon stole his wristwatch a few months ago. He chased it in his pajamas, but it went up a tree and peed on his head." She giggled, and Melanie giggled with her. "And we go to Disneyland a couple times a year."

Melanie sighed enviously. "I've always wanted to go there."

"You've never been to Disneyland? Even though you stayed in Los Angeles for a whole spring?" Karin sounded horrified. "It's the best place in the world. We'll have to tell Mr. Newman." She scribbled something on a pad of paper. "Let's see, he wanted to know where you've lived. I've written down Boston, New York, Los Angeles...and where else?"

"I've lost count—it's too depressing. Everybody keeps saying how lucky I am to travel so much, but how would *they* like to move every few months? And I usually don't get to see much of a place when I stay there. I was in Brisbane with one of my mother's friends for four months, and we never left the city. Worst of all, they have a different school year in Australia, and I had to start in the middle of a term when they sent me back to the States."

"I know, but Mr. Newman still wants a list."

Melanie sighed and began telling her the different towns. It really *was* depressing. Staying with Aaron was turning out okay, but it was only until June, which left another whole year and two months after that before she turned eighteen.

She just had to do something to change things.

CHAPTER TEN

"I DIDN'T KNOW there was another restored riverboat in Old Sacramento," Skylar commented after dinner as they strolled along the river. The brightly lit Delta King riverboat was ahead of them, and the hotel and restaurant added ambiance to the historic district.

The breeze off the water was pleasantly crisp compared to the warm restaurant, and she adjusted her wrap over her shoulders.

"The Dixie Damsel is small compared to the Delta King," Aaron said. "But the atmosphere is great."

He tucked her arm around his elbow. It was another old-fashioned courtesy, reminding Skylar of her thoughts driving into the city. She didn't enjoy remembering how it had felt as a kid, being cocky and afraid at the same time.

"I always thought it would be fun to stay at the Delta King, or take a riverboat cruise up the Mississippi. When I dreamed…" Her voice trailed and she pressed her lips together.

"You dreamed what?"

"Nothing."

Skylar didn't want to share her childhood dreams with Aaron. It wouldn't interest him anyhow, and she could imagine what he'd think about the rebellious girl she'd been, secretly wishing for a romantic honeymoon. Talk about conflicted—on one hand she'd defiantly tried to live down to people's expectations, and on the other, she'd fantasized about ideal families and happily-ever-afters. And until Jimmie's accident she'd gotten her fantasy…a loving husband and the Gibsons and Karin.

They strolled past a street musician, and Aaron tossed a ten-dollar bill into his open violin case.

"I used to wish I had one iota of musical talent," he said as they walked on.

Skylar was grateful he hadn't pushed for an answer. They'd had a pleasant night so far, and she wanted to keep it that way. She couldn't remember the last time she'd had an evening out that didn't include a pizza and teenagers. Her daughter was a terrific kid, but there was something to be said for adult conversation, and Aaron was an interesting companion when he forgot to be a pain in the ass. Of course, it helped that they'd agreed not to discuss business or Melanie's request to move in with her.

Still, Aaron was more complicated than Skylar had thought. He was intelligent, well-informed, and his rare smiles lit his entire face, the same way her daughter's frequent grins filled *her* face. But he also seemed lonely and isolated, despite having a large family.

As it turned out, neither one of them had warm memories of childhood.

"I love Old Sacramento," Skylar murmured. "We used to bring Karin to the railroad museum every year, then we'd eat lunch and get ice cream."

"The museum wasn't my speed, but once I had my Mustang, I started going to the music festival."

"Which Mustang?" she asked flippantly, only to wince. Her mouth used to get her into trouble regularly, and seemed determined to start the same pattern over again.

"Both."

"I guess it isn't that far from Cooperton."

"Especially when you drive a hundred miles an hour. And can you believe it—my father wants to give Melanie a car?" Aaron told her indignantly. "After everything he's seen with the rest of his kids. I realize it's hypocritical of me to object, but I don't want Melanie *driving,* much less having her own car."

The corner of Skylar's mouth twitched, though she didn't think it was funny. "I'm not letting Karin drive until she's thirty."

"Good decision. It was strange, but my father didn't insist. I just told him that Melanie doesn't have her driver's license yet and needs more experience before getting her own ride."

"Maybe it's because she's a girl."

Aaron snorted. "Sexual bias? You could be right. He thought I'd get laid easier driving a Mustang—the glove compartment was stuffed with condoms when the first one arrived."

Skylar turned her gaze forward. Getting laid wasn't

a subject she wanted to discuss. Or condoms. Especially condoms that failed. It wasn't Aaron's Mustang that had appealed to her; it had been the allure of a normal family that looked so much cleaner and nicer than her own.

"If your grandparents were as strict as you say, I'm amazed they let you have a car." Feeling unaccountably colder, Skylar tucked her wrap closer.

"Now that you mention it, that *was* odd."

"Maybe they felt bad, wishing they'd been less demanding, and didn't know how to show it."

He shrugged. "Who knows?"

AARON LOOKED AT the city lights reflecting on the broad river. Earlier that afternoon, he'd regretted telling Skylar about his childhood with the Coopers, yet it didn't seem to matter now. She must hear gossip about her neighbors, but for all of her wild background, he doubted she ran around revealing information about other people—maybe *because* of that background. Her parents had regularly caused scandals in Cooperton, and she'd told their classmates to take a flying leap whenever they tormented her over it.

A faint frown creased his brow.

While he'd resented his grandparents as a kid, what would it have been like for Skylar, growing up with *her* mother and father? He recalled the times she'd come to school with a bruised cheek or a split lip. The teachers had sometimes asked about it, and she'd given them a sassy reply that didn't invite further questions—just a trip to the principal's office for using inappropriate language.

A sick sensation went through his stomach.

Things were a lot less complicated when he'd seen Skylar only as a bad influence for his sister.

Shrugging off his coat he laid it over Skylar's shoulders. It was a belated bit of chivalry...fifteen years late.

"That's not necessary," she said, looking startled.

"You're shivering, and I'm the one who suggested taking a walk."

"I agreed."

She started to take it off, and Aaron caught the lapels between his fingers, trapping her. He looked down, and the breath caught in his throat.

God, she was beautiful.

She'd joked about her daughter calling her outfit a "mom dress," yet it was anything *but* motherly. While it didn't reveal much skin, the soft fabric clung sensuously, showing every curve and hollow of her body, and the dark green was a delicious contrast to her rich auburn hair.

"You never had freckles," he said absentmindedly. "Even when we were kids."

"Some redheads don't."

"No." And he knew she was a genuine redhead. They'd only dated for a few weeks, but he'd reveled in the sight of Skylar, naked against the leather seats of his Mustang, her body seeming practically perfect.

While it hadn't been his first time with a girl, it was the first time the girl had looked like *that*.

Without thinking, Aaron leaned closer and kissed Skylar's mouth. There was a hint of sweetness on her lips from the cheesecake she'd eaten for dessert, and he deepened the caress, his senses reeling. For a brief moment she kissed him back, then with a quick intake of breath, she stepped backward, breaking free.

Aaron swallowed and hoped his arousal wasn't visible in the low light. How in hell could such a chaste kiss turn him inside out so quickly? He wasn't a hormone-crazed teenager any longer; he'd kissed plenty of women, and had made love to his share of them, as well.

Skylar pulled off the coat and handed it to him. "Was that part of your apology?"

Apology?

It took a moment before his befuddled brain remembered why they'd had dinner together. "Sure, kiss and make up," he muttered.

A boisterous group of diners spilled from a nearby restaurant and headed in their direction. They appeared to be tourists, based on the "I love Old Sacramento" and other T-shirts they wore, and he was grateful for the commotion.

"If the tickets aren't sold out, there's a play starting at eight in a theater up the block—Shakespeare's *A Midsummer Night's Dream,*" Aaron said. "The waiter at the Dixie Damsel mentioned that it's gotten excellent local reviews."

"We shouldn't. It would put us quite late getting back." Despite her refusal, Skylar seemed tempted.

"Are you worried about the girls? You called once already during dinner, and everything was all right."

"I'm not used to being out of town and having Karin home alone."

"She isn't alone—Melanie is with her. But I know how you feel. How old is old enough? Aren't teenagers their age doing babysitting?"

"Yup. But I still worry and have trouble letting go when I should. Especially since my...for the past year or so."

He guessed Skylar was referring to the time since her husband's accident, and the shadowed expression in her eyes was sobering. If anything, he'd assumed her marriage was based on practicality, yet the look on her face wasn't that of a woman who'd lost her meal ticket—more like someone who'd lost the love of her life. For some reason the thought made his stomach turn over.

Aaron cleared his throat. "I gather Karin has been taking her father's death hard."

"They were so close. He adored her from the day she was born. I've never seen anything like the two of them together, whether it was watching baseball or going bicycle riding. From the moment she could crawl, she followed him around as if he was the Pied Piper."

"But you didn't have any more children."

"Oh, well, we considered it." Skylar's gaze shifted

away from him, and once again Aaron got the feeling she was hiding something.

"Would it help if you checked on her again? And I can phone Melanie, too." He was unexpectedly reluctant for the evening to end. "We could also watch part of the play and leave at intermission."

"I'll see how Karin sounds."

She stepped a few feet away and Aaron pulled out his own cell phone. Melanie answered after three rings and seemed distracted.

"How is everything?"

"Fine. We're watching TV."

In the background noise of the television, Aaron heard dramatic music and figured the on-screen action was at a crucial point. He didn't get it—Melanie had watched *Star Trek* so much she had to know the episodes by heart, and yet she got swept into the story as if it was entirely new.

"How would you feel if we stayed later than I first thought?"

"That would be awesome! Karin and I ate so much pizza that we haven't had ice cream yet, and we'll have time to get hungry again. Oh, can I sleep over with Karin? The Gibsons have an extra bedroom, you know."

Of course, Aaron thought, resigned. What was that old saying—the problem with cats is that they have kittens? By letting his sister spend the evening with Karin, she just wanted more. She might even think it would actually lead to her moving in with Skylar and her daughter.

"I'll think about it."

"Aaaaaronnnn."

"Mellllannnie." He mimicked her exasperated tone. "I said I'd think about it, and that's all you're getting right now."

Her sigh resonated loudly through the cell phone speaker. "Okay."

"I'll talk to you later."

"Uh…drive carefully."

The caution took Aaron by surprise, and warmth crept through him. "I will. We'll see you later."

Skylar was still talking to Karin when he disconnected. A minute later she was off the phone, as well. "I think they don't want us to come back."

"I got that impression, too."

They walked toward the theater and Aaron bought tickets. Inside, the lights were just coming down, and they were finding their seats as the play began.

It was a small stage, and the director used the same actors to play the king and queen of the fairies as well as the Duke of Athens and his betrothed, with a simple switch in aspects of their costuming to denote their shift to the other character. That, along with a less visually complex set design, allowed the audience to concentrate on the rich humor of Shakespeare's language. Aaron found he was enjoying the play far more than the elaborately staged production he'd seen elsewhere.

At intermission he got bottles of imported spring water for them to drink, while Skylar called home again.

"The girls are eating ice cream and told us to take our time," she said as she slipped the phone back in her purse. "It should be all right to stay for the rest of the play."

"Great. I got sparkling water, but they have wine if you're interested."

"Not for me. Go ahead if you'd like some yourself, I'll be the designated driver. It might be fun seeing what your Mercedes has under the hood." She smiled wickedly, and he saw a hint of the old outrageous Skylar.

"Hey, I know what you *really* think of my car. Stuffy, right? But I have to be a responsible citizen now."

His comment notwithstanding, it was sobering to think that in a few short years he'd gone from a bright red Mustang to a black Mercedes sedan. A Mercedes commanded respect, but the model he favored was a long way from a sports car.

"I wouldn't dream of criticizing your taste in cars. Remember, I drive a twelve-year-old truck." Yet even as Skylar laughed, a flash of another, darker emotion filled her eyes.

They went back into the play, and the second half was as entertaining as the first, though he could tell Skylar was getting edgy toward the end, unconsciously fingering her cell phone. He shifted uncomfortably, as well—perhaps her feelings were contagious, or maybe he was simply becoming more aware of what it took to be responsible for another person.

"Do you think something is wrong?" he whispered, tapping her restless hand. Aaron had never encountered a woman with genuine motherly instinct, but there was always a first time.

Skylar looked down at the phone she held, smiled ruefully and put it away. "No. Occupational hazard of being a parent."

The final act ended, and they clapped enthusiastically with the rest of the audience. Though it didn't take long to get outside, Skylar was on the phone before the theater doors closed behind them.

He supposed her caution was inevitable after losing her husband. Melanie had mentioned it was from an accident. In a car? That could be why his sister was concerned about his safe driving—her shy urge to be careful had been very sweet.

Skylar seemed embarrassed when she put her cell back in her purse. "No problem, other than exasperation," she said to his raised eyebrow inquiry.

Aaron didn't laugh. There were many times he'd wished his own parents had checked up on him more often. At least he would have known they cared… or even remembered he existed. He was still uncertain about Melanie spending so much time at the Nibble Nook, but he couldn't deny that Skylar was a good mother.

The wind was sharper, and over Skylar's protests, he put his coat back around her shoulders on the walk to the Mercedes. They were both quiet as they left the city, and Aaron focused on the road, deep in thought. A few weeks ago it would have been inconceivable that they'd spend a pleasant evening together, but he'd enjoyed himself.

When they got close to Cooperton, Aaron glanced at Skylar.

"Melanie asked if she could spend the night. I told her I'd think about it."

"Karin asked, too. They'll probably be asleep in front of the television when we get there."

"Provided you don't call again and wake them up."

Skylar made a face at him.

"Look, let's not disturb them," Aaron decided. "I'll see you in and pick Melanie up in the morning."

"No. We'll drop her off on the way to church," Skylar offered, almost seeming alarmed.

"If it isn't too much trouble."

"No trouble at all."

Once again there seemed to be an undertone to the conversation that Aaron didn't understand. Or was he just being paranoid?

KARIN GOT A note from Melanie in geometry class on Tuesday morning. It had to be important—it was the very first time Mellie had *ever* passed her a note. She was too afraid of getting in trouble.

They met by Mellie's locker at break.

"What's up?"

Melanie looked around to be sure no one was close by. "I went for a walk yesterday afternoon and saw Nick Jakowski," she whispered. "Did you know he lives two blocks over from Aaron's house? *Just two blocks.*"

"No." Karin gulped. Nick liked Melanie, she was sure of it. And if he lived that close, Mellie probably wouldn't want to move across town.

"Nick was washing his dad's car and saw me. He asked if you'd thought any more about being on the soccer team next year. Isn't that great?"

"Yeah, but he *likes* you," Karin said, determined to be honest.

"Not that much. He goes to the school dances with Tiffany."

Karin frowned. "I don't know. Nick dances with her, but somebody said she comes with her dad. Coach Baldwin is always one of the chaperones."

"Whatever. I just wanted to tell you he asked about you. Nick loves soccer. I told him more about seeing the World Cup and he wants to go someday."

Karin lifted her chin. "Uh, do you want to stay with Aaron, then? Since Nick lives so close?"

Mellie looked shocked. *"No."*

"Even if he asks you out?"

"Of course not. I told you, it's awful moving around all the time and Aaron is just supposed to keep me until June."

"Okay." Karin felt better. "Do your folks know about the letter from Mr. Newman yet?"

Mellie shrugged. "Aaron didn't say when he was going to tell my mother and father."

It was funny. She never said *mom* or *dad*.

"Do you think they'll be mad?"

"I don't know. My mother might be happy about it—she almost had to send me to boarding school this year because nobody would take me until Aaron said yes."

"Yuck."

"Tell me about it."

AARON DIDN'T GET a call from his father until Wednesday morning after getting to the office. Spence usually called during regular business hours—he had little respect for someone who worked.

"What's up, son? Your email didn't say much. Just that you wanted to talk about Melanie."

"Yeah, three days ago."

"You didn't say it was urgent."

True enough. His email to his father had played things down, saying to call when he had time. The one to Eliza had a similar low-key tone. Aaron's preference would have been a conference call between the three of them, but for all his charm, Spence didn't have cordial relationships with his ex-wives—they took a dim view of his casual attitude toward marital fidelity, even when they weren't paragons of virtue in that area themselves.

"Melanie has become friends with a girl from school," he said. "A Karin Gibson. And she's decided she wants to move in with Karin's family. I refused when she asked, and she was upset about it, so she contacted a lawyer. The attorney's letter mentioned her wanting to file for a parent–child divorce."

Spence let out a hearty laugh. "She's starting young, that girl."

"What?"

"Getting divorced."

Aaron drew a sharp breath. "Melanie is *not* going through the revolving divorce-court door—you can't possibly want that for her. Why aren't you more upset? Your daughter wants to sever her relationship with you as her parent."

"All kids go through a rebellious stage. And I don't see any reason she shouldn't move in with Skylar. She's done a fine job with our Karin."

Skylar?

Our Karin?

Aaron knew he hadn't mentioned Skylar's first name, and every nerve in his body tensed. "What in hell do you know about Skylar? And Karin…*our* Karin? What is that supposed to mean?"

"Come on, boy. You haven't done the math? Little Karin Grace Gibson was born nine months after you and her mommy were having fun in your Mustang."

Nine months…the timing was right. And it was as if he'd been punched in the stomach. "That isn't possible. I used a condom, and Skylar had a reputation."

Spence began laughing so hard he was practically choking. "She wasn't the only one, boy. I had a couple of folks on my payroll sending word about you back then—a teacher and a local cop. I heard your nickname was Randy Andy. You're a real chip off the old block."

Randy Andy...? Aaron abruptly sat down in his office chair. His buddies had kidded around, calling him that, but he hadn't thought anyone else knew. And how could dear old Dad have paid people to spy on him when he couldn't be bothered to show up for graduation?

"So you assumed Karin was my daughter, simply because Skylar and I dated a few times," he said after Spence had stopped laughing again.

"I thought it was interesting that she dropped out of school a couple of months after you did a horizontal dance together. Why? If she'd stayed until June, she could have graduated. Then she promptly hightailed it to the next town over and turned up pregnant. So I got someone to check the hospital records where Karin Grace was born and the blood types matched."

"Hospital records are private."

"Not when you pay enough to have someone make copies."

Hell. Aaron didn't want to know if violating medical privacy was a crime—the legality wasn't likely to bother Spence, anyway. "Blood types aren't proof."

"Nope, but you were off to college and too young to be a father. Just in case, I offered Skylar money to help out. I may have my faults, but I would never let my grandchild go without."

Aaron didn't know who he was angrier with—Spence for playing God and not telling him about Karin, or *Skylar*.

Of course, she might have known Karin wasn't his, so why say anything? Just take the check and run. For that matter, if she'd believed Karin was his daughter, she would have come to him for support. That meant Karin *couldn't* be his child.

"How much did Skylar take you for?" he demanded.

"Nothing. She ripped the check in half and told me to take a hike…in much stronger language, of course. That little gal is a real firecracker." The admiration in Spence's voice was hard to swallow.

"You liked her?"

"Hell, yes. There was a big number on that check and she wouldn't touch a penny."

"So you turned your back on a child you thought was your granddaughter."

"I did no such thing. Every few months I've sent someone to get a report on Karin and Skylar to make sure they were doing all right, and would have stepped in if needed. A shame about that husband of hers—he seemed like a decent fellow."

Aaron's gut was churning. The fact he might be a father himself was the biggest shock, but Spence's role in it was also hard to credit. "Did you really believe I wouldn't care that Karin could be my daughter?"

"If you'd cared, you would have figured it out when

you met her," Spence said. And for the first time that Aaron could ever remember, his dad sounded dead serious.

CHAPTER ELEVEN

SKYLAR COULDN'T BELIEVE IT.

She'd worked in the garden the afternoon before and somewhere, somehow, her wedding ring had gone missing. Worse, she hadn't noticed until the next morning—thoughts of Aaron had kept her mind occupied. She hadn't said anything to Karin to keep from upsetting her, instead waiting until after she'd left on the school bus. But as soon as she was alone, Skylar arranged for an extra employee to cover at the Nibble Nook and raced outside.

Jimmie had gotten her the ring when she was still pregnant, planning to propose after the baby was born. The thought that it could have gone out in the trash, picked up that morning by the disposal company, was too awful to think about. It *had* to be in the yard.

Skylar tried to calm down and hunt through the soil she'd dug up in the vegetable garden. An hour later she was in the front of the house, still searching, when she glanced over at the hydrangea bush and saw a glint of gold on the ground beneath a branch.

Breathing a grateful prayer, she snatched the band, remembering how she'd shaken her gardening gloves out; her ring must have come off then. It was loose on her finger—she'd lost some weight since Aaron's reappearance in her life.

It was so annoying.

Why hadn't she slapped his face when he'd kissed her? No matter what, she couldn't afford to get involved with him, even in a small way. She had to think of Karin. And she'd felt guilty ever since, remembering her husband. How could she have responded to Aaron when she still missed Jimmie?

Skylar rocked back on her heels and looked around at the yard. However annoying, Aaron *had* been making her think about things lately. She loved gardening, but maybe it was particularly important to her because of the way she remembered her childhood home…a front yard filled with weeds and rusted-out cars. The brief time she'd dated Aaron she had refused to let him pick her up there, ashamed she lived in such a horrid place.

But the truth was, she'd never had anything to be ashamed about—children weren't responsible for their parents. She'd survived a violent childhood with a deeply troubled mother and father. Maybe her rebellion in high school had simply been part of that survival— emotionally, at least, though it had taken pregnancy to make her wake up and turn her life around.

"Skylar, we have to talk."

She jumped.

Aaron was standing in front of her as if he'd materialized out of her thoughts, and he looked angry. Not that there was anything new about that. Being pissed was his usual condition, and she wondered if Melanie's lawyer had sent him another letter.

"What?"

"I talked to my father this morning. He claims Karin could be my child."

Skylar felt the blood leave her face. "I'll show you her birth certificate—Karin is Jimmie Gibson's daughter."

"Biologically?"

"After fourteen years it isn't any of your business."

"*Damn it*. I deserve a straight answer."

"You don't deserve anything."

She got up and marched into the house with Aaron at her heels. Her worst nightmare had come true, but she wasn't going to let him get the best of her. She spun around and poked him in the chest with her forefinger.

"If you don't get out, Aaron, this time I *will* have you arrested for trespassing."

"You have to talk to me. Let's sit down and work this out." It was strange. Although he was plainly upset, he was obviously trying to sound calm and rational.

"We have nothing to work out."

"Look, I know condoms can fail. Let's just clear the question up by having genetic tests done."

"Absolutely not."

"Be reasonable. With a test we can sort out whether it was me, or someone else you were seeing at the time."

Skylar wanted to kill him. After all these years, he still believed she'd slept around.

"I wasn't seeing anyone else," she hissed. "But I don't care if you believe me. Why should I agree to tests? I don't need you or your messed-up family, and I refuse to tell Karin right now. If you have a shred of decency, you'd realize how devastating that would be for her. She's still having a terrible time dealing with Jimmie's death."

"I don't want to hurt her—I just want to have a part in her life if she's actually my kid. I'm sure there's a way we could do the tests without Karin knowing why."

"I can't take the risk. If my word isn't enough, you can just walk away."

WALK AWAY FROM his own child?

Aaron was appalled.

"Why didn't you tell me you were pregnant?" he asked, holding his temper with an effort.

"Because you wouldn't have believed me. I never slept around, but you believed the lies told by your toadying, weaselly friends without question…lies that I had sex with any guy that came along. Then you spread your own tales, making me sound like the worst tramp who ever lived, which is ironic since you're one they called Randy Andy."

Hell. It was the second time in less than two hours that Aaron had heard the nickname he'd hoped was long forgotten.

"Even so, why not tell me you were pregnant?"

Skylar raised her chin. "Maybe I should have, but I didn't want anything to do with you after the way you acted…as if I was a piece of roadside trash. Do you know how miserable you made my life? Every boy in school thought they could get lucky with me after your stories. Besides, since your father knew about Karin, why would I believe that you *didn't*? I doubt any court would believe it, either."

Aaron ground his teeth.

"Skylar, I didn't—"

"Don't you dare claim you treated me well. You didn't want to be seen with me and you know it."

Her accusation hit uncomfortably close to the mark. She was right about the shabby way he'd treated her. And it hadn't been that long since he'd acknowledged he couldn't have introduced Skylar to his grandparents.

As for his mother and father…?

Celina wouldn't have noticed, and Spence obviously thought well of Skylar. Of course, since he had never had an ex-wife who didn't demand a fortune in divorce court, he'd appreciate any woman who refused to take a penny. His father also had an eye for beauty and feminine curves, and must have appreciated Skylar from that point of view.

"Why not take the check my father gave you?" he asked.

"Because I didn't want anything to do with your family then, any more than I do now."

"You wanted to meet my grandparents when we were dating."

"Yeah, and you were so eager to introduce us," Skylar said sardonically. "But that was before I learned that having wealth and being publicly respectable didn't make a person admirable. You taught me that."

Aaron instinctively opened his mouth to defend himself, only to shut it again. Earlier, he'd started to explain that he wasn't the one who'd spread stories about her, but it wasn't much of a defense—he *had* told his closest buddies. They'd gone about, telling tales and embellishing them far beyond anything he'd said. And he hadn't stopped it. He had shrugged and figured it wouldn't bother a girl with Skylar's reputation, never admitting that his own reputation wasn't particularly admirable, either.

"I'd better leave before we both say something we'll regret," he said finally.

"Fine. You know where the door is."

SKYLAR WAS SHAKING as Aaron disappeared. What would happen if her daughter had to face this?

She'd worried that Karin would think she was a hypocrite, but that wasn't the worst part.... The worst part would be having the foundation of Karin's world shattered again. Maybe when she was older it would be all right to tell her, but not now. Not when she still cried herself to sleep sometimes with her dad's picture under her pillow.

Skylar suddenly remembered the lawyer Melanie had consulted. She quickly dialed the attorney's number and asked if he was available.

"Hello, Mrs. Gibson," Jeremy Newman said a minute later. "Did you have more questions for me?"

"More than just questions. Are you interested in a new client?"

"I suppose you want your free hour, too?"

"My what?" Skylar asked, confused.

"Oh, nothing. Sometimes my sense of humor gets me in trouble. I'm happy to get new clients. What can I do?"

"Whatever I tell you has to be confidential. From everyone. Especially Karin and Melanie."

"Of course. I'm bound by law to protect your privacy."

Her mouth dry, Skylar quickly explained. About her daughter and Aaron and Jimmie. About Aaron finding out and the pieces of the check from S. S. Hollister that she kept in the safe deposit box. *Everything.*

"If Aaron tries going to court," she said, "I want to have someone I can call for help."

"Mr. Hollister will probably realize his best interests are served by working outside the legal system. There are no guarantees, but I believe a local court is unlikely to support any action he might attempt. He's surely intelligent enough to realize that."

"You have no idea how stubborn Aaron is, Mr. Newman."

"So am I. Now, try to relax. I know your primary concern is Karin finding out, but it may not happen. We have to prepare for any eventuality, however, so when you have time, bring me a copy of that check you ripped in half. It's an excellent piece of evidence."

"All right. Thanks."

The lawyer's calm assurance helped. After they got off the phone, Skylar pulled herself together and headed toward the Nibble Nook. She probably wouldn't do much good there, but she had to try and act normally.

AARON PACED THE floor for the next two nights.

Was Karin his child?

He tried to think if she bore a resemblance to the Hollisters or the Coopers, but Karin was such an individual in her own right, it was hard for him to see her as anything except herself.

Then Eliza called on Friday, after he'd finally managed to fall asleep.

"Aaron, *sweetheart*," she exclaimed. "I'm sorry it took so long to phone, but I told you we were going to be out of touch, didn't I?"

He yawned. "Yes, that's one of the reasons I emailed."

"Is Melanie all right…? She hasn't gotten sick again?"

"She's fine, but she wants to move in with a friend and live there until she's eighteen."

"Really?"

Eliza didn't sound horrified by the idea, more speculative.

"It's probably just a bid for attention," he added quickly. "Though she's consulted with an attorney."

"Goodness, an attorney?" Eliza laughed, obviously not concerned. "She didn't ask you first?"

"Well, yes. She asked if she could move in with the Gibsons, and naturally I refused.

"Are they nice people?"

Aaron thought about the way he'd tried to keep Melanie away from the Nibble Nook, believing the worst of Skylar. It wasn't something he could explain to Eliza.

"I'm still getting to know the family," he hedged. "Melanie's friend is fourteen and very smart, well ahead of her classmates. The mother owns a local hamburger stand, and the girls study there after school."

"What does Mr. Gibson do?"

"Mrs. Gibson is a widow. Her husband died last year in an auto accident. They used to run the hamburger stand together."

"How terrible." For once Eliza didn't sound blithely cheerful. "Taking Melanie would be too much of an imposition under the circumstances, even if Mrs. Gibson is willing."

Aaron sat up in the bed. It was a shock to realize that his flighty ex-stepmother was showing more sensitivity toward Skylar than he ever had. "Yes, of course."

"You'll have to get Melanie to understand."

"I don't know if she will. She's tired of being moved from place to place," Aaron said bluntly.

"But she doesn't want to go to boarding school, and I need to travel with John," Eliza protested. "You see, there was a scare with his health shortly after we were married. It turned out to be nothing, but I was frightened and promised to always be with him. And I... Well, I knew John wasn't interested in being a father."

So she was admitting she'd made the choice between her husband and her child. An image of Skylar rose in Aaron's mind, fighting like a tigress in Karin's defense. She was a good mother, though a few weeks ago it would have galled him to admit it. And despite his nights of pacing the floor and trying to decide the right thing, it had never occurred to him that Karin should be anywhere but with her mom.

"I can talk to Melanie," Aaron told Eliza. "But you need to speak with her, too."

"I'll call her right now... Oh, *dear,* I just realized what time it is in California. You must have been asleep. I'll try getting Melanie tomorrow or the next day."

Or next week, or next month, he thought, resigned. *If ever.*

Eliza had bared her soul briefly, yet it was plain that she wasn't going to wallow in self-recrimination.

It was easier to retreat into that pretty world she lived in, removed from everyday troubles. She probably felt that if a problem was ignored long enough it would simply go away.

"I'm sure Melanie will love hearing from you," he murmured.

"You're a dear, Aaron. I've always been very fond of you—that's why I asked you to be Melanie's god-father. Take care."

Aaron said goodbye and turned off his cell phone, frowning. Why hadn't he told Eliza that Spence was in favor of Melanie moving in with the Gibsons? However flighty and good-natured Eliza might be, she wasn't on good terms with her ex-husband; she probably would oppose anything that Spence supported.

Putting an arm behind his head, Aaron lay back and gazed at the ceiling. He wasn't like Eliza; he couldn't ignore reality. And he'd found that problems usually got bigger if you ignored them.

What in hell was he going to do about Skylar's daughter?

If he tried to get a court order for genetic testing, it could cause a public spectacle that would be rough on everyone. Once he wouldn't have cared, but it was different now.

Pictures filled Aaron's head…Karin and Melanie giggling. Karin defending her friend. A pair of blue eyes that sparkled with mischief and determination—

eyes that turned wary and suspicious when they looked at him, just like her mother.

He sighed.

Whether Karin was his daughter or not, he couldn't do anything that hurt her. His pride would have to take a backseat to any decision he made.

"Mooommm," Karin said. "The traffic light turned green ages ago and now it's yellow again. I don't want to be late."

"Sorry, sweetheart." Skylar waited until the next green light and drove forward. It was Saturday, and they were on the way to the church for the second half of the painting project.

She'd been tense before, wondering if Aaron would find out about Karin, but it was worse now that he knew. What was he going to do—be sensitive, or act like a testosterone-crazed grizzly bear with wounded pride? Her kid's well-being was at stake, and it was making her a nervous wreck.

If only she hadn't lost her temper—she'd said all kinds of things to Aaron that she wished she hadn't... things that might make him angrier. Her temper had been a problem her entire life. Jimmie had known how to calm her down, but Aaron seemed to take pleasure in striking the match and lighting the fuse.

"Do they have any idea how long you'll be painting?" she asked absently.

"Probably the same as last week. But you don't have to pick me up. Mrs. Hashima and Mr. Calderas are driving the kids home," Karin said, getting out at the church. She was dressed in her old clothes again, and Skylar's only consolation was that the other kids who were arriving looked equally appalling.

"What about lunch?"

Karin grabbed her backpack and slung it over her shoulder. "They're ordering pizza."

"All right, I'll see you later." Skylar watched her daughter dash over and greet her friends and Mrs. Hashima. Luckily, Karin hadn't realized there was anything going on. Her thoughts were taken up with Melanie and her classes at school and the failure of her team to make it to the World Series.

Skylar had expected worse anguish over the pennant race and World Series than during the play-offs, but Karin's hopes of Melanie living with them seemed to have eased the emotional trauma of watching the games without her father. Or at least they had provided a distraction. Thankfully the baseball fall classic had also come to a swift end, with one team sweeping the series.

Skylar's eyes widened as she saw a familiar black Mercedes pull in ahead of her. Melanie bounced from the car, and Aaron got out, as well—tall, well built, looking casually gorgeous in jeans and a white shirt with sleeves rolled to the elbow. It really wasn't fair for men to get better looking over the years.

Karin appeared surprised to see her friend and began introducing her to the other kids while Aaron shook hands with Mrs. Hashima. They spoke for a couple of minutes and then the youth leader nodded. Aaron pulled his wallet from his back pocket and held out several bills. Mrs. Hashima seemed reluctant to take the money, but she finally did and hurried the kids into the building.

Skylar frowned. What was Aaron doing?

He turned and walked straight to the driver's side of the truck. Skylar grudgingly rolled down the window.

"Yes?"

"We need to talk."

She couldn't tell anything from his face except that he looked tired; if she hadn't known better, she'd think he was minus a few nights' sleep. But what did he have to fuss and fume about? He didn't believe Karin was his biological child in the first place.

"About what? I haven't changed my mind. I'm not agreeing to any tests."

"Please, Skylar, let's go somewhere private. Melanie asked this morning if she could help with the painting, and I thought it would give us a chance to talk. Mrs. Hashima gave permission for her to stay and work with the others."

"What was the money for?"

"I offered to pay for everyone's lunch."

"You can't buy your way into popularity, Aaron."

He lifted an eyebrow. "What is that supposed to mean?"

"Come on, you must know that half the youth group's parents work for you—it's a statistical probability. But paying for their kids' pizza won't make up for the way you've been treating them at the factory."

"I haven't cut pay or benefits, Skylar. All I've done is change a few rules and enforce some of the others so they stop taking advantage."

She snorted. "You tripled prices in the cafeteria and shortened lunch so they almost *have* to eat there or at the Nibble Nook if they didn't bring something. Who is taking advantage of whom?"

Aaron frowned. "The cafeteria was losing money— my grandfather has been subsidizing it for years. And a good number of employees were abusing their hour lunch break, stretching it even longer. They were also taking Cooper Industry products home with them, sometimes by the trunkload. And those are just some of the problems."

"I'm sure there were abuses, but not as many as you think. Did you ever consider that a lot of them had permission? At the very least, I know Mr. Cooper encouraged people to take factory seconds home— now you're just incinerating them."

There was a peculiar expression on Aaron's face. "I'll look into it, but this isn't what I wanted to talk about."

"You ought to talk to *somebody* about it."

"One thing at a time. I hope you don't mind, but I've asked Mrs. Hashima to drop Melanie at your place when they're done. Then I'll come get her."

Skylar's pulse jumped. "No, I'll bring her over myself."

"I realize you don't want me around Karin, but that's part of what we need to discuss."

"Fine, just not at my house," Skylar said stubbornly.

A ghost of a smile creased Aaron's mouth. "Then we'll go to mine. I'll put on a pot of coffee."

"*Your* place? You should show better judgment. I might contaminate it with my shocking reputation." Lord, her mouth was completely out of control.

"Give me a chance," he said quietly. "Boys can grow up and recognize their mistakes."

"That remains to be seen. But go ahead, I'll meet you there."

Skylar jerkily put her truck in gear. While there wasn't a "bad" section of town any longer, there definitely was a "nice" one, with larger, more expensive homes. On a map it was roughly bell-shaped, with the Cooper mansion forming the clapper. The house Aaron had leased was at the top of the bell. It was the second-largest home in Cooperton, and had been built by a Sacramento banker who'd wanted to live in a quiet community, only to discover that quiet drove him crazy. He'd moved back to the city and rented out the house whenever possible.

She parked behind the Mercedes on the driveway. "I see you got the lawn mowed," she murmured as Aaron opened the truck door for her. "In front, at least."

"Yeah." He smiled ruefully. "I must have looked like an idiot, trying to start the mower the wrong way—too much on my mind, I guess, to think it through. It took most of Sunday to finish the job, and I already need to mow again. They have a strict neighborhood association in this part of town."

The pleasant chitchat was increasing Skylar's tension, but she tried to play along. "The weather is extending the growing season. I can't remember the last time it was this warm so late in the year. My summer vegetables have slowed down, but they're still producing well. And I've gotten a second crop of lettuce and spinach and sugar snap peas."

"Melanie was quite impressed with your home-grown salad. Come on, you haven't been inside, have you?"

"No."

Skylar looked around curiously as she followed him. While the living room was furnished and there were chairs and a table in the spacious breakfast area in the kitchen, the formal dining room was empty, along with the large family room opening off the kitchen.

"The house is too big," Aaron explained, gesturing to the room a step down from the kitchen. "But I needed a place after Eliza asked me to take Melanie for the year and didn't have time to look. I was living in an apartment over the business offices in Cooper Industries—hardly suitable for a teenager."

"In the middle of a factory? No. Your view here is much nicer."

The back of the house was almost entirely windows.

A large yard was edged by a creek and a wooded strip of land designated as protected green space by the city council. It didn't surprise her that Aaron had rented a house too big for his and Melanie's needs—after the Cooper Mansion, this place was the showiest home in town.

"Do you prefer decaffeinated or regular?" Aaron asked, pulling out the coffeemaker.

"Either is fine."

"In that case, I'll make decaf—Melanie fixed breakfast this morning, and her coffee is stronger than Mississippi mud—it could kick-start a mule. But don't tell her I said that. She's been charming, trying to cook for me every now and then."

Skylar sat at the table and wondered if Melanie was cooking out of sheer self-defense. Takeout got tiresome, and Aaron probably wasn't a cook himself. Other than the coffeemaker, there were no kitchen gadgets or utensils on the limestone countertops— just a pile of menus by the telephone.

"Cream or sugar?" Aaron asked after a few minutes, setting two steaming mugs of coffee on the table.

"Black is fine."

He dropped into a chair opposite her and tapped his finger on the side of his cup. But he didn't say anything, and the silence was more than Skylar could take.

"This was your idea," she prompted. "What did you have to say to me?"

A spasm of emotion crossed his face. "I've been awake the past three nights, trying to work things out in my mind. It boils down to one thing—regardless of whether Karin is my daughter or not, she's a nice kid and I don't want to hurt her."

"And?"

"And we'll do it your way. Karin believes Jimmie Gibson was her biological father, so I won't push for genetic tests, at least for a while. But I want us to get better acquainted."

The relief that had filled Skylar faltered. "What do you mean by that?"

"I want to spend time with her, doing things that she and Melanie will enjoy. That way I can get to know her, and she can get to know me. I'll be able to get a better grasp of the situation that way."

"Oh." Skylar didn't say anything else for a long minute.

Aaron's comment about getting a "grasp of the situation" sounded like a typical businessman, but he wasn't as bad as she'd thought. Still, there were a number of ways her daughter could be hurt by him or his family. And while she didn't have any more right to judge the Coopers and Hollisters than Aaron had to judge her background, she didn't want Karin to be touched by their lifestyle.

"Skylar, I honestly didn't know there was a chance I might be a father," Aaron murmured, leaning forward. "My dad admitted he had some people in Cooperton sending him updates on me. One was a teacher, the other a police officer. Apparently they found out you were pregnant, and he took matters into his own hands."

"Yeah." Her ire rose with the memory. "He tried to pay me off as if I was a cheap nobody who'd taken advantage of his innocent son. I don't know when you stopped being innocent, but *I* didn't have anything to do with it!"

"That wasn't it at all. Spence has his issues, but he's always provided for his children financially. He says he felt I was too young to be a father, so he offered money to help with Karin in case she was really his granddaughter."

Skylar didn't know if she believed Aaron or not. And it didn't matter. Protecting Karin remained her first concern, both then and now.

CHAPTER TWELVE

AARON COULDN'T TELL what Skylar was thinking…but he could guess. She didn't want him near Karin for fear of what he might say or do.

"What do you think?" he prompted.

"Things are busy now, with school and the holidays coming up. Maybe when everything settles down—"

"I was thinking we could do something tomorrow," Aaron interrupted. He didn't want Skylar to hope he'd lose interest over time. "As you've pointed out yourself, the weather is unseasonably warm. We could take inner tubes down a few miles of the American River tomorrow. Karin swims, doesn't she?"

"Like a fish, but you aren't taking my daughter anywhere without me."

"Of course not," he agreed quickly.

It hadn't occurred to Aaron to go someplace with the girls by himself. Skylar was the experienced parent; he wanted her there to run interference. He struggled enough to communicate with Melanie.

Skylar sat back, and Aaron saw shadows in her eyes and the weary tension around her mouth. He tried to dig up the anger he'd felt upon learning about Karin, but it was hard. *She* was the one who had faced becoming a single mother at eighteen, while he'd gone off to college and a life made easy by his trust fund.

"All right," she murmured finally. "You can spend time with Karin as long as I'm present. But don't overdo it with extravagant plans, or push too hard. Friendship is one thing, but I don't want her becoming fond of you, only to see you disappear from her life."

"You mean if I don't turn out to be her father."

Her gaze narrowed. "I'd appreciate it if you'd stop voicing doubts about Karin's paternity at every opportunity. You can think what you like, but I don't have to listen to it. What I *meant* is that it takes more than DNA to be a father, and I seriously doubt you plan to put down permanent roots in Cooperton. My guess is that you want to get Cooper Industries running solidly again and sell out once the value is up."

Aaron resisted the urge to loosen his collar. Selling the company was one of the options he'd considered, along with having someone manage it while he went back to the city. Still, if Karin was his daughter, it could affect whatever decision he made, at least until she was ready for college.

"Cooper Industries needs to update and expand before anything is an option," he said noncommittally.

Skylar pushed her coffee cup a few inches away. "Your expansion plans are a separate issue, and I want them to stay that way. Much as I'd like to use my position on the city council to keep you out of

Karin's life, I can't do it. My decision on your proposal will be based on its merits and what's good for Cooperton. The main thing holding it up is that I'm waiting for your response to my concerns, along with any new blueprints that might be needed."

Curiously, Aaron believed her. He didn't even think she would reject his proposal out of hand if he *didn't* take her suggestions.

"I've sent your ideas to the industrial engineers who worked on the original plans. I'm waiting for their evaluation."

"Fine. Call the mayor's office at city hall when you have anything to discuss, and Micki Jo will let me know."

He'd prefer contacting Skylar directly, but knew that she was trying to distance herself from him in any way possible. She'd drawn the line at discussing Cooper Industries at the Nibble Nook, now she was trying to limit it further.

"All right. So how about tomorrow?"

She swallowed visibly and shifted in her chair. "We could be ready to leave by 10:00 a.m. Shall I pack a picnic lunch?"

The flicker of emotion in Skylar's green eyes told Aaron she was far from being as composed as she sounded. "I don't want to put you to any trouble. We can stop at a restaurant."

"A picnic would save time if we want to be on the river during the warmest part of the day. I'll figure something out. I know Melanie's allergies and her likes and dislikes—what are yours?"

"No allergies, and I eat practically everything except anchovies or bell pepper on my pizza."

Skylar flinched. Aaron wondered about it until he remembered that Karin's favorite pizza was "everything except anchovies and bell peppers." It wasn't a genetic test and hardly an unusual dislike, yet it tightened his stomach.

He'd never wanted kids, not wanting to risk repeating his father's mistakes. Skylar's words had stung when she'd said his family considered child rearing to be someone else's responsibility...mostly because she was right. His flighty mother had sent him to live with his grandparents after he'd been bounced between her and Spence for years. And while he'd spent part of each summer with Celina and his stepfather in New York, his father had usually been too occupied with finding a new wife or getting rid of the old one to see him.

Lord, what a mess.

And Skylar had said something else that was bothering him...about it being hard for his grandparents to raise a young child at their age. He'd given lip service to the challenge they'd faced taking him, but had never really thought about it. They had been settled into a gracious life of middle-aged comfort when he'd come along with his boyish energy and resentment against the world. That *couldn't* have been easy.

He'd have to visit his grandparents soon.

It might be time to look at them in a whole new way.

"WE'RE DOING WHAT, MOM?" Karin asked. She scratched at a streak of paint on the back of her hand. The work was done in the church basement, and it looked awful nice. Mrs. Hashima and Mr. Calderas had worried that the brighter colors underneath would show through the primer and a single coat of enamel paint, but so far, so good.

"We're going rafting with Melanie and her brother tomorrow," her mom said. She was fixing dinner, along with a picnic to take on the rafting trip.

"Melanie didn't say anything about it."

"Her brother wanted to ask me first, in case we had plans."

"Oh. Okay."

Inner tubing on the river sounded like a blast. The youth group had wanted to do it last summer, but it never worked out. It would be odd doing it with Mr. Hollister, though.

"If you don't want to go, I'll call and tell him."

Karin blinked. "No, it'll be fun. And I'm sure Mellie has never swum in a river like me. Remember when we…" She stopped and bit her lip.

She'd started to talk about the time they'd gone camping in Yosemite National Park. They'd found a river to swim in near a covered bridge, and the water had been really deep and clear with giant boulders that were twice as tall as her dad. She'd loved diving down near the bottom and letting the current sweep her downstream. It was so free and cool, gliding along that way. Mom and Dad had loved it, too, and they'd done it over and over while Grandpa Joe and Grandma Grace sat with their feet in the water and watched.

"Remember what, Karin?"

Karin shrugged. "Nothing." Whenever she talked about her dad and the things they used to do together, it upset people. "Should I get the sunscreen?"

"It's in my bathroom. I already put the swimsuits away in a box of summer clothes, so I'll go up to the attic for them later."

Karin went into her mom's bathroom and got the sunscreen from the medicine cabinet. They used an unscented kind because perfume had given her dad headaches, and she tried not to get sad again as she put it in the backpack on the kitchen counter.

"Do you think this means Mr. Hollister is going to let Mellie move in with us?" she asked, brightening with the thought.

"I think he's just being friendly."

"I don't know. Nobody likes him. At school they think he's awful mean—that's why the kids wouldn't talk to Mellie at the mixer in August, just because he's her half brother. You shouldn't be mean to someone because of their family."

Her mom snapped a lid on a bowl of chicken salad and put it in the refrigerator. "Why don't you decide on your own about Aaron? That's what Grandma

Grace says to do, isn't it? 'Don't pay attention to gossip and make up your own mind about people.' You did that with Melanie. You saw your classmates weren't being nice and went to talk to her. And now you're best friends."

That was true. Her parents had never required her to "like" someone just because they were a grown-up, though they'd expected her to be polite. There was a sourpuss old lady at church that her mom didn't care for, but she was nice to Mrs. Delinsky and even brought her food when she wasn't well.

"Okay. Are you making pretzel rolls?" she asked, noticing the bowl of rising bread dough on the counter.

"I thought they'd be good with the chicken salad tomorrow."

"*Yum.* I'm going to call Mellie and tell her. She's never had pretzel bread before." Karin happily went to her room and flung herself on the bed with her cell phone.

It had been grand to have Melanie show up to help with the painting, and now they were all going inner tubing.

Awesome.

THE SEASONAL BUSINESSES renting rafts and inner tubes had mostly closed down, but by late Saturday afternoon, Aaron had located someone willing to provide five—one for each of them, and one to carry supplies.

The casual rafting he'd done as a teenager with his

friends seemed a long way off as he worried about things he hadn't considered before—like emergencies and life jackets. While he didn't think either girl would appreciate wearing them, he arranged to have four new life vests available. At least Melanie's education in swimming hadn't been neglected in the places she'd lived—she had even won medals at one school when she joined their swim team.

He was almost glad when Sunday dawned gray, thinking they'd be able to cancel the outing, but the overcast sky cleared quickly and it was comfortably warm by the time they arrived at the designated starting point on the river.

"Mr. Hollister?" said the man waiting by a truck filled with giant inner tubes. The logo on the tailgate said, Gordo's Fun in the Sun Water Equipment.

"Yes. Do you have everything?"

"Everything you asked for, and a bit more. I brought watertight containers to use for food and cell phones and such. Also ropes to connect the inner tubes so they don't get too far apart."

He cheerfully began unloading everything at the water's edge, no doubt delighted to have an unexpected customer who was willing to pay a premium for service.

"Shall we eat first, or find a place along the river?" Skylar asked when the vendor had driven away with a friendly assurance that he'd be waiting at the pickup point in a few hours.

"Later," the girls said in unison. They were hastily rubbing sunscreen on their skin, anxious to get started.

"All right."

Skylar shimmied out of her jeans and shirt and Aaron's mouth went dry. She wore a one-piece blue swimsuit cut high on the hips that was guaranteed to turn a man into a raving lunatic. He'd never been especially partial to bikinis—they revealed rather than teased—and at the moment he didn't care if he ever saw a woman in one again.

She joined the girls in applying sunscreen, and Aaron had another difficult moment, watching her hands slide over her neck and shoulders, arms...legs. He deliberately turned away, reminding himself that Skylar would sooner put a knee in his groin than consider him as a potential lover. And there was another issue that he couldn't ignore—Karin's and Melanie's presence. It didn't seem appropriate to have those thoughts with the teenagers nearby.

Before they could complain about the life jackets, Skylar fastened one on and put an oversize shirt over it. Part of her was covered as a result, but it did nothing to restore Aaron's peace of mind—the sight of Skylar's curves and long, long legs was burned onto his retinas.

"Do we have to, Mom?" Karin asked, her small nose wrinkling at the life jacket.

"Yes, you have to."

Skylar's firm reply ended additional protest. Melanie and Karin put them on, giggling as they looked at each other in the brightly colored safety gear.

"I just realized...what about the water wing things?" Aaron asked Skylar in an undertone. "I saw kids wearing them this summer—the air-filled things that go on the upper arms. Should they have those?"

"At their age? Not unless you want wholesale mutiny," she replied in the same soft voice. "Anyhow, my mother-in-law is convinced they could actually push a very young child's head under the water, so we never used them for Karin, even when she was small."

She obviously respected her mother-in-law, and Aaron had a sudden urge to meet the Gibsons. Karin mentioned her grandparents on a regular basis, and they'd obviously had a good deal of influence on her. If Karin *was* his daughter, he should know everyone important in her life. Though not right away. He was adjusting to a whole new reality and needed to take it a step at a time.

All at once Skylar grabbed his arm and pulled him farther away. "I just remembered something I should have said yesterday," she whispered. "Don't make an unusual effort to talk to Karin or get too close to her. You'll creep her out. You're a stranger, and she has no reason to trust you."

Aaron wanted to ask whose fault that was but figured Skylar would tell him to look in a mirror...or something earthier. And it *was* good advice.

"I won't," he promised. "I'm not sure how this should work, so I'll take it slowly."

"Good."

They returned to the riverbank and stowed the food and other gear in the watertight containers. One of the inner tubes had a net to hold everything and they fastened it around their supplies before pushing off.

The water was much colder than Aaron remembered from teenage rafting trips, though whether it was because he was older now, or due to the late time of year, he didn't know. Melanie and Karin didn't seem to mind, and Skylar lay with her legs and arms draped over the inner tube, looking relaxed as they drifted along.

Aaron had hoped their positions would shift around with the slow current, giving him a chance to be close to Karin and engage her in casual conversation, but the teenagers kicked and paddled with their hands to stay together.

Frustrated, he finally rested his head on the inner tube and listened to their innocent chatter. They complained about one of the teachers at school being dull, worried about a test coming up and speculated about who was going steady with whom. Karin made a couple of references to finding a cure to diseases, so when Aaron's inner tube bumped against Skylar's, he lifted his head.

"She wants to go to medical school?"

"And become a scientist," Skylar murmured without opening her eyes.

"When did that interest start?"

"After Joe, her grandfather, was treated for prostate cancer several years ago. It was caught early, but it scared the hell out of the family. That's when Grace and I got serious about organic foods."

"You seem very close to your in-laws."

"They're wonderful people."

"What about your own parents?"

Skylar instantly tensed and looked toward her daughter. Melanie's and Karin's inner tubes had drifted ahead the full length of the connecting ropes, and they were griping about the paint they hadn't been able to get out of their hair.

"I have no idea where my parents are, and don't want to," Skylar muttered. "They've never even seen Karin. Girls," she called in a louder voice, let's paddle toward that low place on the riverbank and have our picnic."

On shore they unpacked lunch from the cooler, Karin excitedly explaining to him that the five-inch rolls were pretzel bread her mother had baked the night before. Aaron bit into a thickly loaded sandwich and understood why Karin was so enthusiastic. None of the food was fancy or gourmet, but the chicken salad was crunchy with diced celery and tangy with dried cranberries, and the soft rolls were delicious. Fruit and chocolate brownies finished the meal, and he lay back in the sun feeling stuffed and lazy and half-asleep.

How long had it been since he'd just enjoyed an afternoon?

There always seemed to be something that needed doing. Not just at Cooper Industries, but in each of the executive positions he'd held around different parts of the country. Actually, he had something to do now, too…talk to Karin. The question was how to engage a teenager in conversation without "creeping her out" as Skylar had warned.

"Mr. Hollister?" said a voice.

Aaron opened his eyes. "Yes, Karin?"

"Thank you for inviting Mom and me to come today."

"Not at all. It's…uh…much more fun with company. And please, call me Aaron."

"Okay."

"Karin, I've wanted to apologize for the way I acted about Melanie going to the Nibble Nook to study," he said awkwardly. "Please understand, it had nothing to do with you."

"That's what Mom said."

"What else did she say?"

"Mostly that you had the wrong idea about the Nibble Nook and would figure it out sooner or later." She looked over at her mother and Melanie, who were taking a walk along the river. "Mellie says you went to college at UCLA. That's where I want to go, too."

"It's a good school. You'll do great there."

"That what my dad always told me. He used to…" She stopped and bit her lip.

"What about your dad?" Aaron prompted. He wasn't certain he wanted to hear about Jimmie Gibson, but if that was what Karin wanted to talk about, he was going to listen.

"He…he used to say dreaming is important, but *doing* can change the world."

"He sounds like a great guy."

"Yeah. Whenever I think of him, he's smiling. Dad laughed a lot, and he made Mom laugh, too." Karin glanced quickly toward Skylar again and sniffed. "I sure miss him."

Aaron wished he had something comforting to say, but he'd never lost someone special and couldn't pretend to know how she felt. "I guess…that is, it doesn't seem fair, does it?"

"No." She let out a huge sigh. "And sometimes I get awful mad."

"I don't blame you. I'd be angry, too."

Skylar and Melanie were walking back, and Karin leaned closer. "Don't tell Mom I was talking about my dad. It makes her sad. Promise?"

It seemed important to her, and Aaron figured it wouldn't do any harm to keep the small confidence from Skylar. "I promise. Why don't we get ready to go?"

Karin nodded, and they had everything packed within a few minutes, so all his sister and Skylar had to do was help push the rope-linked inner tubes back into the water.

Aaron was grateful that Skylar and the girls didn't

say anything to him as they got underway. He had more than his lunch to digest, including a disturbing conviction that Jimmie Gibson had been a better father than he could ever hope to be.

SKYLAR HOPED SHE hadn't made a mistake, going with Melanie on a short walk to give Aaron a chance to talk with Karin. He probably believed she'd prejudiced her daughter against him, but she hadn't, at least not consciously. If anything, she'd wanted to avoid talking about him altogether.

She didn't know what to think of Aaron's father, though she *did* believe S. S. Hollister was capable of contacting her without telling anybody. His motives were less clear—he hadn't mentioned wanting to help her and Karin; he'd just acted smug and condescending.

The afternoon air was losing its warmth as they neared a broad bend of the river, where the man from Fun in the Sun Water Equipment was waiting. Melanie and Karin obviously wished the rafting could go on forever, but Skylar was glad to get out and wrap up in a beach towel. Autumn had been unseasonably late arriving, but there was a bite in the air that told her it was finally here.

However, at the sight of a stretch limousine waiting, she turned to Aaron and raised an eyebrow.

"We needed a ride back to my car," he explained. "I said nothing extravagant."

"It's just a limo, and it was easier and more practical than calling for a taxi and having to wait."

She decided to let it go, and the teenagers instantly scrambled into the luxury vehicle to explore the "bar," obviously stocked specially for underage riders, with a hot-chocolate maker and snack foods. They quickly made cups of cocoa mounded with real whipped cream and sprinkled with cinnamon, laughing as it got on their noses when they tried to drink. If their other friends had been there, they might have felt compelled to act blasé, but with just the two of them, they were free to enjoy.

"Hey, you two, first things first," Skylar said, tossing beach towels and their clothes into them.

They took their time, sipping cocoa and eating junk food, in between drying themselves with the towels and squirming into their jeans and T-shirts.

Skylar shimmied into her own outer garments and gestured toward the limo. "You think that's practical?" she asked. "They're going to be on a sugar high for the rest of the day."

"I ordered a few extras, that's all."

She buttoned her jeans and blotted the damp length of her French braid with a towel. "You can't help it, can you? A fully stocked limo for a drive of a few miles—that's the sort of thing you think is normal."

"I'm not spoiled—I work hard," Aaron said seriously. "I could live extremely well on my trust fund, but I earned my way into a top CEO position, in companies unconnected to my family. Taking over

Cooper Industries is rather like being asked to become Captain of the Titanic ten minutes after hitting the iceberg."

Skylar folded the towel over her arm. "Are things that bad?"

"They're bad enough. Damn it, Skylar, I can't figure out why my grandfather didn't keep the factory updated—the equipment, the buildings, *nothing* done for thirty years. He wasn't saving a fund for the future, either. George is a smart man—he surely knew that was a poor way to do business."

"Maybe it was his age. He worked twenty years past the time when most people retire."

"Maybe."

Aaron sat on a fallen log and ran his fingers through his damp hair. He looked so endearingly young and perplexed that Skylar couldn't help seeing the resemblance to Karin. Her tension level, already high, shot skyward.

She sat on the other end of the log and gazed at the river flowing by. It was beautiful and tranquil, oblivious to human concerns, and for a brief moment, drifting along in the sunshine on the inner tube, she'd been at peace.

"The factory has gone through multiple transformations over the years," Aaron muttered, "with every Cooper president adjusting to changing times. Why not George? He did it as a young man when he took charge after his own father's retirement."

"Ask him."

"We aren't exactly close, but I'm having dinner with them on Tuesday. I'll add that to the things I want to discuss. Is there any chance Melanie could spend the evening with you and Karin? It would be more fun for her to hang out with Karin than sit around the house alone."

"Of course," Skylar agreed, at the same moment thinking wryly of how hard Aaron had tried to keep Melanie away from both her and the Nibble Nook. "She can go home with us after school and sleep over."

"Thanks. My grandparents invited her, but they'd be painfully proper and polite to cover how they feel. She'd be miserable."

Skylar got up and gathered the cooler and other containers from their picnic at the edge of the river. "How *do* they feel?"

"Well, my parents' divorce was ugly, and Melanie's only connection to them is through their ex-son-in-law."

"That shouldn't be important," Skylar said thoughtfully. "You're their grandson and Melanie is your sister. Doesn't that count for something?"

Aaron frowned. "It should. I'm just not sure they agree. Oh, before I forget, how about going to the Sacramento Zoo next Saturday? Is that something Karin would enjoy, or is it too childish? Melanie loves the idea—apparently she's never been to a zoo."

"I think Karin would be okay with it. She used to

want to be a veterinarian and adores *All Creatures Great and Small* and the other books by James Herriot."

"Great. We'll pick you up at nine, if it isn't too early."

"That's fine."

Aaron put a hand out to help her up, then slung the picnic gear over his shoulder. "By the way, thanks for giving me some time with Karin."

"Is that what I did?" Skylar said, keeping her face blank.

She still didn't want her daughter having anything to do with the Hollisters, but Aaron obviously wasn't going away anytime soon, and she was trying to be fair.

CHAPTER THIRTEEN

AARON DROPPED MELANIE at school on Monday and hurried to the office. In spite of their disagreement and her threat to resign, Peggy was at her desk, still sending him disapproving looks.

"Your father has phoned several times this morning," she said ominously. "It's bad enough speaking with him once in a while, but he keeps calling me 'Sunshine' and asking for my physical...*dimensions*. He claims I sound like a Playboy bunny and could make a fortune working at a dial-for-sex 900 number."

"Damn." Aaron could strangle his father for acting like an irreverent lecher. Peggy unquestionably had a husky, melodic voice which sounded far younger than her actual years, but that was no excuse. "Please accept my apologies. That sort of thing is unacceptable. Check caller identification from now on and don't answer if it's from him."

"But he's your father."

"Who behaves like an X-rated Peter Pan who will never grow up or realize that he should have respect for other people. I'll talk to him, but believe me, he isn't going to change."

Peggy's expression softened. "That's all right. I can handle him."

"You shouldn't have to. I'm serious—you have enough to do without that nonsense."

The woman actually smiled, dropping decades from her appearance. "All right. Shall I get you a cup of coffee?"

Aaron was taken aback. She had never offered to get coffee, and he didn't expect an assistant to wait on his personal needs. "Only if you're getting one for yourself."

She dimpled. "Cream or sugar?"

"Black. And thank you."

Peggy was back with the coffee so quickly he barely had time to sit down at his desk. "Here you are. Let me know if there's anything else you need."

She left, still smiling, and Aaron shook his head. He hadn't been sure she had teeth, she'd been so tight-lipped their entire acquaintance.

He opened the bottom drawer in the desk and withdrew the file she had given him over a week before. Occupied with thoughts of Skylar and Melanie, he'd tossed it there, intending to forget it altogether. But the things Skylar had said about his employees were bothering him.

He started with the oldest memos, dating back to a few years after he was born. Mostly they were general, this and that about equipment and processing, issues that applied to the functioning of the factory. Then he found photocopies of the leases his grandfather had signed with several farmers for the land east of the factory, the land Aaron had been hoping to develop.

In the margin of one was a note in his grandfather's handwriting.

> *Spoke to John Isaacs and others this morning. Assured them leases would be renewed at reasonable rate if organic venture is successful. New age nonsense or cutting-edge idea? Time will tell.*

Aaron stared. He'd read the original paperwork, and it said nothing about a guaranteed renewal. An unsigned, handwritten bit of text might not be legally binding, but his grandfather's note suggested a verbal agreement had been made. And whether it was legally enforceable or not, Aaron wasn't going to break his grandfather's word—if George had promised to renew the leases, that's what would happen.

He set the annotated photocopy on the corner of the desk and continued reading.

A polite petition from the employees for a one-hour meal break came several memos later, along with George's reply, approving the request. Halfway through the folder, Aaron found a notice to the employees discussing permission to take home factory seconds. Pain began throbbing in his temples as he read George's private note written in the corner.

Longtime custom started by Grandfather during the Depression when we were only producing canned goods. Decided formal memo should be issued.

Then Aaron found material supporting a seven-and-a-half-hour day for "employees with a compelling reason to need an extended meal break." Another handwritten note appeared in the margins.

Not a good policy for assembly-line jobs and may affect production output, but Sarah will never forgive me if I don't support working mothers.

The idea that his grandmother was aware of the demands placed on working parents was hard to fathom.

When he'd finished reading the last document in the folder, Aaron pulled out a bottle of aspirin and swallowed several tablets.

Hell. He'd come into Cooper Industries and seen scandalous employee behavior and blamed it on a workforce taking advantage of their aged employer. It was more complicated than that, however. George Cooper had made the kind of people decisions you made in a small family business, forgetting that Cooper Industries wasn't small, and allowing abuses to grow out of his decisions because he didn't monitor the results. The trick would be finding a way to mix the past and present in a way that would keep the company viable.

In the meantime, Aaron wrote a note to the shift foremen and forewomen, saying he was reinstating permission for employees to take home a reasonable number of factory seconds. He asked them to monitor distribution until a process could be established to properly identify and label safe-to-consume food items not meeting Cooper Industries retail standards, and which ensured employees were able to share equally in the benefit.

Stepping into the outer office, he handed Peggy a signed copy and asked her to issue it immediately.

"The employees will be so pleased, Mr. Hollister," she said, looking surprised. "But I thought you didn't approve."

"I'm not sure I do, but I'll survive."

"I'll get it right out."

Aaron's second memo, to the general employee population, was more difficult to write. Skylar had suggested his lack of trust was affecting employee relations, but how could he fix it when he *didn't* entirely trust them? After all, there had been abuses, and a variable-length meal break didn't work well in factory positions—the people who were back at a certain time often had to wait on the ones who weren't. He finally wrote out a draft that didn't express everything, but might be a start.

To Cooper Industry Employees:
I am evaluating the standardized meal-break policy established several months ago. Produc-

tion output significantly increased with the new policy, but concerns have been expressed, especially on behalf of working parents with childcare issues.

Your ideas are welcome in identifying a solution that maintains productivity, but also supports a positive working environment.

I also wish to form a committee to evaluate the feasibility of a day-care facility. Please submit your name to a foreman/forewoman if you are interested in working on this committee.

Aaron saved the memo on his computer so he could review it over the next week before sending it out. He had other calls to make, and he might as well get to them. His father was first—Spence probably wasn't going to listen to reason, but there wasn't any harm in trying. As for why he might have called…Aaron wasn't overly curious. Spence rarely called about anything important.

MELANIE PUT A nightshirt and clothes in her backpack on Tuesday morning so Mrs. Gibson…*Skylar,* wouldn't have to go by Aaron's house on the way home. Mrs. Gibson had told her the day before that it was okay to call her Skylar. It was nice, because Karin was getting to call Aaron by his first name.

"Do you…well, have what you need?" Aaron asked as she came downstairs. "For tonight?"

"Uh-huh." It was going to be splendid spending the whole afternoon and night with the Gibsons.

They drove to the school and Melanie got out hastily. She liked Aaron much better now than she had in the beginning, but she still didn't want the other kids seeing them together more than necessary. Once she got her driver's license, maybe she could drive herself. Aaron had arranged for lessons, so it shouldn't be long before she could take the tests.

"Bye," she said over her shoulder as she hurried up the sidewalk.

They were all going to the zoo together on Saturday, and she knew Aaron was making other plans, too. Maybe he figured if she did things with Karin she wouldn't care about moving in with the Gibsons, but she wasn't going to change her mind. She hadn't talked to either her mother or father about it yet, though Aaron had said they'd both called. She had asked him if they were mad at her because of the lawyer, and he'd said they weren't, but wouldn't say more than that, other than her mother being worried for Mrs. Gibson because her husband had died.

"But I can help Mrs. Gibson," she'd said. "I'll do chores just like Karin and volunteer to do extras."

Aaron had just shaken his head, not wanting to talk about it anymore. He was being really nice to her, even though she'd confessed that she *hadn't* asked Skylar for permission to move in with them. Most of the places she'd stayed they'd wanted her to be invisible. It wasn't that they'd *said* she should be invisible, but she could tell when people thought she was in the way.

On Tuesday evening, Aaron drove up the circular brick driveway in front of his grandparents' house. He looked around the brightly lit yard as he got out, marveling at how little the place had changed over the years.

Since his last visit, the summer flowers had been replaced with the winter bedding plants his grandmother favored. They were always the same, spaced equally, with shredded bark mulch giving a uniform appearance to the ground. The trees were bigger and older, but the lawns were precisely cut and the driveway spotless. He knew that if he went to the back, he would see the converted carriage-house garage looking crisp and clean, and the driveway there as perfectly maintained.

"Aaron, please come in," said Sarah Cooper when she opened the door. "We're glad you were free tonight."

He stepped inside and was surrounded by the familiar scent of beeswax polish used for the wood furniture and hardwood floor.

George appeared at the library door and nodded. "Good evening, Aaron."

"Hello, Grandfather."

His grandmother gestured to the formal living room. "Shall we have a glass of sherry? It's already poured."

Aaron didn't care for the sweet wine the elderly

couple enjoyed, but they'd had a custom of sipping imported Spanish sherry as an aperitif since before he was born.

"And how is Melanie?" Sarah asked as she sat down. "Doing better in school?"

"Her grades have improved and she's caught up with her classes." Aaron took a sip from his glass and tried to appreciate the sherry—no doubt it was one of the finest that Spain produced. The stuff was just so damned sweet. If they had liked a dry variety, it might be different.

"Excellent, school is important."

The Coopers were both aged and ageless, Aaron mused. While they were in their eighties, they looked much the same as when he was a boy. Yet their outlook was more Victorian than twenty-first century.

Or was it?

"Grandmother, I understand you have an interest in the needs of working mothers," he murmured in the silence. From the few times he'd visited them since returning to Cooperton, he knew that silence could stretch interminably if he didn't say something.

Sarah's eyes widened. "Why, yes. Despite the so-called sexual revolution, child-care responsibilities seem to fall largely to women, yet they often work, as well. Nevertheless, I believe support should be given any working parent, regardless of gender."

That might be the most she'd ever said to him in a single stream of words.

"Then you'll be pleased that I'm considering an onsite child-care facility at Cooper Industries."

A hint of a smile curved her mouth. "That would be a long-overdue advance."

George let out a faint huff. "Now, Sarah, I believe we've discussed this."

"Obviously *not* sufficiently."

"Very well, my dear." He inclined his head and finished his sherry while Sarah's gaze filled with quiet satisfaction.

Aaron blinked, seeing nuances between them that he'd never caught before. Of course, as a boy he hadn't participated in the formal aperitif ritual, and at dinner he'd put his head down and eaten as quickly as possible so he could get away. Once he'd turned sixteen and had a car to give him freedom, he had gone out whenever possible.

"I've been speaking to a member of the city council about expanding the factory," he said. "Would you like to hear my plans, Grandfather?"

George waved a vague hand. "That isn't necessary. I'm sure the council will approve."

At least he hadn't said his usual "What's good for Cooperton, is good for Cooper Industries." Aaron wasn't sure it was true, but it fit with George's desire to be seen as a benefactor of the community.

"The plan is to expand east of the plant," he said casually.

His grandfather frowned. "East? But that's the land leased to the organic farmers."

"The lease is expiring this coming February."

"Oh. Yes." George clenched his glass until his knuckles went white, and he stared fixedly at the small amount of wine it still contained. "Organic products have become quite popular. The...the farmers are expecting their leases to be renewed."

Aaron gulped the remainder of his sherry in a single swallow. While they weren't close, his grandfather's tension was hard to watch. He was about to explain the alternate plan to expand in a different direction when George's glass suddenly broke.

Both Aaron and Sarah jumped to their feet.

"*George,* you're bleeding," his grandmother cried.

"It's nothing, my dear."

"I'll get something," she said, rushing out of the living room.

Aaron took the broken pieces of the glass and set them aside, shaken more by the depth of emotion he'd seen in his grandfather than by the small trickle of red on the old man's hand. How many times had he thought of George as a cold fish, doing the right thing because of image and pride in his family heritage, rather than any real concern for the people of Cooperton?

George took out his handkerchief and dabbed his fingers. "I realize that I no longer have a say in the matter, but I would greatly appreciate you renewing those leases," he breathed. "The farmers have spent large sums getting certified organic. They...they have worked very hard on their endeavor."

"Of course, Grandfather," Aaron said gently. "It may be more logical expanding south, anyway, since the town has plans for a new sewage treatment plant in that direction. And the city council has expressed concerns that we would be building over prime farmland with my primary plan. The land is more marginal on the alternate site."

"A superb idea." Unbelievably, George patted his hand. "I've watched your progress in business over the years. Exceptionally well-done. I realize it was a sacrifice returning to Cooperton."

Aaron had felt that way initially; now he wasn't so sure. There was Karin to consider, and the Coopers were another question mark. Perhaps getting to know them better wouldn't be such a bad thing. They were certainly talking to him more than they ever had, as if a logjam had suddenly cleared.

"I'm doing all right here," he said. "I admit Peggy has been a challenge. Until this morning, that is. I must have said something she appreciated because she suddenly can't do enough for me, though who knows how long it will last."

"Ah." George nodded. "Getting along with her is really quite simple—let Peggy know she's needed and she'll move the world for you. You'll never find a more loyal employee. Her husband is a foreman in the fruit-cup division, a fine man. And her son was shaping well for advancement when I retired."

"I'll keep that in mind."

Sarah returned to clean and bandage the small

wounds on George's hand. She seemed more upset about it than her husband, so when the cook came in a few minutes later and announced dinner, Aaron tried to leave so they could relax.

"No," they declared in unison.

"You must stay," Sarah added, fidgeting with the first aid supplies. "Cook fixed pot roast because she remembered it was your favorite."

"All right. It's been a long time since I've had Mrs. Ryland's pot roast."

The meal went more smoothly than Aaron could recall any meal going with the Coopers, though it was a long way from comfortable. He had planned to ask more questions, but he didn't want to risk anything else dramatic happening.

Besides, he had more than enough to consider already.

SKYLAR PEEKED INTO Karin's bedroom. She was on the floor in her sleeping bag, with Melanie on the bed. They hadn't wanted to be in separate bedrooms, saying it was more like a slumber party this way. Slumber party or not, it was a school night, and Skylar had insisted they be in bed with the lights out by ten o'clock. Predictably, they'd giggled and whispered until a stern warning had gotten them to settle down.

She was folding laundry when a faint knocking at the front door caught her attention. Peeking through the curtain, she saw Aaron.

"What are you doing here?" she asked, opening the door. "Melanie is supposed to spend the night."

"I thought I'd stop by and see how you were doing." His mouth was taut and there was a troubled look in his eyes; obviously this was more than a status check on his sister.

"I take it dinner with your grandparents didn't go well."

He shrugged.

Skylar cast a quick glance toward the back of the house, then grabbed a jacket from the coat closet. "Let's go out on the porch so we don't wake the girls. We can sit on the swing."

"Good idea."

The porch swing under the old wisteria vine was dark and private with the light off and they sat there for several minutes in silence.

It was a chilly night, and while Skylar regretted the end of summer, there were compensations. Thanksgiving would soon come with the rich scent of sage and roasting turkey and apple pie. And then Christmas, with the lights and color and hum of music. She'd talked with Grace and Joe, and they were all determined to keep the holidays from being as sad this year.

She'd also told them about Aaron.

They had instantly declared that he'd better not try to take Karin away or he'd be sorry. Their staunch support was so much like Jimmie that she'd almost cried. Some people wouldn't have considered their son's adopted child to be a "real" grandchild, but her in-laws were ready to go to war on Karin's behalf.

"Wouldn't the Coopers talk to you?" Skylar asked at length.

She felt, rather than saw, Aaron's shrug. "Questioning them is harder than it sounds. My grandparents were distant when I was a boy—they took me out of duty and lost few opportunities to remind me of it. That isn't the best basis for communication."

Duty sounded like a lousy way to be raised—perhaps the loneliness she'd seen in Aaron's eyes years ago had been real. The old saying, "to understand all is to forgive all," could be going too far in his case, but understanding his childhood better did explain a great deal.

"The Coopers are very proper whenever I've seen them in public. Mr. Cooper is usually the Grand Marshal of the Founder's Day Parade, and very popular for ribbon cuttings, such as the rededication of city hall."

He let out a short, humorless laugh. "My grandparents are proper, all right, but they aren't as unemotional as I've always thought. Grandfather was so unnerved at one point, he broke a glass in his hand."

"Was he hurt?"

"A small cut and a few nicks. Grandmother was rattled, as well. I didn't try to get any more information after that—it's obviously going to take a while to get the answers I want."

Skylar put a hand on Aaron's arm. "But didn't

tonight already answer some of those questions? You thought they were unemotional, and they aren't. And if they *do* have strong feelings, maybe your questions need to change."

"Could be. They asked me to Sunday lunch. I've avoided them as much as possible since coming back to Cooperton, but I'll have to go."

She thought of the countless family meals she'd eaten with the Gibsons, looking forward to each one. They talked on the phone several times a week, visited back and forth, and she'd often wished they lived in Cooperton instead of Trident because seeing them was a pleasure, not a chore. Then again, the Gibsons were nothing like the Coopers. She'd loved them before she had ever thought marrying Jimmie was a possibility.

"By the way," Aaron said. "I've decided to renew the organic farmers' leases. Why in hell didn't you tell me my grandfather made promises to them about the land? You knew, didn't you?"

"I knew," she admitted. "I buy direct from the growers, and we talk. They've been worried since they hadn't heard whether you were going to let them stay. Two have invested in hydroponics facilities so they can produce crops year-round, and it was going to be a bad blow if they couldn't continue."

"You didn't tell them about my plans for the company?"

"Nope, I was hoping you'd change your mind, and I didn't think hysterical phone calls would help."

"It wouldn't have." Aaron's laugh was more genuine this time, and he stretched out his legs. "God, I'm tired. Doing anything with my grandparents is exhausting. The negotiations when I took over the company were bad enough to get through, but having a meal with them is like being flattened by a steamroller."

"I take it Mr. Cooper didn't tell you about the leases when you became president."

"Not a word. We've had a number of phone conversations since, along with a few meetings, and he's obviously getting reports on the company from someone, but all he says is, 'What's good for Cooperton is good for Cooper Industries.' The odd thing is, I think he's trying to let me run the place without interfering. I thought he'd drive me insane, calling and demanding things be done a certain way, even though he'd signed everything over."

Skylar didn't say anything for a moment. Two months ago she couldn't have imagined having a civilized conversation with Aaron, but here she was, talking to him on her front porch.

"Mr. Cooper's retirement was years overdue," she said finally. "Though I don't think anyone thought it was strange because he looks so much younger than his age. And they knew he was expecting you to return one day and take his place."

"Some people don't want to retire, but I never would have guessed George cared about anything beyond his public image. It was rough watching him tonight. He's always seemed a stern authoritarian whose pride meant more to him than breathing."

A queer sensation went through Skylar. Obviously they'd both had lousy parenting growing up, in radically different ways. Her poor childhood was one of the things that had scared her when Karin was born. After all, what had *she* known about being a good mother? She'd struggled with being overprotective, and only Grace Gibson's sensible advice had kept her from making more mistakes.

Aaron shifted in the swing next to her and gently tugged a lock of her hair. He didn't say anything else for a while and neither did Skylar, but it was a companionable silence. The swing rocked back and forth, and she closed her eyes, listening to the faint sounds of the night. A dog down the street barked once, a friendly yip, as if pleased or excited—it was Itty, the Takahashis' German shepherd. The breeze ruffled the leaves of bushes and trees around the house. She could even hear the faint sound of Aaron breathing.

"I suppose I should get home," he said without moving.

"And I should get back inside in case the girls need something." She shivered and Aaron tugged her close.

"You should be wearing a heavier jacket."

"It doesn't matter if I'm going back into the house."

"No, it doesn't." His fingers were splayed along her

rib cage, and she swallowed. A few more inches and he'd be touching her breasts; the alarming part was that she *wanted* him to touch her. "What is it about you that always gets to me?" Aaron whispered. "You drove me crazy when we were kids." He kissed the corner of her mouth in a tempting caress.

"Reminding me about the past isn't the best idea right now," she warned.

"Okay." He kissed her more deeply, and her body, unaccustomed to the newly arrived autumn chill, heated abruptly. Aaron's tongue flicked between her lips, teasing playfully, and Skylar acknowledged that he'd learned something about kissing since he was seventeen.

"You aren't concentrating," he whispered, tipping her backward on the seat of the swing and flicking his thumbs across her nipples.

Every cell in her body was suddenly at attention and he took advantage of it, kissing and coaxing a response with expert precision.

She didn't know where it might have gone if she hadn't heard a low, urgent voice from the sidewalk saying, "*No,* don't…come back here," followed by a cold nose thrusting itself into her neck and a canine tongue swiping her check.

"*Itty, stop.*" Skylar nudged the German shepherd's head away and scrambled upright. She pushed Aaron back onto the swing as he started to stand, whispering, "You stay here," before grabbing Itty's leash to lead him back to his waiting master.

AARON TRIED NOT to groan as he waited for Skylar to return.

Damned dog, he cursed silently.

He looked around. The front and side of the home was banded by the wide farmhouse porch, and the swing was tucked into the deep shade of a climbing bush. It was already a dark night, with no moon, so the velvet black surrounding him provided near-perfect privacy.

Except to dogs, apparently.

A few words from the quiet roadside conversation drifted in, though not enough to get the gist of what they were saying. Soon Skylar laughed, and he heard her returning up the walkway.

"That was Itty," she said, remaining out of arm's reach.

Obviously, she was no longer in the mood for snuggling.

"Itty?"

"Short for Itty Bitty."

"Itty Bitty?" Aaron repeated in disbelief. "That animal is huge."

"He's tiny compared to the Saint Bernard they used to have. Their daughter was four when they got Itty as a pup, and Wendy kept calling him Itty Bitty. The name stuck."

He reluctantly stood up as she yawned. "I'd better get home. You were probably on your way to bed."

"Actually, I was doing the laundry. Teenage girls go through a lot of clothes in a week."

"Tell me about it."

Laundry was the one domestic task Aaron could muddle through with a minimum of damage, which was a good thing because the woman from Trident who cleaned house for him had adamantly declared, "No windows, no laundry and *no litter boxes.*"

Melanie had looked wistful when she heard the words "litter boxes" and he'd worried that she would want a cat. Now he was bothered that she hadn't asked. Poor kid, aside from periodic moments of sass and defiance, she was afraid to ask for much of anything. Requesting permission to come live with the Gibsons must have taken a huge amount of resolve on her part...and a good push from Karin.

"I'll let you get back to work," he said. "Thanks for hosting Melanie tonight."

"She's always welcome."

Skylar had said that more than once, but it no longer irritated him. If nothing else, Melanie needed to know, beyond a doubt, that there was a place where she was welcomed and wanted...he just wished he'd done a better job of making certain that place was *his* house.

Aaron waited until Skylar was inside with the door locked before walking to his car. He got in with a dissatisfied frown. The plush interior of the Mercedes and the fashionable house he'd leased were a far cry from porch swings and farmhouses, but as he looked at Skylar's front door, he couldn't help wishing he was on the other side of it.

CHAPTER FOURTEEN

"Can you believe it?" Greg asked as he helped wipe down the Nibble Nook counters on Friday. "Mr. Hollister is letting employees take factory seconds home again."

Skylar froze. She didn't want to think about Aaron, much less talk about him. Letting him kiss her the other evening had been foolish. What if Karin had woken up and seen them on the porch? She wasn't ready to see her mother with another man.

"He is?" Skylar asked, trying to sound casual.

"Yes. Apparently Mr. Hollister is working on a process for it to be given to employees equally, rather than whoever grabs the stuff. You know my sister... She'd never be pushy, so she rarely took anything. The foremen are monitoring it until everything is settled, and Katie's received several items over the past few days. Anything extra helps on their budget."

Skylar nodded. Greg's brother-in-law had been injured the year before, and he was finally back to work as a mechanic, but the family was in debt and struggling to keep their heads above water.

"Do you think she'll be happier at Cooper Industries now?"

"It's too early to know for sure, but Katie likes that things are being done more fairly. She said Mr. Hollister walked through their division this week and was really friendly. Mr. Cooper used to do that, except Mr. Hollister asked what they thought would help make the factory run better."

"That's nice."

"It sure is. She was getting awfully fed up with the place."

Deep in thought, Skylar went outside and began cleaning out the half whiskey barrels she used as flower planters. In the summer, petunias and lobelia and other flowers crowded the planters, spilling out in a riot of color, but a hard frost the night before had singed the lingering blossoms.

Normally she was able to clear her mind while gardening, yet she couldn't stop thinking about what Greg had told her. Was it possible that Aaron had changed his factory-seconds policy because of what she'd said the previous weekend? It would be nice to think he had, but it was just as likely that he'd finally realized he needed to do something to improve his employee relations.

Annoyed with herself for caring what Aaron did, she finished her task by piling pumpkins and gourds on top of the barrels for decoration.

A few late customers came and went, and at two-thirty, Greg put up the Closed sign on the three cashiers windows. The windows had rarely been in simultaneous use until Aaron took over Cooper Industries; now they needed all three during the factory meal breaks in order to handle the influx of patrons.

Unfortunately, while night-shift employees often stopped for breakfast after work, the Nibble Nook was only open for the daytime meal break. The two later shifts had to rely on food they'd brought with them, or the Cooper Cafeteria since the nearest fast-food stand was several miles away near the highway.

Karin and Melanie arrived from school and promptly sat down to study.

"You're dedicated," Skylar said as she brought them a tray of snacks.

"If we finish our homework today, we won't have to think about it at the zoo or anything," Karin declared.

"You don't have any tests next week?"

The girls exchanged a glance. "Uh, one for history," Karin admitted. "But it isn't until Wednesday. We can study for it on Monday and Tuesday."

"All right, if you're sure."

Skylar went inside to finish counting out the cash registers. Greg took the deposit to the bank for her on Fridays, and she didn't want to hold him up.

"We're done," he told her a few minutes later.

Skylar handed him the deposit envelope. "Me, too. I'll see you next week," she called out. "Thanks, everyone. Great job this week, it was crazier than usual."

A chorus of agreement came from the departing employees.

Tired, Skylar rolled her shoulders to release the

tension. She'd tried to keep Aaron out of her work life, now that Nibble Nook employees were talking about him. The customers, on the other hand, had complained less about Cooper Industries this week. She'd sensed a difference, and Greg's comments had just confirmed that things might be improving at Cooper Industries.

Sighing, Skylar went into the back room and looked at the picture hanging there. The informal family portrait was one of her favorites, and it was particularly good of Jimmie. After the funeral, small messages had begun appearing on the plain white wall, written there by employees.

Best boss EVER.

I never knew anyone like him.

Made you want to try harder.

Greatest laugh in the world... She always smiled when she read that one and Jimmie would have loved it as a tribute. He'd believed food was less important than laughing, because food just fed the body, while laughter fed the soul.

Skylar looked down and realized she'd been unconsciously twisting the wedding ring on her finger.

What would Joe and Grace think if they knew she was attracted to Aaron Hollister? A few months ago they'd rather awkwardly explained that nobody expected her to be alone for the rest of her life…and that Jimmie would say the same thing. Skylar wasn't sure if they'd been suggesting she get remarried one day, or talking about her starting to date, but at the time, dating had been the last thing on her mind. How could she think about an adult social life when she was busy with the Nibble Nook and had a teenage daughter at home? Besides, she would have sworn that part of her life was over.

She touched Jimmie's face in the photograph, but it was a poor substitute for real touching and real conversation. Was it possible that Karin was having so much trouble letting go of her father because her mother was having the same problem? Jimmie would have wanted to be remembered with love, not pain.

"Mooommm," Karin's voice called from outside the Nibble Nook, and Skylar jerked guiltily.

"Yes?" she said, stepping outside.

"I don't get why we have to read this," her daughter complained, pushing a small book across the table. "We're already learning about the Civil War in history class."

"The American Lit class always has students read *The Red Badge of Courage* when they're studying the Civil War," Skylar murmured, feeling almost nostalgic for her high-school days.

"Isn't there a movie we can watch instead?"

"That wouldn't be the same. But it's a great book—supposedly the first time color was used to describe emotions."

"Really?" It was Melanie, and she looked at her own copy of the novel with greater interest. She'd confided in Skylar that she wanted to be an author, except she didn't want anyone else to know in case they thought she was being bigheaded. "You mean like, 'I feel blue' or something?"

"I don't remember if that's one he used, but yes," Skylar said, smiling. "I think the author only lived until he was twenty-nine, but he's considered one of the best writers of the eighteen hundreds. Imagine changing literature and being so well-known that young."

"Twenty-nine is *old,*" Karin objected.

"You won't feel that way when you're twenty-nine," Skylar advised, hiding a smile. "When are you supposed to finish the book?"

"In a couple of weeks."

"It's an exciting story. May I borrow it this weekend since you won't be studying?" she asked casually.

Karin shot a look at the novel as if she now couldn't bear to let it out of her sight. "I might start it tonight after all."

"Just let me know."

All at once both Melanie and Karin looked alarmed, and Skylar turned around to see Aaron pulling into a parking space. The girls began whispering together, probably because his presence at the Nibble Nook had usually meant trouble. Perhaps it was Pavlovian, but her own heartbeat raced faster, as well.

She walked to the Mercedes as he got out. "Is something wrong?"

"No, but I wanted to suggest going to the zoo in San Francisco tomorrow, instead of Sacramento. That way we could go to Ghirardelli Square for ice cream and eat at Fisherman's Wharf. The girls would like that, wouldn't they?"

"Sure, but there's a two-night school trip coming up to San Francisco," Skylar said. "Isn't Melanie going? Karin has been talking about it for weeks and the consent forms are due on Monday."

"I haven't heard about a trip."

"Melanie?" she called.

"Yes, Mrs. Gib…Skylar?" the teenager said, coming over with a worried expression.

"Aren't you in one of the classes going to San Francisco week after next?"

Melanie shifted from one foot to the other. "Uh…yes."

Aaron frowned. "Why didn't you tell me about it?"

She bit her lip. "I don't know."

"Give me the consent form tonight, and whatever information they gave you about the trip so I can look it over," he said, looking harassed.

"Okay." She hastily rejoined Karin, and they diligently bent over their textbooks.

Aaron leaned against his car and groaned. "It's as if she was afraid to ask if she could go. I thought we were getting along better. What am I doing wrong?"

"I wouldn't read too much into it," Skylar advised in the same low tone. "I can't tell you how many times Karin told us she needed us to sign a consent form on the day it was due. Or that she was supposed to bring cupcakes to school the next morning, usually after the store was closed. I learned to keep supplies on hand for those occasions. When she was younger I went through her book bag every night to see if the teacher sent something home, but at her age I hate to invade her privacy."

"Thank God. I thought it was just me."

"No. You just haven't built up immunity to the bursts of adrenaline kids put you through."

She didn't tell him that a few weeks ago she'd also made cookies for Melanie, who'd planned to buy them at a bakery to avoid telling her brother that she needed to bring something for a school bake sale. Hearing that wouldn't bolster his confidence about how he was doing in his quasi-parental role—though why she should care how he felt was another question.

Aaron gave her a lopsided grin. "What about the class trip—do you think it's all right?"

"They have parents going along to chaperone, and the teacher in charge is very strict. It wouldn't be fair to leave Melanie out."

"I know."

"As for tomorrow, the Sacramento Zoo is nice," Skylar said. "And if you want to do something else in town as well, we could visit Sutter's Fort."

"I remember that place from school field trips. California gold-rush history, right?"

She nodded. "Along with pioneer and Native American."

"Sounds good. How about going to dinner tonight,

too? There's a new place out in the country—a Victorian converted into a restaurant. I'm curious since it's in the original home my great-great-great-grandfather built for his family. If we go by six, we can still get an early start in the morning."

It sounded tempting. Skylar had read about the grand opening of the elegant restaurant in the newspaper, though the article hadn't mentioned that the property once belonged to the Cooper family. The place was closer to Sacramento than Cooperton, and the building had been abandoned for years before being bought by an entrepreneur. The out-of-town location was a bonus—she wasn't sure she wanted to be seen with Aaron. For one thing, anyone who'd known them in high school might start speculating about things she didn't want anyone thinking about.

"All right. I have to finish here and need to change my clothes, but we could be ready by five-thirty. Karin," she called over her shoulder, "we're going to dinner with Aaron and Melanie. You'll need to wear something nice."

The two teenagers grinned happily.

"Sounds like a plan, then," Aaron said. "I'll help so you can leave sooner."

Skylar raised an eyebrow and gave him a visual inspection. He was wearing one of his expensive suits and another pair of leather shoes which likely cost more than an average family's mortgage payment. "Dressed like that? I don't think so."

"What's wrong with my clothes?"

"Nothing if you don't mind belonging to the Old Fuddy-Duddies club."

AARON TRIED NOT to be insulted. His sister and Karin giggled—they'd obviously heard Skylar's comment— and he gave them a mock glare. They giggled again.

"For your information, *Mrs. Gibson,* I'm supposed to look a certain way as president of the company."

"Says who? You want to modernize Cooper Industries, so modernize your look. Be original. An innovator. Show them you don't have to think the same way as everyone."

He opened his mouth…then shut it.

Skylar didn't seem to notice his speechlessness; she went into the Nibble Nook and came out a few minutes later with a bucket of soapy water.

"You're still here?" she asked, looking genuinely surprised.

"Of course I'm here. I said I'd help." He took off his jacket and tossed it into the Mercedes.

"Hmm."

She took a hose from a cabinet on the wall and screwed it onto the faucet. Aaron cleared the trash from the tables as she scrubbed, then grabbed the hose to spray everything down behind her. It was strangely comfortable, and they kidded back and forth as they worked.

His shoes got wet and the leather would never be the same, but Skylar had started him thinking. Even if she was joking about the Fuddy-Duddies club, he couldn't deny there was truth to it. He'd adopted conservative business attire early in his career in an attempt to get people to take him seriously. The Hollister name *wasn't* an advantage if you wanted to do something more than throw a wild party and drink champagne—not with his father and Matt being infamous for their playboy ways.

But he wasn't working in the computer industry any longer; he ran a factory complex. If his grandfather's formal mahogany office furniture didn't fit the image, neither did his own tailored suits and ties.

"Hey. Watch where you point that thing."

Startled, Aaron looked up and saw that he'd absentmindedly sprayed Skylar with the hose. "Sorry."

She wiped the water dripping from her chin. "Oh, well, I probably wasn't going to have time for a shower before dinner, anyway."

He laughed. There weren't many women who'd put up with getting doused without becoming angry. "You're entitled to squirt me back."

"Naw. I prefer getting revenge in my own way. Preferably when you aren't expecting it."

She went back to scrubbing tables, and he tried not to focus on her shapely rear end. It wouldn't do for Karin *or* Melanie to see him leering.

Aaron could almost forget that Skylar had gone all those years without telling him he might be a father. He didn't understand it, any more than he understood why she hadn't accepted Spence's money. She'd claimed she didn't want her daughter around his family, but while the Coopers and Hollisters had their problems, they weren't monsters. If nothing else, Karin's education could cost a small fortune, and however good they might be, Nibble Nook hamburgers wouldn't pay for something like medical school.

Of course, Skylar also hadn't wanted Karin anywhere around *him*. It was a bitter pill to swallow—he'd never had much trust in women, but Skylar didn't trust him, either. And he couldn't deny that he should have treated her better, both when they were kids and after he'd returned to Cooperton.

So why was he messing around with her?

He'd nearly lost his head the other night on the porch swing. There was no escaping the fact that she still reached into his gut and made him go irrational…and that he enjoyed it.

Deep in thought, Aaron continued spraying down the eating area. The girls automatically moved to one of the front tables and dried it off with rags from the storage cabinet, before settling down to their studies again. Karin must have been doing that for years, coming here after school while her parents finished up for the day—shifting around while everything got done, playing or studying inside once the weather became too unpleasant. She must have been a cute little thing—stubborn and fiercely independent like her mother.

A shaft of sorrow went through him.

He'd never wanted children, but if Karin was really his daughter, he'd missed a hell of a lot.

THE NEXT MORNING Karin rolled over and blinked at the clock on her bedside table. Oh, good, she could sleep longer. It was before seven, and Mellie and Aaron weren't coming until nine.

Last night had been awesome. She'd never eaten at a fancy place like the Meadowlark Inn. Well, except the Blue Bayou restaurant—*it* was super fantabulous, being in Disneyland. But the Meadowlark Inn was dandy, in an old house fixed up with sparkly cut glass in the windows and crystal chandeliers. It sat on a low hill, and all the trees around it were strung with little white lights.

She and Melanie had gotten her mom and Aaron to let them eat at their own table across the room and they'd felt grown-up, ordering hors d'oeuvres and salad and stuff. They'd gotten extravagant fruit drinks in funny glasses, and the waiter had brought piles and piles of French bread and butter.

Karin pulled the quilt around her shoulders and snuggled down, imagining going on a date at the Meadowlark Inn with a guy like Nick Jakowski. It was terribly romantic, and outside under the trees was the perfect place for a first kiss. Just because she was going to be a famous scientist and never get married, it didn't mean she was going to ignore boys.

She heard the front door open and close and figured it was her mom, going out to work in the garden.

Jeez.

Mom *never* slept in, no matter what.

It was nearly eight when Karin woke up again. The house was quiet and she got out of bed, yawning. "Mom?" she called.

There wasn't an answer, so she peeked out the window and saw her mother in the driveway.

She stumbled outside in her pajamas. "Whatcha doing?" she asked, blinking sleepily.

"I've washed the truck, and now I'm waxing it."

Karin was suddenly wide-awake. Her mom hadn't washed the truck in...well, she'd *never* washed the truck. It was Dad who'd always taken care of the cars, and the last time he had done it was the day of his accident. He'd said it was *his* job and that he always wanted them to look nice for his family.

Then that 18-wheeler had hit him.

"But..." She stopped. It hurt to see her mother polishing the fender.

"You'd better go inside and start getting ready, Karin. Aaron and Melanie will be here before long. Let me know when you're ready for breakfast, and I'll fix something."

"Okay."

She ran back into the house, gulping big breaths of

air, wanting to cry. Nobody would understand why she was so upset, not when she didn't understand it herself.

AARON LOOKED AT Karin and Melanie as they hurried through the Sacramento Zoo entrance and veered left following a short, whispered consultation. As usual, both girls were more interested in going off by themselves than hanging around the adults. His plan to "get to know Karin" was moving slowly because of it; he'd have to think of an activity where they all did something together.

"Karin was quiet on the drive into the city," he murmured. "Didn't she enjoy herself last night?"

"Very much."

He glanced at Skylar; she'd been quiet herself. "You're pale—is everything okay? We shouldn't have come if you aren't feeling well."

Her smile seemed forced. "I'm not sick. I just have a lot on my mind."

Aaron figured part of her problem was having him around Karin so much. There was an edge of watchful tension in her, as if she was worried about what he might say or do—the tension should have been a clue that she was keeping a secret from him, even *before* his father let the cat out of the bag.

What had Spence claimed...that if he'd cared Karin might be his daughter, he would have figured it out when he met her?

Aaron's jaw hardened. He *did* care; it just hadn't

occurred to him to question the situation with so much going on at Cooper Industries, and with Melanie. Not to mention Skylar rattling his brain. Besides, Skylar had named her daughter after her mother-in-law, which was pretty close timing if Jimmie Gibson *wasn't* Karin's biological father.

But Aaron knew there was something else he hadn't considered. Over the years he'd had so little faith in people, he'd never questioned whether they had any reason to have faith in him. He could try to keep dismissing Skylar's actions as proof that women were untrustworthy, but *should* he blame her for not telling him about Karin, especially after his family offered her money?

He *had* treated her badly. He *hadn't* thought she was someone he could introduce to his family. And he probably *would* have told her to take a hike if she'd told him she was pregnant, certain the baby couldn't be his.

They stopped at the jaguar enclosure, and Skylar leaned on the railing, gazing at one of the big cats, sitting alert and watchful in the late-morning sunshine.

"They're such powerful animals," she said. "But as beautiful as they are, I hate seeing them in captivity."

"There's controversy over zoos," Aaron acknowledged. "One faction argues it's cruel to confine animals that should be free, and another claims zoos and wildlife preserves are important to conservation efforts."

"I've heard that someday certain species may *only* exist in confinement."

"One of my brothers talks about that—he's a photographer who specializes in exotic locations."

"Jake Hollister, right?" Skylar said, turning her head. "He won the Pulitzer for his work in Iraq."

Aaron grimaced. "Don't mention that to Jake. He never wanted to be a war photojournalist and doesn't feel awards should be given for pictures of violence. Going to the Middle East was a onetime thing."

"I'm not likely to ever meet him."

Aaron wasn't so sure. If Karin was his daughter, then his brothers and sisters were her uncles and aunts. Maybe they should consider having some sort of central gathering, like an annual reunion.

"You never know," he said noncommittally. "Oh... speaking of photographs, would it be possible to see some early pictures of Karin? Perhaps you have an album I could borrow."

Skylar tensed visibly with the question. "There are several family albums you could look at when it's safe. Wait until you see the ones of Karin in her Halloween costumes."

She went on, describing the costume choices Karin had made over the years, her face relaxing as she talked. Karin had never wanted to be a princess like her friends; Skylar's maternal challenge had included creating costumes for a robot, an alley cat and a skunk. He enjoyed the account so much it was a while before he looked around for Melanie and Karin, only to find they'd disappeared from view.

He sighed. "Should we catch up with the girls?"

"It's a small zoo—they're not going to get lost."

"I suppose."

They wandered on, and Skylar pointed out the tiger exhibit, saying a Sumatran tiger had been born in the zoo in early spring, then began talking about a place she'd heard of called Tiger Island where they hand-raised the cubs, and visitors were able to interact directly with the animals.

Skylar's knowledge had surprised Aaron several times in the past few weeks. For all that she'd dropped out of school, she seemed to be well-read, often knowing more about a subject than he did. Of course, she'd dropped out because she was pregnant, not because she couldn't handle the academics.

"By the way," he said, "I've been thinking about Karin's education. If she sticks with her current plans, the cost for postgraduate school will be huge."

"It's more or less taken care of."

"Skylar, you may have saved, but—"

"It's taken care of," she said sharply, yet a moment later gave him an apologetic smile. "Sorry. Touchy subject. We've had a college fund since Karin was a baby, and I deposit all of her Social Security survivor's benefits into the account, as well. And…" She hesitated. "There was a settlement from the trucking company after Jimmie's accident, not to mention a life-insurance payment. I paid off the mortgage and

have enough set aside for a new truck and emergencies, but the rest is there and should be enough."

"You could be using that money to make things easier. If nothing else, you could hire more employees and cut your hours at the Nibble Nook."

Skylar shrugged. "I like working. We have enough to be comfortable, and this way Karin will have choices."

They walked through another section of the zoo and found the girls in front of the giraffe exhibit. Aaron's gaze moved between his sister and Karin. They *did* look alike, but was it anything more than similar coloring? Karin definitely didn't favor Tamlyn or April; they were the image of their flamboyant mother, but Oona was another matter.

He made a mental note to email Oona in Italy, asking if she would send a photo of herself as a teen. Then again, she might wonder why, and he couldn't explain.

Aaron sighed as the girls dashed away to another exhibit. For Pete's sake, getting to know Karin was like chasing a hummingbird.

"What am I doing wrong?" he muttered to Skylar. "I thought going to the zoo was a family group activity...we'd walk around together and talk. But it's as if they can't wait to get away from me."

"It isn't you—it's the age they're at," Skylar assured softly. "Friends become more important than parents when you're a teenager. It doesn't mean anything. They're establishing their independence and individuality."

Aaron cast her a long sideways glance. "Somehow, I don't think individuality has ever been a problem for Karin."

Skylar laughed and hooked her arm through his elbow. "Not really. Come on, let's go see the kangaroos, and I'll tell you about the time she was three years old and didn't want her sandbox getting wet in the rain."

Her eyes were merry, and Aaron grinned in spite of himself. "I have a feeling she did something drastic."

"Boy, did she. And it was a hell of mess to clean up."

CHAPTER FIFTEEN

KARIN SAT ON a bench and kicked her legs as she waited for Mellie. They'd eaten lunch at the zoo and were planning to go downtown to Sutter's Fort, but her mom and Mellie had wanted to visit the zoo's gift shop before leaving.

Usually Karin loved going into stores, but she hadn't felt like it today.

"Is something wrong, Karin?"

It was Aaron. She shrugged.

"You've been quiet this morning."

She eyed him, and remembered how nice he'd been when they were rafting, letting her talk about her dad and stuff. "You'll think it's dumb."

He sat down on the bench. "I promise I won't."

"Well…uh…Mom got up and washed and waxed the truck this morning." Heck, even *she* thought it sounded dumb.

"Yeah, I thought it looked shinier."

Karin kicked a stick of gum someone had dropped on the ground. "Nobody's washed the truck since…" She stopped and swallowed. "You see, my dad washed and waxed it the day he…he…you know."

Aaron nodded, and she could tell he knew what day she meant, but he wasn't all wigged out or worried or anything. That was the nice thing about talking to Aaron about her dad—it didn't upset him the way it upset her mom or Grandpa Joe and Grandma Grace.

"We haven't washed it since then," she added. "I felt real funny when I saw Mom had done it. And it's silly, because Dad wanted things to look nice."

Aaron sighed. "Karin, I've never lost anyone special like your father, so I'm a little foggy on this stuff. But maybe it was like you had to say goodbye to him again. Or seeing your mother doing it was another reminder that he isn't here."

She scrunched up her nose, thinking it over. "Kind of both, I guess."

"You should talk to her about it."

"No." She shook her head vigorously. "It makes people sad when I talk about Dad. And he was so terrific. You should have seen him when we went anywhere, having fun and getting people to join in."

"You can tell me about your dad whenever you want."

"You don't mind?"

"Of course not. I'd love to hear your stories."

Karin thought that Aaron meant it, so she told him about the time her father had climbed the tree to rescue Bennie when he was half-grown and had escaped out of the house. Bennie had inched away, staying just out of reach, until her mom had come out, shaking a bag of cat food.

"What happened?"

"Bennie jumped on my dad's shoulder and used it as a launching pad down to the ground. Dad yelled, then laughed so hard he fell out of the tree."

"Was he hurt?"

"Just his pride. He said most of it was in his butt, so it kept him from breaking his tailbone."

SKYLAR LOOKED AT the stuffed animals in the gift shop window, keeping a covert eye on Aaron and her daughter outside. Perhaps she shouldn't have washed the truck that morning—it had upset Karin more than she'd expected, but it had seemed symbolic. Karin had to move on, which meant *she* had to move on. Neither one of them would ever forget Jimmie or stop missing him, yet there was no pretending he wasn't gone. In a way, that's what the truck had represented.

No matter what she'd thought or said about being too busy, Skylar knew she could have kept it washed and waxed. But as long as she didn't do it, it was as if Jimmie had just taken a trip or something. Or that it really hadn't been months and months, and now more than a year, since he'd held her. It was the same thing with his T-shirt drawer—she'd gotten up at two in the morning and packed the contents into a box. Keeping that drawer untouched wasn't going to bring him back; it just reminded her he was gone.

"What do you think about this one, Skylar?" Melanie asked, holding up a pretty necklace.

"It's very nice. You have excellent taste, Melanie."

The teenager blushed as she put it on and looked at herself in a mirror. "They have two of them. Do you think Karin would like it, too? Aaron gave me money, and we could wear them at the same time and be like twins."

"I'm sure she would, but a gift isn't necessary."

"I know. I just want to get her one."

Melanie happily went to the counter to buy the two necklaces, and Skylar looked out the window again. Karin looked happier. She was chattering away and Aaron was smiling at her. They really *did* look alike, particularly their eyes and smiles. Aaron had smiled so little since returning that Skylar had rarely been reminded of the resemblance.

"Mrs…uh, Skylar?" Melanie said again.

Skylar turned guiltily. "Yes?"

"This is for you." She held out a bag from the gift shop.

"You shouldn't have gotten me anything."

"I want to thank you…for being so nice and helping with school and stuff. Even if I don't get to come live with you and Karin, it's really great being wanted. See if you like it," she said eagerly.

Inside the bag was a pendant on a silver chain…a mother tiger with two babies at her feet. Skylar understood the message behind the gift, and her eyes burned as she hugged the teenager. She could strangle Melanie's mother and father for not seeing what a terrific kid they had.

Parents didn't have to knock their kid across a yard to wound them. Sometimes ignoring them was just as hurtful.

AARON WOULD HAVE preferred doing something with Skylar and the girls the next day instead of having lunch with his grandparents, but he needed to understand more about the Coopers and why things were a mess at the company.

The door opened as he walked up the steps of the Victorian, and they were both standing inside as if they'd been waiting for him to arrive.

"How are you, Grandfather?" he asked, gesturing to George's bandaged hand.

"Fine, fine. A foolish thing to happen."

"And where is Melanie?" queried his grandmother as she ushered him into the front living room.

"Spending the afternoon with a friend."

Sarah touched the cameo pinned to her throat. "You should have brought her with you. We'd love to meet her."

Aaron found that hard to believe, considering their attitude toward his father. "I'll talk to her about it."

"Of course, meeting two old people can't be exciting to a child her age, but she's an important part of your life." Sarah handed him the inevitable glass of sherry. "We can tell how fond you've become of the child."

"She's a great kid and has been bounced around too much."

"Perhaps you should think about giving her a home until she's eighteen," George suggested.

Aaron blinked. While it wasn't a new idea, he hadn't expected the Coopers to support the idea. Eliza, on the other hand, was certain to agree. She had run out of people she could ask to take her daughter, making boarding school the only remaining option.

"I'm already considering it."

"You were always a good boy," approved his grandmother.

Good?

Aaron nearly choked on his sherry.

George and Sarah had acted as if he was a juvenile delinquent who needed to be whipped back into shape. "That's not how you treated me," he said bluntly.

His grandparents exchanged glances and George cleared his throat. "We've been talking, and…well, you should understand the reasons we were so strict when you came to live with us."

"Oh?" Aaron raised his eyebrows. This ought to be interesting. Another lecture about duty, perhaps?

George tapped his fingers on the arm of the chair, seeming nervous. "You see, by the time your mother came along, we'd given up hoping for children. We married young and thought we'd have a large family, but it was ten years before Celina was born. The doctor felt she would be our only child."

Sarah set her untouched glass on a tray. "I fear we indulged her. We just couldn't say no to whatever she wanted. So you see, it's *our* fault she became such an unhappy, restless woman."

A light began to dawn in Aaron. "So when she sent me here…"

"We promised ourselves that we wouldn't make the same mistakes." His grandmother twisted a handkerchief between her fingers, looking at him unhappily, yet it was the loneliness in her eyes that bothered Aaron the most. "We went too far, but we wanted you to have a better life than your mother, and felt the only way was teaching you to be different from either of your parents."

"If you want to be hard on someone for what we did, be hard on me," George said, his chin jutted forward. "I was the one who insisted we take a strong, disciplinary line."

"I don't want to be hard on either one of you," Aaron told him, and he meant it. He'd grown up lonely, but his grandparents were just as lonely—they didn't seem to have friends, and their only daughter never visited.

A dizzying vision went through his head of how he might look in thirty years if he kept on the way he was going—stuffy and friendless, too busy running Cooper Industries or some other damned company to have had anything more.

Sarah smoothed her crumpled handkerchief on the palm of her hand. "Thank you, Aaron. That's very generous."

George nodded. "At least we got out of debt with the company intact and could sign it over to you free and clear."

"Debt?" Aaron asked, confused all over again.

"From your mother. Before she remarried she ran up huge debts. We assumed them, of course, though we first had to repay the…" His grandfather stopped and pressed his lips together.

"Tell him, George."

"Sarah, he doesn't need to hear all this."

"Yeah, I think I should," Aaron countered, his curiosity mounting.

George's face was haggard as he spoke. "Your mother also tapped into your trust fund. It wasn't exactly…legal. She was going to be arrested, but we made an agreement with the district attorney to repay everything and insisted she send you to us. Your father had no choice but to go along with the plan—while he enjoys the spotlight, it wasn't the kind of attention he wanted."

Hearing that his mother had raided his trust fund wasn't the shock the Coopers obviously expected it to be; she was so egocentric, she probably hadn't thought of it as stealing from her son, just using available funds. It was a far cry from Skylar, who worked hard and saved money for Karin's education that she could have rightfully used for herself.

"So the debts are why you didn't retire," Aaron said. "You should have told me. I would have helped."

"It wasn't your responsibility. And besides, we wanted you to have time away from Cooperton before coming back."

Aaron wished his grandparents had confided in him earlier—while their revelations didn't change anything from his childhood, it was nice to know they weren't quite as cold as they'd seemed. And it wasn't any wonder that the factory hadn't been updated if they'd been restoring his trust fund and paying off his mother's old debts.

Mrs. Ryland stepped in and announced lunch, to Aaron's great relief. The meal was delicious as usual, and he deliberately shifted the conversation to lighter topics.

He still had questions, but at the moment, he didn't think he could handle any more answers.

THAT'S WEIRD, KARIN thought when Aaron came by the Nibble Nook again a few days later.

He waved at her and Melanie, but didn't come over, instead waiting until her mom came out with a bucket to start washing the picnic tables.

"Aaron, what are you doing here?" she asked.

His answer was low, and they couldn't hear it, even though they were trying to listen without being obvious.

Her mom laughed before stepping back and looking Aaron up and down. The other times he'd come to the Nibble Nook he'd been wearing a stuffy suit, but today was different. He had jeans on for one thing, and even if he was wearing a jacket and tie, it was cute in an older, good-looking-guy sort of way.

"What's up with him?" she asked Mellie. "He's... like, wanting to do all this stuff together. I mean, it's fun and all, but weird."

"In the beginning, I thought he was just trying to make me forget about moving out. Of course, I'm pretty sure he *also* thinks your mom is sexy," Mellie said matter-of-factly.

Karin froze.

Her mom wasn't sexy—she was a mom. Sure, Dad had wolf-whistled at her a lot, but dads were supposed to do that.

She gulped and looked down at her history assignment. Well, her mom *was* pretty. And last week when Mellie was sleeping over, she had gotten up for a glass of milk. She'd gone into the living room and heard Aaron and her mom on the front porch. It was almost as if they'd been smooching out there.

Or maybe they'd just been talking.

That was probably it.

Her mom was on the city council and supposed to be approving Aaron's plans for his dumb factory, so he was trying to convince her to say "yes" by being nice to them both.

Except...it seemed like he was being truly nice, not just for show. Karin remembered how carefully Aaron had listened to the stories about her dad and had made her feel better about the truck getting washed. And he hadn't even acted like she was silly for being upset.

A minute later Aaron walked over to their table and grinned at them. "I'm taking us out tonight for a surprise. Is that okay with you?"

Melanie bobbed her head. "It's okay with me."

"Uh, me, too," Karin added.

"Great." He went over and took the bucket of water from her mom. "I'll scrub this time," he said.

Karin chewed on her lip as they started cleaning the Nibble Nook tables together. It was supposed to be her dad there, making her mother laugh. And now Aaron was taking them out for a surprise on a school night…? He hadn't liked Mellie coming to the Nibble Nook, and now he was around all the time.

Mellie nudged her.

"At least they aren't yelling," she whispered.

No. And her mom hadn't smiled this much since the accident. When Karin closed her eyes at night she could still see her mother's face at the funeral, pale and frozen, as if she wasn't alive anymore, either.

She squared her shoulders.

Mom just enjoyed having someone around she could argue with, and Aaron was just helping so people would like him better. It was nothing more than that.

TWO HOURS LATER, Skylar felt bad for Aaron as he watched Karin and Melanie leave to talk with schoolmates on the other side of the ice-cream parlor. Honestly, he really *was* trying with Karin, and the child wasn't cooperating in the least.

"So, was dinner and sundaes at Duffy's the surprise?" Skylar asked lightly.

"What… Oh, no, it isn't." Aaron shook his head. "It's still coming. I had no idea the food was so good here—I just thought they'd enjoy the ice cream."

Despite her best efforts, he hadn't told her what he had planned. He'd just said to wear jeans and had taken them to Duffy's for dinner and dessert.

Skylar couldn't resist glancing at the high ceiling, remembering Jeremy Newman's law offices were located in the second floor of the building. She'd photocopied the pieces of the check from S. S. Hollister and brought them to him, despite Aaron's assurance he would respect her wishes about Karin. After all, it was better to be safe than sorry.

So why did she feel bad for not trusting him? Aaron had never done anything to earn her faith, and she didn't know what to think about his determined efforts with Karin. She'd expected him to quickly lose interest in his supposed fatherhood, but if anything he seemed more determined than ever.

The ice cream in her bowl was melting and Skylar pushed it away—after one of Duffy's deluxe club sandwiches with homemade coleslaw, she had no appetite left.

Aaron checked his watch. "If you're done, why

don't we go on? I know it's a school night and we shouldn't be out late."

"Sure."

They collected the girls on the way to the door, and Aaron drove out of town toward Trident.

"Aaron, where are we—"

"It's still a surprise," he said.

But when they pulled into a parking lot on the outskirts of Trident, Skylar winced, wishing he'd consulted her first.

It was a bowling alley.

And bowling had been Jimmie and Karin's special thing to do together.

AARON'S FRUSTRATION GREW as the evening wore on. Karin was unusually quiet and seemed to be on the verge of tears most of the time. He'd tried to come up with an activity that would keep them all together, without the girls running off to do their own thing. Bowling had seemed perfect, but it was turning into a disaster.

Finally he sat next to Karin. "Hey, what's wrong?"

"Nothing," she said in a muffled voice, hunched over and staring at her shoes.

Melanie finished with her second throw, so Karin got up and sent her ball down the middle of the lane. Every pin went flying and he raised an eyebrow. She was very, *very* good.

When she returned, she sat down on the other side of their area, obviously avoiding him.

He gave Skylar a helpless glance, and she shrugged. Worst of all, she looked sorry for him. It was a hell of a thing when your ex-girlfriend, who might be the mother of your only child, felt pity for you.

"Your turn, Aaron," Melanie reminded him.

Discouraged, he got up. But after sending his own ball sailing into the gutter, he turned around and saw Skylar was alone.

"Where are they?" he asked, resigned. Dealing with disgruntled employees was nothing compared to getting acquainted with a teenager.

"To the restroom, probably with a detour through the arcade."

"Damn. Where did I screw up?"

"It isn't you."

He dropped onto the bench next to her. "Yeah, right."

"Karin and her dad used to go bowling together, that's all."

Aaron's shoulders slumped.

Jimmie Gibson, *again*. He respected what he'd learned about the other man, but it was hard to compete with a ghost.

"They'd probably have ended up in the arcade, anyway," Skylar murmured after a minute. "I told you, kids their age hang out together, preferably without their parents around. It was hard when Karin started pulling away from us, but we had to let go."

That was reassuring to hear, and there were worse things than getting paired up with Skylar and hearing stories about Karin's childhood. It was ironic. How many times had he hidden his impatience as people talked endlessly about their kids? He hadn't been able to believe parents could drone on and on about the "cute" things their darling had said or done, when they weren't cute or interesting in the least.

Yet now he wanted to know everything about Karin, the littlest shred of insight into her life. He'd missed it all, her first steps, the loss of her baby teeth, the first report card with a wry comment from her teacher about her boundless curiosity...everything.

When Skylar forgot to be wary and was herself, she was a natural storyteller—rueful, often humorous, sometimes frustrated, and always filled with love for her child.

The stories would be enough, but watching her was a reward by itself. How could this be the girl that his teenage friends had once sniggered over, saying her thighs were as loose as her mother's...that any guy with a pulse could screw her? And why would they have dared him to make it with Skylar if she was that easy?

The answer?

She hadn't been "easy."

They'd lied, and he hadn't seen the obvious inconsistency because he was so hot to have her. It didn't change the fact that Skylar hadn't told him she was pregnant, any more than it meant Karin was his biological child. But it was hard to ignore the very real likelihood that he'd been a father for fourteen years and hadn't known it.

"KARIN, YOU DON'T need to take eleven T-shirts," Skylar said late on Sunday afternoon as she sorted through the clothes and other items piled on the bed next to her daughter's duffel bag. They were packing for her school field trip, and as usual, it was like preparing for a polar expedition.

"*Moooommm,* I can't wear the same T-shirt at night as I wear during the day."

"You're only going to be gone for two nights and three days, and you *do* plan to wear something to the bus on the first morning, don't you?"

Karin rolled her eyes, refusing to dignify the question with a response.

"You don't have enough room for everything," Skylar pointed out. The stack of clothes and other "necessities" Karin had chosen were far more than would go into the duffel bag.

"I'll bring two bags."

"No, the instructions from your teacher said *one* duffel or suitcase up to this size, and no bigger. The only other thing you can bring is a small backpack. And by the way, it also says you are *not* allowed to bring a personal DVD player, a video game or enough snack food to feed a small country."

Karin plopped onto the bed and pouted.

"Start weeding things out," Skylar ordered as her cell phone rang. She hurried into the kitchen and grabbed it from the countertop without looking at the caller ID. "Yes?"

"You sound harassed."

It was Grace, and Skylar leaned against the wall with a sigh. "Karin is packing for her field trip to San Francisco. She wants to take enough clothes to last a year. You know, just in case the bus breaks down and they get to stay an extra day."

Her mother-in-law chuckled. "With Jimmie it was the opposite. He didn't want to take anything."

"He never changed. His idea of packing was stuffing two shirts and a pair of jeans into a paper sack. Underwear optional."

"Joe, too. Equipment on the other hand..."

"Ouch. Don't remind me."

Her father-in-law was the gadget master. If there was a new and improved piece of camping equipment or fishing gear out there, he had to have it. And everything went with them on vacation, no matter how long they planned to be gone.

"I was just calling to see how things were going with Aaron Hollister."

Skylar straightened and stepped outside, carefully closing the door behind her. She should have known the discussion would turn private—Grace only called the cell phone when she wanted to be sure that Karin couldn't accidentally pick up the extension.

"It's better than I expected," she said, "though his idea to go bowling was a disaster. He didn't tell me ahead of time—it was supposed to be a surprise—

and I actually felt sorry for him the way it bombed. Because of it, he backed off doing anything this weekend so he can regroup." She walked to the far end of the backyard, keeping a watch on the house.

"Oh, dear."

"Aaron *is* trying. I don't think he's convinced about Karin one way or the other, but he's making an effort."

"I'd sooner he *didn't* believe Karin is his daughter, though I'd still be furious with him for thinking you'd lie."

Skylar smiled, warmed by Grace's staunch support. She got food for the fish in the pond and tossed it in the water. "With everything that's been going on, we haven't seen you since the school carnival. How about coming to dinner on Sunday? We can talk about what we're doing for Thanksgiving."

"We'd love to. What can I bring?"

"Joe. He'd hate being left behind."

"Victoria Skylar Gibson, you *know* what I mean."

Skylar grinned. "Dessert would be fine. And I should never have told you my first name."

"You can tell me anything, you know that, don't you?" Helen's voice had gone serious.

"I know. I'm sorry I didn't explain about Aaron Hollister before, I just… With my background, I used to be ashamed of the way I'd grown up."

"Not any longer, I hope. Just to make it perfectly clear, Joe and I couldn't be prouder of you. And nothing could change that. Got it?"

"I've got it."

"Good. Now go make sure my granddaughter doesn't pack her entire bedroom for a three-day visit to San Francisco."

Skylar swallowed hard to keep from crying as she turned off the phone and slipped it into her pocket. She might have stopped beating herself up for her background and the mistakes she'd made as a girl, but it didn't change the facts—things could have turned out quite differently if she hadn't gone to work for the Gibsons. A pregnant eighteen-year-old high-school dropout didn't have many options, but they'd taken her into their hearts from the beginning.

IT WAS MUCH later in the evening when Skylar heard a familiar tap on the front door. She checked to be sure it was Aaron, and opened the door. His face was an odd mixture of exasperation and victory.

"What *are* you doing here?"

"Come out for a minute so we can talk."

Wary, she undid the dead bolt on the security screen and found herself instantly pulled into the shadows of the wisteria, where a very thorough kiss was planted on her lips. She wasn't entirely displeased, though kissing Aaron ought to be off-limits.

"Uh...what was that for?"

"I deserved a reward after getting Melanie packed for that field trip."

Understanding dawned. "Ah...I see."

"It was like running a marathon. First it was the

suitcase. The other kids were bringing duffel bags, so we went to two stores to find one the right size and color. And then she couldn't find her favorite T-shirt, so I took her into Sacramento to find a place that was still open. Sunday evening is *not* a good time to go clothes shopping, even in the city," he said gloomily.

"You didn't."

"Well...*yes*. She has her moments, but she's usually so accommodating about everything and I want her to enjoy herself."

"Of course." Skylar clasped a hand over her mouth to keep from laughing. Yet it was sweet, too, imagining the big brother being run ragged by a teenage girl's angst over her travel wardrobe.

"We finally found several she liked, but of course, the new T-shirts had to be run twice through the washing machine so they wouldn't look new. Apparently *that's* a bad idea, as well. They're hanging over the heat vent right now to dry."

"They could have gone in the dryer."

"And risk having them shrink or melt after going through all that?" Aaron sounded horrified. "I wouldn't dare."

"Oh. Okay."

He leaned forward, no more than a faint shadow in the darkness. "You're laughing at me, aren't you?"

"Technically, I'm trying *not* to laugh."

"Oh, God. What did I do wrong this time?"

"Nothing. I just ran the same marathon with Karin..."

though I probably wouldn't have driven into Sacramento for a T-shirt. That one is all yours."

"Are all girls their age like that?"

Skylar shrugged before realizing it was too dark for him to see the gesture. "Got me. Anyway, Karin's bag is packed, and she's in bed, asleep."

"Melanie is, too. I left a note and ran away from home."

"You'd better run back," Skylar advised before she was tempted to let him kiss her again.

In his own inept way, he was trying to do right by both girls. She'd been impatient, watching his awkwardness with Melanie, but it was difficult to learn parenting when you were starting with a teenager. Heaven knew how *she* would have done getting thrown into it suddenly. She should have been more sympathetic—he hadn't gotten his nerves conditioned the way most parents do by the twelve years of chills and thrills that led up to a child *becoming* a teen.

"By the way," Aaron said. "Will you go into Sacramento with me tomorrow after you close the Nibble Nook? I need to do more shopping and would appreciate your advice."

"Isn't one trip to the city this week enough?"

"It's for furniture. I want to fix up the family room so it's comfortable for Melanie. I'm sure you have a better idea of what's needed than me—I've always just called a decorator to take care of that kind of thing."

Skylar pictured the large room opening off the

kitchen. The empty space was cold and uninviting, and for Melanie's sake, it definitely needed fixing up.

"All right."

"Thanks."

Aaron tugged her close, and his hands crept down her back, cupping her bottom and pulling her snug to his body as he kissed her thoroughly.

Damn him.

He really did know how to do it well.

CHAPTER SIXTEEN

"I UNDERSTAND, Mr. Newman," Melanie said into her cell phone. The teachers had made them turn off their phones on the bus, but she'd checked once they'd arrived in San Francisco and discovered the lawyer had left a message.

Karin couldn't listen to what the lawyer was saying—they didn't dare put the phone on loudspeaker in case the other students came close enough to hear them.

They were visiting the old Spanish Mission, and she and Karin had gone out to the cemetery to return Mr. Newman's call. It was creepy being there, and she tried not to look at the gravestones. What if there were ghosts? Would they be angry because they got woken up by a bunch of kids?

"Be sure to call if there's any problem or you decide you want to file the papers to be emancipated," said Mr. Newman. "And I'll let you know if I hear anything. Your brother or parents may still respond to my letter."

"Thank you."

"You're very welcome, Mellie. Good luck."

She disconnected and looked at Karin. "Mr. Newman hasn't heard anything from Aaron or my parents. He mentioned filing to be an emancipated minor again and said he'd help if that's what I want to do, but I can't make up my mind. I don't want my family to think I don't love them anymore."

"Yeah. I hadn't thought of that."

Melanie wrinkled her nose. "He isn't going to charge anything—he probably wrote the letter because he felt bad for me. But I have another idea. If we're nice to my brother and I don't make trouble, he might let me stay until I finish high school."

Karin brightened. "That's better than boarding school and you'd still be in Cooperton."

"Lots better. And you know, Aaron is trying really hard to take care of me, much more than anywhere else I've lived. I like him a lot."

"Yeah, he isn't so bad now that he's not arguing as much with my mom and saying the Nibble Nook is a bad place."

"Uh-huh." Melanie didn't understand why Aaron had acted that way. "Maybe he's just too old to understand teenagers."

"That must be it."

Melanie saw Mr. Rosecrans, one of the teachers on the trip, coming their direction and quickly hid her smartphone.

"Don't forget you're doing a paper on the San Francisco Mission in my class," he reminded them. "You'd best get moving or you won't have time to see it all."

"Yes, sir."

He hurried away, and they decided to visit the little museum first. It was beautiful and interesting and sad, because the Native Americans weren't always treated so well at the Missions and got sick and died with diseases the settlers brought with them. Melanie was glad it had happened a long time ago, or it would be too awful to learn about.

"You'll like this," Karin said when they got to the gift shop and she was reading something off a shelf. "It says the first California book was written at the Mission, the *Life of Junipero Serra.* I bet it's short—they didn't have computers back then."

Melanie wavered over what to buy and finally got one of the books about the Mission, and postcards to send to her mother and father. It was strange not being able to spend as much as she wanted, but the school had only let students bring a certain amount of cash with them, and using the credit card her father had sent her probably wouldn't be allowed.

Still, it was okay being normal like the other kids and having to pick and choose.

SKYLAR GAVE A pained smile to Aaron as they entered their third furniture store on Monday evening. She should have warned him that she didn't put up with unctuous salespeople easily. So far she'd kept from losing her temper, but if they got shown another ugly, overpriced living room set, she couldn't guarantee what would happen.

"Hello," said an eager voice before they'd gone ten feet. "My name is Gary. What can I do for you?"

"I want to furnish a large family room," Aaron replied. "Suitable for my teenage sister. Right now it's a blank slate. No couch, nothing."

"I'm sure we have just what you need. Come this way."

Gary led them to various displays of furniture better suited to a baroque mansion than a house in Cooperton, and when Aaron shook his head, kept moving to new displays. Frustrated, the salesman finally pointed to a formal couch that looked hideously uncomfortable. "I'm sure you'll like this one. It's my favorite piece in the store."

Aaron looked at Skylar. "What do you think?"

She thumped the solid cushions. "Uh…how about something softer?"

"Like pink or a pattern with flowers?" he asked doubtfully.

"No. *Softer,* with cushions that don't break bones if you throw yourself down the way teenagers fling themselves onto a couch. It should squash a little, for long chats on the phone or movie marathons." She looked at the discreet price tag and rolled her eyes. "And it shouldn't cost so much that spilled nachos are a problem," she added.

The salesman glared at her from behind Aaron's back. He had pegged the situation instantly—Aaron carried the platinum credit card with no spending limits, while she was a working gal on a budget. She could practically hear him thinking, *She's not even a girlfriend.*

"Quality will tell, sir," Gary said smoothly. "What your friend doesn't realize is that we can apply a treatment to the fabric to resist stains. You needn't worry about spills."

"You don't have teenagers, do you?" Skylar asked drily.

"I...no."

"I didn't think so. A teenager can stain *anything.* And they never keep their shoes off the couch. Tar, chewing gum, grease—it all goes on the upholstery."

The corners of Aaron's mouth twitched.

"Well, *really.*" The salesman didn't make an effort to hide his glare this time.

"Yes, really. Stop trying to palm off overpriced stuff you haven't been able to sell. I can guess how long this couch has been sitting here as a display model—it took time for that much dust to build up in the corners."

"I beg your pardon, that's the latest style we car—"

"Don't fight with her—you'll lose," Aaron interrupted. "And I think you've misunderstood the situation—you mess with Skylar, and you mess with me. Send someone else to help us." He put an arm around her waist and tugged her close.

Gary loosened his collar. "Yes, sir."

Skylar glanced up at Aaron once they were alone. "I didn't need you to defend me, but it was very gallant."

"No problem. I didn't like him anyway."

They probably *did* appear incongruous together. Aaron was no longer wearing suits to the office; instead he'd adopted a new style—a white shirt, tie and sport jacket topped well-used jeans, and his shoes were understated tan suede instead of polished leather. A fashionista would probably call it shabby chic, but whatever it was called, it looked fantastic... or maybe it just looked fantastic on him.

She, on the other hand, was dressed in her usual jeans—with mustard smeared on one knee—a faded T-shirt and athletic shoes that had seen better days... three years ago. Dressing up to sling hamburgers did *not* make sense.

"What did Peggy say when you ditched your fancy suits?" Skylar asked as they wandered around without waiting for the next salesperson to find them. He'd told her a few things about the executive assistant he'd inherited from his grandfather, and she sounded formidable.

"Nothing. She had a heart attack when she saw me and has been in the hospital ever since."

Skylar dug an elbow into his side, and he laughed.

"All right, all right. I think she likes it. I've noticed she's relaxed her own dress code and looks twenty years younger."

It was more comfortable without a salesperson hovering over them, and it wasn't long before they found everything needed for the family room. Aaron had already purchased a huge flat-screen television and other assorted electronics, and was able to convince the furniture store to deliver his order to Cooperton the next day...for a hefty bonus.

It seemed an awful lot of money to spend so quickly, but Aaron didn't look at price tags, so Skylar supposed he could afford the expense. And it was endearing that he wanted to create a cozy space for his sister.

"I'm hungry. Is a steak house okay with you?" he asked as they were heading out of town.

"Sure."

He pulled into a restaurant parking lot. "I've eaten here before—the food is decent and they have a variety of choices."

Skylar knew she should have insisted on going straight back to Cooperton. With Karin on a school trip she could be doing something useful like mopping the kitchen floor or cleaning out the freezer, but it wouldn't be a disaster to take a night off. Of course, it would likely end up being *two* nights, since she'd promised to come over before Melanie got home to be sure the new furniture was properly arranged.

AARON SHOVED FURNITURE around the family room for more than an hour the next evening, trying unsuccessfully to keep Skylar from helping with the heavy lifting. When they were finally done, he looked around and smiled—the room was warm and inviting, just what he wanted for his sister.

Aside from his grandparents, he hadn't told anyone that he might keep Melanie longer. He still had misgivings, but how could he let her be sent to a boarding school when she dreaded it so much?

Karin was another question he hadn't resolved.

He was quite fond of the teenager. She was smart and funny and a loyal friend. She deserved the best future, and Skylar was working to give it to her. When it came right down to it, the kid didn't need him, but if she was his daughter, he should be part of her life.

Turning abruptly on his heel, Aaron went into the kitchen. He'd always said he didn't want to be a father and had religiously avoided women with baby booties on their minds. Now he didn't know what he wanted…or if he'd screwed up any chance he'd had of getting it.

"I picked up food from Vittorino's," Aaron said gruffly. "It just has to be reheated."

"Sounds good." Skylar leaned her elbows on the broad counter providing separation between the kitchen and family room, or *great room,* as the rental agent had called it. No doubt she'd think *great room* sounded pretentious.

He took a container from one of the bags and pulled off the covering. "Have some appetizers. We also have chicken piccata, pasta primavera, lasagna, something made with polenta that I can't pronounce and various desserts."

"What were you trying to do, feed an army?" She came around and began putting the foil containers in the oven.

Aaron's breath caught in his throat. Her hair was mussed and her face flushed from moving furniture, yet she'd never been more beautiful. Their chaste goodbye kiss the night before had left him awake half the night. Cold showers were woefully ineffective when it came to a woman like Skylar.

And now he was aching again...which was exactly what had gotten him into trouble almost fifteen years ago, Aaron reminded himself grimly. He might have been trying to win a bet with his buddies, but he'd wanted her before they had challenged him. The contrast between Skylar's passionate nature and his grandparents' reserve had been nearly irresistible.

And she was still passionate, still quick to anger, and electricity still hummed whenever he was near her. And she was *still* nearly irresistible.

"What?" Skylar asked, her eyes narrowing at his silence.

"Nothing."

It was a lie. He was wondering if he'd missed out on something important when he was a teenager... something that could have changed his life if he'd recognized it at the time. And he wondered if there was any way to get that something back

"The food shouldn't take that long to heat—it was still warm," she said.

"Shall we inaugurate the television and watch a movie while we eat? We can see if that stuff they put on the furniture really helps keep it from staining."

Skylar laughed, just as he'd intended. "Actually,

stain repellant works well, but kids have a gift for demolition—food, Kool-Aid, bicycle grease—you name it. And don't get me started on what they can do with a hot glue gun."

"And you didn't mind it a bit, right?"

"Not really. I wanted Karin to have a happy childhood, and all of that was trivial. Heavens, you should have seen the time she painted her grandparents' cat."

She went on, recounting how her four-year-old daughter had used black paint to put zebra stripes on the elder Gibsons' white alley cat. The feline hadn't scratched her once, saving his venom for Joe and Grace when they were giving it a bath.

"That poor animal had blotchy, grayish stripes for weeks," Skylar said, shaking her head. "And it took almost that long for the scratches to heal."

"I hope the paint wasn't toxic."

"No, but it wouldn't have been healthy to ingest. Oh, I brought one of the family albums. You could look at it after the movie," she said. "It's in my backpack."

"Forget the movie. I'd like to see it now."

Aaron sat next to Skylar on the new sectional couch and opened the book. The album started with a photo of Skylar in a hospital bed, looking young and scared and happy, holding a bundle in her arms with a tiny pink face barely visible within the blankets. He gazed at it a long time, a painful sensation in his stomach; he'd missed so much.

Next to the picture of Skylar was the usual "first"

baby picture of Karin, also from the hospital, with hair swirled into a peak on her head. Two plastic envelopes were affixed to the page, the first containing a tiny curl of white blond hair, the second holding one of rich auburn.

"She was beautiful."

"We always thought so."

We?

We, as in Skylar and the elder Gibsons? Or *we,* as in Skylar and her husband? And would a phantom Jimmie Gibson be forever included in everything Skylar thought and did? Aaron involuntarily looked down and saw her wedding ring was gone.

"Uh…where's your ring?"

She put her hands together, running her right thumb over the indentation of pale skin on the third finger of her left hand. "I put it in my jewelry box a few days ago. It's too loose and got lost in the garden once already."

It was odd that he hadn't noticed the ring's absence before; he'd looked at it often enough over the past weeks, thinking about her husband and what they'd had together. It was a hell of a thing to envy a dead man.

Aaron glanced at Skylar. Her green eyes were faintly melancholy, and he wanted to wipe the expression away. Hell, might as well be honest…he wanted her to forget Jimmie Gibson and everything he'd meant to her. But that wasn't possible, and it was damned selfish, considering how well the other man had raised Karin.

"I've been thinking about what we could do on Saturday," Aaron murmured finally. "Since bowling was a disaster, I thought we could do something less ambitious here at the house, like barbecuing or getting pizza and watching movies."

Skylar lifted an eyebrow. "Do you barbecue?"

"No, but it can't be that hard."

She chuckled. "Get pizza. Barbecuing for the first time is *extremely* ambitious."

"How tough can it be?"

"Let me put it this way—one of our neighbors set fire to his deck two summers ago when he was grilling and it spread to the side of the house. His wife will never let him forget it—his birthday present this year was a fire extinguisher."

Aaron reluctantly gave up the idea of a barbecue and visions of everyone having fun in the backyard. He didn't want to look like an idiot in front of Skylar or the girls, and trying to douse a flaming steak would look pretty idiotic.

"All right. Then on Sunday I thought we could—"

"Not Sunday," Skylar interrupted. "We're busy. Joe and Grace are coming to dinner."

"Oh." Aaron didn't bother trying to get an invitation, as well. He wasn't ready to meet Skylar's in-laws, and it was unlikely she would go for it, anyhow.

He turned his attention back to the photo album. He didn't find any wedding pictures as he turned the pages, but there were shots of Jimmie Gibson scattered here and there. The man had been rangy, with broad shoulders, sandy hair and a perpetual smile—and he'd looked at Skylar and Karin as if the sun rose and set in them.

James Gibson's blondish hair wasn't dissimilar from Karin's, but hair color didn't guarantee anything. After all, Spence had brown hair and eyes, while Melanie was quite fair…just like Karin. Aaron counted back, for the hundredth time, the weeks and months between when he'd dated Skylar and Karin's birthday. *Nine months*. It was inescapable.

He didn't need genetic tests. If he accepted that Skylar hadn't slept around when they were together, he had to accept that Karin was his daughter.

SKYLAR TRIED NOT to watch Aaron as he looked through the album. She was torn between wishing he'd become bored with his attempts at fatherhood, and hope that he was starting to genuinely care. Life was uncertain, and having someone else who loved her daughter wasn't such a bad thing, was it?

Aaron gestured to a photo of Karin in her junior-high-school soccer uniform, kicking a black-and-white ball. "Karin hasn't mentioned that she used to be on a team. Not that she's talked that much to me," he said wryly. "Does she still play?"

"She quit last year after her father died. Being a teenager is hard enough without losing someone you love, and it was so sudden the way it happened. But you don't need to hear the details."

"Maybe I do. It's something that affects Karin profoundly."

"All right." Skylar drew her legs up under her and tried to control her breathing. "It…it was on a Saturday afternoon and Jimmie went to Trident to have his dad install a toolbox on our new truck. He wasn't supposed to be gone long, and I was wondering what was keeping him when the doorbell rang. It was the highway patrol."

"Hell."

"That sums it up perfectly. They didn't want Karin to stay in the room, but she'd already guessed the truth. It was a terrible accident, halfway between Cooperton and Trident—an 18-wheeler was speeding and ran a stop sign. I couldn't protect her from it…couldn't let her be a child for a little longer. I was in so much shock, I didn't even know what to say."

Skylar shivered. The grief was easing, and she was starting to remember the happy times before she remembered the loss, but nothing could soften the memory of that afternoon when the world had fallen apart.

"You'd just lost your husband, Skylar," Aaron said slowly. "And you couldn't have said anything to make it easier for Karin. I don't know much about kids, but I know that. Nothing could have made the truth easier. Do you really think telling her an hour later would have made a difference?"

"I suppose not. We sat on the couch, and I held her until Jimmie's parents arrived, and a thought kept beating at the back of my mind, making everything even worse. You see, Karin wanted to go with Jimmie, then at the last minute a friend called and she went swimming instead."

"God." Aaron had gone white around his mouth, and she knew that he'd grasped how close Karin had come to being in the accident with her father.

She took his hand and squeezed it. However uncertain she might be of him, she'd experienced that plunging sensation in her stomach too often not to understand.

The timer on the stove went off, reminding her of the food in the oven, and she scrambled to her feet, grateful for a distraction. "I think our dinner's ready," she said. "Shall we eat?"

Aaron set the photo album on the coffee table with slow, deliberate movements. "Sure."

AARON BARELY NOTICED how the meal tasted. Vittorino's served excellent Italian cuisine, but the food might as well have been sawdust.

He'd hoped for a nice, light evening with Skylar in front of a cheerful fire, and instead he had gotten an emotional sucker punch. Karin had talked about how it felt when her father died, but she hadn't said she'd planned to go with him.

It was unthinkable that she could have died, and Aaron breathed a silent prayer of gratitude that his daughter been spared along with her mother, because it was chillingly plain that Skylar could have been in that truck, as well.

CHAPTER SEVENTEEN

RESTLESS, SKYLAR PUT her empty plate on the coffee table and got up to look at the movies on the shelves.

"I wouldn't have pegged you as a classic-movie fan," she said over her shoulder.

"They're for Melanie. Her tastes are eclectic, especially for a teenager—old films, ghost-hunting reality shows and science fiction. I ordered those a couple of weeks ago and have been waiting for the best moment to surprise her."

"The family room is going to be such a big surprise, she may not notice a few dozen movies." Skylar scanned the titles. "*Desk Set* with Hepburn and Tracy, *The Adventures of Robin Hood*..." She grinned as she saw a film she'd loved as a girl. "Ohmigod, *Hobson's Choice*. I haven't seen that since I was a kid. It's a great romantic comedy set in the 1800s."

"You mean a chick flick."

"*No.*" Skylar took out the DVD and threw the plastic case at him. "For a comment like that, you're going to have to watch it with me."

She popped the disc in the machine. In the movie, a widowed father haunted the local pub while his feisty eldest daughter ran his boot shop before striking out on her own. Skylar returned to the couch and settled down. Perhaps she'd loved *Hobson's Choice* because the daughter made her own destiny, despite her drunken father and the barriers of class and expectations about women in Victorian England.

She was quickly drawn into the familiar story and didn't object when Aaron draped his arm around her shoulder. The tale was romantic and wickedly amusing at the same time, and it was a relief to have something less intense taking their attention. By the time the movie ended they were curled up together, their bare feet stretched toward the crackling fire.

"I withdraw my chick-flick remark. That's a terrific movie," Aaron declared.

Skylar yawned lazily. "Uh-huh. I love the old films, but I didn't know this one had come out on DVD."

"It's yours."

"But you got it for Melanie."

"I'll get her another."

Skylar thought about refusing, but she really did love the movie and it wouldn't be the end of the world to accept a gift from him.

Aaron stroked her hair. "You were also right about this couch."

"Oh?"

"It's *awesome,* as Melanie and Karin would say. Do you remember saying *awesome* and *gross* that much when we were their age?" he asked with a perplexed frown.

"I don't know—it feels like a long time ago. The other day Karin announced that twenty-nine was *old*. I didn't remind her I was three years older than that."

He kissed her forehead. "You're too beautiful to worry about getting old."

Skylar blinked. It seemed forever since she'd thought much about her appearance and it was nice to think she still had something to recommend her. "That's nice of you to say."

"Not nice, just honest."

She still felt pleasantly mellow from the movie and firelight and soft couch. "Hmm. Give me your honest opinion on something."

"Sure."

"Do you think bustles were sexy?"

Aaron cocked his head to one side. "Bustles?"

"Yeah, they talked about it in the movie. The two younger daughters were wearing bustles to catch male attention, and their father thought it was immodest."

"Oh. Well, they really aren't the fashion any longer."

"But let's say it's 1880 and you're a gentleman around town. You see a lady walking down the street with her skirt pouffed out in the rear. Bustles *did* draw attention to a woman's backside, and they wagged when she walked. Eye-catching, don't you think?"

"I can't say they do anything for me. I prefer tight jeans." He kissed her forehead.

"But they didn't have tight jeans in Victorian England. They had bustles."

"They also had corsets, child labor and no airplanes. However, I'm sure I would have appreciated a fashionable lady as much as the next guy. Especially if the lady looked like you." They had slid downward to the point she was lying on the couch, and he was resting his weight on his elbow, gazing at her with a smile. "You get loopy when you're sleepy, don't you?"

"A little. Sometimes."

"I like it."

"I'll have to wake up to drive home."

"Don't go yet." Aaron traced the line of her jaw, and a warm, quiver went through her abdomen. She might be out of practice, but she recognized the look in his eye.

She shifted her leg so she could run her toe along his calf. "If I stay, I might end up sleeping on the couch. What will the neighbors say if my old truck is in your driveway all night?"

"You didn't used to care what the neighbors thought."

"No, I just *pretended* not to care. There's a difference," Skylar said quietly. "But since I couldn't be respectable, I was determined to prove everything the gossips said about me and my parents was true."

AARON HATED SEEING the shadows in Skylar's eyes.

"I'm sorry," he whispered.

It was amazing that she'd grown up to love Cooperton...especially since Cooperton had failed her when she was a child, letting her parents hurt her. He traced her mouth with the tip of his finger, remembering the times he'd seen her with a swollen, split lip or a black eye. The abused girl, who'd grown up with gossiping fingers pointed at her, had become a remarkable woman.

Her beauty took his breath away as much now as it had when they were seventeen. Nobody had forced her to be a good mother; she could have gone to Hollywood or New York to be a model. If anything, that's what he'd thought she was doing when she dropped out of school. And though he wished she'd told him about Karin, he was infinitely grateful she'd stayed close to Cooperton, where he could find her.

Skylar's French braid had tumbled over her shoulder, and he unfastened the band on the end, carefully separating the thick plait. Firelight glinted, sparking gold and fiery red, and he fanned the long strands, enthralled by their brilliance. He remembered how she used to charge into class, hair flying, a glint in her eyes daring anyone to give her trouble. There hadn't been a girl in school who could compete.

"You've never cut it short?"

"I think it's easier to take care of this way."

Aaron opened the first button on her top and waited to see if she'd object. The other buttons followed more quickly and beneath the practical cotton work shirt, he found a lacy peach confection. As bras went, it ranked at the top of his approval level.

"I'm sure I don't need to tell you it unhooks in the

front." Skylar's expression was unfathomable, but he knew she was telling him, in her own way, that she was making a choice to be with him.

"No, you don't." Aaron bent down to kiss her. It was probably a mistake to take this any further, but at least it was a mistake they'd be making together.

He unhooked the bra and groaned at the curves beneath, flicking his thumbs across each responsive peak. In the years since they'd been together, he'd made love to some beautiful women, but none like Skylar, and the hard demand of his body made it difficult to think clearly. At least there were condoms in his wallet—that much hadn't changed since Melanie's arrival in his life.

Skylar's clothes went flying until she was naked and glowing in his arms, and gathering the long waves of her hair in his fingers, he stroked it over her breasts, wanting her to need him more than her memories.

SKYLAR WAS NO longer sleepy, the grabbing need in her belly fueled by Aaron's caresses. She tugged his shirt free from his jeans, and he helped pull it over his head. Part of her hoped to see a businessman's body, going soft from too much deskwork, but the taut planes of his chest were anything but soft.

"What are you thinking?" he whispered.

"I'm not."

"Not what?"

"Thinking."

She wasn't. Instinct was taking over, and she undid the waistband of his jeans. His arousal was so hard against the zipper that she eased her fingers inside, teasing and protecting him as she eased the tab downward.

The harsh hiss of his breath sounded in her ear and she smiled. He kicked the denims away. They were skin to skin and it was both satisfying and arousing. She opened her thighs and felt him probing her slick, hot center...then groaned when he drew away.

"Damn," Aaron muttered, reaching toward the floor as if searching for something. A moment later he grabbed his jeans and fished his wallet from the back pocket.

Of course, a condom.

Skylar's passion cooled briefly as she realized how close they'd come to unprotected sex, but before she could say anything, Aaron drew one of her nipples into his mouth, tugging the hard point gently one moment, the next suckling deeply. Heat streaked through her veins, making her forget everything but the need growing at the apex of her thighs, a need that seemed impossible to satisfy.

His erection was hot against her thigh, then unerringly sliding inside.

Skylar's fingers dug into Aaron's shoulders as he thrust deep. Time lost all meaning as he intensified the rhythm, her hips moving with him urgently. He whispered to her, and she could sense him holding back, waiting for her to climax, and abruptly her body convulsed in a long wave of pleasure.

A few seconds later he followed her.

And as Aaron collapsed on the couch next to her, both of them gasping for breath, an errant thought crossed her mind…he really *had* learned a lot since they were seventeen.

SKYLAR GRADUALLY BECAME aware that it was morning, unable to remember the last time she'd felt so relaxed. The only problem was the fuzzy blanket tickling her nose.

Hmm, fuzzy what?

The comforter on her bed wasn't fuzzy. Reaching up, she flicked at the offending tickle…only to realize that she was cuddled up to a very warm, very naked man. And she was equally naked except for the blanket covering them both.

Aaron.

Memories of the previous night came flooding back, and she raised herself on her elbow, staring at him. The gray light of morning was creeping into the room, and she could tell that he was still peacefully asleep. Dark beard shadow covered his jaw and he was annoyingly attractive, while she must look a fright.

Skylar touched her hair, remembering how Aaron had undone her braid and played with its heavy length. They'd made love twice, the second time well after midnight. The fire had died down into glowing coals, and she'd opened her eyes to see Aaron bending over the hearth, piling wood onto the grate. She'd planned to go home then, only to have him convince her it was too late…and that there were much more interesting things to do than get dressed and drive across town.

"Are you regretting last night?" Aaron asked, startling her. He'd awakened and was gazing at her. "Because of your husband?"

She thought about Jimmie and the happiness they'd shared together, and the guilt she'd felt, being attracted to another man. Yet Jimmie would have said it was absurd. He'd believed in living fully; it was one of the things she had loved about him.

"No regrets."

It was true…and yet still a shock to find herself in bed with Aaron. That is, asleep on a couch.

Okay, he'd changed, and the changes were very appealing. Her heart was becoming far too involved, but she had to think about her daughter. If Karin had grown up knowing Jimmie wasn't her biological father it might be all right, but it would be cruel to complicate her grief with belated revelations now. Besides, just because Aaron was determined to have a role in his daughter's life, it didn't mean he wanted more than that.

Skylar's internal alarm clock told her it was past the time she usually got up and she wiggled upright. The big, comfortable sectional was still a snug fit for two adults, though they'd managed well enough.

Aaron yawned and put a hand behind his head. "Where are you going?"

"I have a hamburger stand to run and want to shower and change before starting my day. And you have a factory to keep you busy. This was nice, but playtime is over."

"Why do I have a feeling you're referring to something besides watching a movie and eating Italian?"

"Because you're a smart man." Skylar found her bra and donned it along with her T-shirt. Her panties, on the other hand, were more elusive. "Get up," she ordered Aaron, exasperated. He was still lying there as if he hoped she'd change her mind.

"Something wrong?"

"I can't find my panties, and I'm *not* leaving without them. Besides, you wouldn't want Melanie to find women's underwear in here, would you?"

The comment galvanized Aaron, who hastily began searching around the cushions. He found them deep in the couch and held up the offending bit of peach silk and lace that matched her bra.

"These do *not* look as if they belong to a woman who flips hamburgers for a living."

She snatched them. "I may have to dress practically on the outside, but there's nothing wrong with being feminine underneath."

"Hey, I approve. You have no idea how much."

Skylar had a pretty good idea—no doubt he was far more conversant with sexy women's lingerie than she would ever be. She pulled the panties over her hips and shook out her shirt. The cotton wasn't as wrinkled as she'd expected since the garment had ended up over a lamp—when sex was involved, Aaron still didn't spare much concern to where clothes landed.

She shimmied her jeans on and went hunting for her shoes and socks. Their location couldn't be blamed on Aaron; she'd kicked them off herself, long before things had gotten hot and heavy.

He just stood there, unconcerned about his nudity, watching her with a faintly appreciative, but mostly worried, expression.

"Don't look so nervous," she told him in exasperation. "I'm not going to get domestic and fix you breakfast or start thinking about decorating possibilities for the house. This was a onetime thing, never to be repeated."

"Maybe that's what I'm worried about."

"*Ha*. I know you, Aaron Hollister. Sleepovers are the closest thing to a commitment you'll ever make. What am I forgetting… *Oh*." She tucked her shirt into her jeans and put the photo album into the backpack.

"Can't I keep that for a while?" Aaron asked.

"And risk Melanie seeing it? I don't want to know what she'd think if she found an album filled with pictures of Karin. And she'd promptly tell Karin, too. Their imaginations would run wild."

"I'll put it in my bedroom. There's a master suite on the other side of the living room. Melanie never goes in there."

Skylar shook her head. "It isn't worth the chance.

Anyway, I told you I'd send the pictures by email. And we have other albums, as well—this one is more of a scrapbook, with certificates and ribbons and such."

"That's one of the things I like about it. Kind of a tour through Karin's childhood. Did she actually stage a rebellion and refuse to dissect a live frog in junior high?"

"No, that was me," Skylar returned drily. "I got expelled for a week, but they *did* stop using frogs in science class. Karin is the one who got the students to go on strike in the cafeteria because they were serving net-caught tuna. They were going to expel her, too, but I told them if they had as much sense as a seventh grader they wouldn't be environmentally irresponsible in the first place. They changed their minds and gave her a citizenship-of-the-month award."

Aaron chuckled. "Like mother, like daughter."

"You'd better mean that in a nice way," she warned.

"I do."

"Well, I've got to get going. I'll see you at the school when the bus arrives, or would you like me to bring Melanie home?" It wasn't easy sounding brisk and unemotional. The sex had been spectacular, and she didn't want to be uncomfortable about it, but this was *Aaron*. The commitmentphobe. The guy who came from a family of snobs who'd despise her background.

He was also the guy she couldn't stop thinking about.

"Why don't I pick up the girls?" he suggested.

"You've spent all your free time the past two days helping me get the family room ready."

"I prefer meeting Karin myself. And I might as well give Melanie a ride at the same time."

Aaron was silent for a moment, and Skylar figured he was annoyed that she still didn't want him alone with Karin without her being there, but then he smiled.

"Okay. I'll see you here at the house. I'll get more food and we can all eat together. And don't say it's not necessary—at the very least you deserve to see Melanie's face when she sees the family room is more than an empty cave now."

It was an argument she couldn't resist. "Fine."

Skylar dug her keys from her backpack as she hurried out to the truck. Yet no matter how much she rushed, she couldn't escape the thought that had been nagging at her for days.

She had to protect her daughter from the truth, but was that fair to Aaron? His growing affection for Karin was unmistakable, and it must be hard for him to think he'd never be more to her than her friend's brother.

THE KIDS WERE tired and noisy on the school bus, but the teachers and parent chaperones didn't try to settle them down except when something went flying through the air. Karin sat with Mellie in the back, and they compared notes on the souvenirs they'd gotten at the different places they had visited.

Mellie had mostly bought books for herself and a glass paperweight for Aaron; Karin had gotten two T-shirts, a ball cap and gifts for her mom and Grandma Grace and Grandpa Joe. She'd also picked out a key ring for Aaron, but wasn't sure about giving it to him.

Funny, in the beginning Mellie had always said *half* brother when she talked about Aaron, but not anymore. Of course, it would be weird saying *half* all the time. And family was family, no matter what. She and Mellie had decided that even if they didn't get to live together, they were going to be sisters.

They got back to the school late, and her mom was waiting with the rest of the parents, but they didn't see Aaron.

"It was fantabulous," Karin said when they'd gotten off the bus and her mom had hugged them both. "Can we go back and walk across the Golden Gate Bridge?"

Her mother laughed. "I guess so. Melanie, Aaron planned to be here, but I told him I'd bring you home. We're going to have dinner together at your house."

Mellie looked relieved, and Karin knew she'd been worried about being forgotten. "Okay."

Karin was quiet as they waited for their duffel bags to be unloaded from under the bus. She didn't think Aaron would have forgotten Mellie, but there must have been times when *somebody* had forgotten her, or she wouldn't have been worried about it.

That was crummy.

Her mom had been extra clingy since the accident, but Karin couldn't remember ever being forgotten, even before then. And she could always call Grandpa Joe and Grandma Grace if there was a problem. Mellie didn't have anyone like that.

"What was that for?" her mom asked when she gave her another hug.

Karin shrugged. It wasn't something she could explain. But as lousy as it was not to have her dad any longer, she had it lots better than Mellie.

When they got to Aaron's house, his snooty Mercedes was in the driveway. Karin wrinkled her nose. Okay, so it wasn't cool like a sports car or a little SUV, but he must be her mom's age. He was probably too old to care about being cool.

They put Melanie's duffel bag in the entryway of the house and went toward the kitchen when Aaron called them to come back there. As they rounded the corner, Karin's eyes widened when she saw the family room.

"Ohmigod," Mellie exclaimed.

"Do you like it?" Aaron asked.

"*It's awesome.*" She went around, looking at everything and smiling.

"I can't take much of the credit—Skylar picked out the furniture. I thought you should have a place to hang out besides your room."

Mellie ran over and threw her arms around his neck. "Nobody ever did anything this nice for me."

"Then it's time somebody did. Go check out the classic movies on the shelves. I hope they're the kind you like."

She sniffed. "I will."

"You could have the *best* slumber party in here," Karin said, plopping down on the couch. Just then she looked up at her mom and saw her cheeks were red. Aaron had a funny expression, too, and Karin realized they'd hardly said anything to each other.

An odd feeling went through her. She was sure her mom had been uptight the past few weeks because of Aaron. They fought an awful lot, but she was sure they'd smooched a few times on the front porch. And now they were acting really funny…as if they'd done *more* than smooching.

Only that couldn't be right. Everyone in Cooperton thought he was obnoxious. Didn't they?

Karin hugged a sofa throw pillow to her chest.

Okay, not *everyone* in Cooperton.

Mellie thought Aaron was okay, and people in town didn't seem to dislike him as much as before. Karin chewed on the inside of her lip. Her mom had said she should make up her own mind about Aaron, and he didn't *seem* obnoxious. He listened, and it was nice to have someone who didn't look sad when she talked about missing her dad, the way everybody else looked because they missed him, too. Well, Aaron had said it was *also* because they were worried about her.

She just didn't know.

And even if she liked him a bunch, that didn't mean she wanted him going to bed with her mom.

CHAPTER EIGHTEEN

WHEN SUNDAY MORNING dawned cold and rainy, Aaron tried to be glad he didn't have plans with Skylar and the girls. Still, even though Skylar and Karin weren't available, maybe he could do something with his sister.

"I can't—I have a test tomorrow," she said when he asked. Though she'd eaten breakfast, she was already munching a slice of leftover pizza. Next to her was a cup of hot chocolate. All in all, he didn't think she minded studying; she was ensconced in the family room in front of a crackling fire and had a well-stocked refrigerator and microwave nearby.

Pleasure filled him. Everything had seemed so perfect the previous evening with everyone enjoying the newly furnished family room. It was nothing dramatic, just a movie night, yet he had never been more contented. All the money and success in the world couldn't buy that feeling, and he'd wondered…he'd never been willing to risk his heart, but was it the only thing that would make him happy?

Maybe.

And maybe he had even more in common with Melanie than he'd thought, because the enticements of home and family were becoming almost as irresistible as Skylar.

"Well, since you have to study, I'll probably go to my office," he said. "Be careful if you put more wood on the fire."

"I will." At the last minute Melanie jumped up to give him a kiss, and the warmth stayed with Aaron as he stepped outside into the damp air. A scatter of dry leaves blew past. Surprised, he looked up at the stately trees arching over the house. They were gilded gold; autumn was finally in full swing.

He drove to the office with the dismal feeling that he was the only person in Cooperton who had nothing better to do. The factory didn't operate on Sundays—a holdover from an era when Sunday was respected as a day of rest—and it seemed forlorn. Skylar and Karin were having the Gibsons over for dinner, and even his grandparents would be enjoying a gracious meal, superbly prepared by Mrs. Ryland. He had a standing invitation to eat with them, but despite the improvement in their relationship, he wasn't comfortable there. While they were genuinely regretful of the cold, disciplined way they'd raised him, the past wasn't easy to undo.

In his silent office, Aaron handled various tasks, ending with a memo for Peggy to distribute when she came in the next morning. It modified yet another employee rule he'd made since returning to Cooperton, and he grimaced as he clicked Send. He ought to have found out *why* things were done a certain way before establishing new policies and radically changing things.

Skylar was right.

He'd founded his decisions on distrust. Hell, many of his employees had ancestors who'd worked at Cooper Industries since the day it started. Generations of families, loyal to their employer, and they'd pulled each other through the Great Depression and two World Wars. He *couldn't* treat them the same as he would an employee anywhere else; they'd stayed through both the good times and the bad.

He figured trust issues also explained the difference between the way the town used to treat his grandfather and the way they treated him. George had been fiercely protective of both Cooper Industries and Cooperton, while Aaron suspected everyone was convinced *he* would sell both town and company to the highest bidder. To turn things around, he'd have to treat Cooper Industries as more than an unavoidable task on his way to something better.

Aaron got up from the desk and paced restlessly.

The truth was, he'd always had an exit strategy— both at work and with the people in his life. Did that make him more similar to his father than he wanted to think? There were different kinds of commitment, and he had avoided them in his own way, at the same time patting himself on the back for not being like Spence.

How had he turned out so different from Skylar, when they'd both seen such lousy relationships growing up? She'd barely survived the horrors of her parents' marriage. She could have taken the money from Spence or given Karin up for adoption and had a more glamorous life. Instead she'd made a happy marriage. And for all the gut-wrenching sorrow Karin and Skylar felt at losing James Gibson, Aaron didn't think they'd trade their years with him for anything in the world.

A few months ago he wouldn't have believed that kind of devotion was real. Now he did. And it would be extraordinary to have someone who cared about him that much.

So maybe Skylar was wrong.... Maybe sleepovers *weren't* the closest thing to a commitment he'd ever make. But there were two sides to the kind of commitment he was thinking about, and she might not have any interest in making one with him.

"Do you think Karin is upset with me for some reason?" Aaron asked Skylar on Tuesday evening.

He'd gotten into the habit of dropping by for a short time after Melanie was in bed, just to sit on the porch and talk. And it *was* just talk—Skylar hadn't allowed anything more intimate than a handshake since they'd slept together. She'd even moved the cushioned porch swing to a less private spot.

"I can't imagine why she would be. Why do you ask?"

"It's just a feeling. I keep wondering if she guessed that we..." He let the words trail.

"Don't even think it."

The swing drifted back and forth, with Aaron occasionally giving a push with his foot to keep it moving. It was cold, reminding him the Thanksgiving holiday was on Thursday, and he was worried that it would be just as disappointing to Melanie as Halloween had been.

She'd wanted full-size chocolate bars for the trick-or-treaters, so they'd gotten stacks of them, and she had sat by the front door in her costume, waiting for each ring of the bell. But while dozens of hobgoblins, fairy princesses and Darth Vader–clad kids had gone by in the street, few had stopped. She'd disconsolately eaten one candy bar after another until the floor around her feet was littered with wrappers.

It was his fault.

Their house was where the *real* ogre lived. He was no longer Cooperton's favorite son…if he'd ever been. Aaron had a growing disillusionment about his popularity when he was younger. Skylar had accused his buddies of being toadying and weaselly, and looking back, he could see they probably *had* been more interested in his money and Ford Mustang than friendship.

"How about us all doing something tomorrow night?" Aaron asked after a few minutes of silence. "Unless you'll be too busy with holiday cooking."

"The Nibble Nook is closing early—I can cook in the afternoon. By the way, I…uh…talked with Grace and Joe about it on Sunday. I know you have reservations to eat at the Meadowlark Inn, but they've invited you and Melanie to come for Thanksgiving dinner."

"How do you feel about that?"

"Fine." She cast him a glance. "Well...not fine, but I'll live with it. They know about you, by the way."

Aaron wasn't sure he should accept, but Melanie would be ecstatic if she could spend Thanksgiving with her friend. "It's very generous of your in-laws. We'd love to come."

"Good. What do you have in mind for tomorrow?"

"Ice-skating. I couldn't believe it when I found out the old rink is still operating. Or is that something Karin used to do with Jimmie?"

"It should be okay. She goes often with the youth group or friends, and one of the parents throws a birthday party there every year. We've only been there as a family once or twice since moving back to Cooperton."

"How old was Karin then?"

"Almost five. When Jimmie and I got married, his parents gave us the Nibble Nook as a wedding gift. We commuted until Karin was school age, but didn't want to be working in one town, with her attending school in another."

The references to Jimmie Gibson were getting easier for Aaron. He still struggled with a mixture of jealousy and resentment toward the other man, but the feelings were fading. Jimmie was the guy who'd stayed up nights when Karin had a tummy ache, soothed her tears when she skinned her knee and loved her with all his heart.

What Aaron mostly felt now was gratitude. James Gibson must have been one hell of a guy, and in a curious way, Aaron was sorry they'd never met.

AT THE SKATING rink the next evening, Skylar could see what Aaron meant about Karin. Her daughter was distant. Not exactly angry, but acting as if she didn't know what to make of him.

It was probably to be expected.

Aaron had vocally disapproved of Melanie coming to the Nibble Nook and had a lousy reputation in Cooperton—then all of sudden they were going rafting and taking trips to the zoo? Karin was smart and *had* to be wondering what was going on.

Skylar tied the laces on her skates snugly, making sure they weren't loose around the ankles. Karin and Melanie were already circling the ice.

Aaron finished tying his own skates and tried to stand up, only to promptly sit down again.

"*Crap.* I just remembered that I hate ice-skating."

She patted his arm consolingly. "You'll hate it even more the first time you fall."

"That isn't funny."

"Neither is bouncing on your butt. But you'll survive."

"Don't expect sympathy when you go flying," Aaron said darkly.

"I'm not going to go flying—I'm going to sit here and look cute in my jeans and parka and stay away from the ice. I'll wobble to the snack bar—that's it."

"No, you don't." Aaron pulled her to her feet. "If I skate, you skate. And I'll bet twenty bucks that you fall first."

Fifteen seconds later Aaron pulled out his wallet and extracted a twenty. He looked quite sexy lying on the ice, and Skylar spun in a circle around him before snatching the bill from his fingers.

"You cheated," he said crossly. "You can skate."

"I never said I couldn't. I used to come here when I was a kid and my…"

He lifted an eyebrow. "And your what?"

"When my parents were fighting. It was safer to find somewhere else to go," she managed to say matter-of-factly. She gave Aaron a hand to help him up. "We lived a few blocks away, and the owner felt sorry for me. Hank let me skate without paying as long as he didn't have a private party in the rink."

"Maybe you should have gone professional."

"Don't get any ideas of a great talent gone to waste. I was never in danger of becoming that good. Anyhow, Hank died when I was twelve, and his grandson took over. *He* didn't believe in freebies, so my trips to the rink were over."

"Twelve?"

"Yes. Coincidentally, about the same time I started getting into more serious trouble."

"You didn't get any breaks."

"Yes, I did," Skylar said seriously. "I had Hank, even though he was just a gruff old guy who didn't talk much. I'd help clean up the snack bar, and he'd feed me a hot dog or nachos. And later I had the Gibsons and Jimmie and Karin. I don't feel sorry for myself, Aaron, and I don't want anyone else to, either."

"All right."

They stayed close to the outer edge of the rink, where Aaron could grab the railing if needed. The girls called "hi" a few times as they passed more quickly. And as Aaron got more comfortable, he was willing to go farther out on the ice. He only fell two more times the rest of the evening, which was an accomplishment for a guy who hadn't worn ice skates in over fifteen years.

Karin seemed to have forgotten whatever was bothering her as they turned in their skates and headed for the Mercedes. She was giggling with Melanie when a dog in the dark cab of a pickup suddenly leaped at the half-open window, snarling fiercely.

Karin and Melanie both let out a shriek, jumped awkwardly and tumbled to the ground.

"Hell." Aaron got to them first. "Are you guys okay?"

"I think so, 'cept my hand hurts." Melanie got to her feet and flicked at the gravel stuck in her palm.

"Me, too," Karin added. She sat up and let out another yelp. "Uh, maybe not."

Skylar knelt next to her and smoothed her hair back. "What's wrong, sweetie?"

"My arm." She held it to her body. "I think it's broken."

Broken?

Aaron was horrified, but he could barely hear himself think because the damned dog kept barking its head off and throwing itself against the truck door.

"All right," Skylar murmured. "Does anything else hurt, like your head or neck or back?"

"Nothing except my pride."

Skylar smiled faintly and then looked at Melanie. "How about you, hon?"

His sister shook her head. "I fell on Karin."

"And I just fell on my arm." Karin was obviously trying to be brave, but her eyes were bright with pain.

Aaron pulled out his cell phone. "I'll call for an ambulance."

"No!" Karin shrieked so fast he was astonished.

"I think it's okay if we take them to the emergency room ourselves, but she needs a splint on her arm," Skylar said. She stood up, marched to the shiny black pickup, and slammed her fist on the door. "Shut up!" she yelled. "Or I'll rip your lungs out, you miserable beast."

The noise switched off abruptly.

"Hey, lady, what the frig are you doing to my truck?" yelled a man as he ran across the parking lot.

Aaron stepped between the irate man and Skylar. "Take your animal and get out of here," he ordered.

"Who are you, her daddy?"

"No, I'm the guy protecting you from the woman whose daughter just broke her arm because of your vicious dog. Trust me, you don't want to mess with her. *Or me*."

The man backed off. "All right, all right. I'm leaving."

Aaron got the first aid kit from the Mercedes. "It's okay, Karin. You're going to be fine." He hoped he sounded calmer than he felt.

"Yeah, but it *sucks*."

He wasn't sure it was language Skylar wanted her using, but it *did* suck. "You bet."

A small crowd of onlookers gathered as they splinted Karin's arm and used a sling to immobilize it against her body. Melanie kept saying she was okay, but Skylar insisted on wrapping her hand with sterile gauze before leaving.

Aaron marveled at her composure.

The hospital was just a few minutes away, and he stopped in front of the emergency room door.

"I'll get them inside while you park the car," Skylar said.

"I don't need a doctor," Melanie protested.

"Yes, you do."

"Don't bother trying to get out of it," Karin told her resignedly. "It's a mom thing."

If Aaron hadn't been so stressed, he would have laughed. But all he could think was that his daughter and sister were injured, and he couldn't fix it.

By the time he got the Mercedes parked, both the girls were in examination rooms. The martinet at the front desk was sympathetic, but determined to get his information and signature on several forms. How had Skylar gotten in so quickly? He finally escaped and found her sitting with Melanie in the waiting room. His sister's hand was neatly bandaged and he took off his coat and wrapped it around her. Poor kid, she looked terrified.

"How are you doing?"

"Okay," she said in a small voice. "The nurse washed my palm with some stuff."

"Are you sure you aren't hurt anywhere else?"

"No. They checked me out, like my reflexes and all that."

"Thank goodness. What's happening with Karin?" he asked Skylar.

"They sent us out while they're doing an X-ray."

"Just an X-ray? It should be an MRI, or a CAT scan at the very least."

She sighed. "Aaron, they aren't even sure it's broken. There wasn't any obvious bone displacement, and they don't usually do MRIs or CAT scans on a simple fracture."

"We'll see about that."

He promptly headed back to the reception desk.

"I'M SO SORRY," Melanie whispered when Aaron was gone again. "It's my fault for falling on Karin."

"Nonsense." Skylar put an arm around her. She would have stayed with her daughter, but Melanie hadn't been allowed to remain and Karin hadn't wanted her friend to be alone. "It was an accident. If you want to blame anyone, blame that dog for barking."

Melanie sniffed. "I just never had a real friend before. What if she hates me?"

"She *won't* hate you. I know my daughter. Besides, a broken arm heals…*if* it's even broken, which they weren't sure about. They'll put a cast on, and you'll probably be the first to sign it unless the doctor beats you to it."

"Really?"

"Really."

The teenager rested her head on Skylar's shoulder, and her slow, silent tears were heartrending. Lord, the child's parents should be arrested for ignoring their daughter and making her so uncertain and anxious for love—of all people, Skylar knew what stupid decisions could come out of such a basic, desperate need. Slowly, the tears quieted, replaced by the regular breathing rhythm of sleep.

Skylar looked up and saw Aaron watching, and his white, strained face made her ache. If anything, she'd expected him to jump ship at the first crisis. But he was still here, and she didn't think it was just his concern for Melanie.

Beneath that cool, distant facade he was so good at showing the world, Aaron Hollister had become a pretty decent guy…a guy she'd fallen for, all over again. Except this time it was a love capable of tearing her apart.

It was almost funny. She'd worried about Karin getting hurt, and then about Aaron's feelings. But she'd forgotten to protect her own heart.

He walked over and sat next to her.

"You're right—they won't consider a CAT scan unless there's an indication it's needed," he said softly. "How can you be so calm?"

"Practice. Kids have accidents, and you have to deal with them. When Karin was born I wanted to protect her from everything. But I couldn't. Banged elbows and knees and broken arms are part of growing up. You do your best and thank God they're resilient. I'll go home and fall apart once Karin is in bed—I can't afford to until then."

"Well, you were amazing." Aaron rubbed the back of his neck. "And how did you get past Dragon Lady so fast?"

"Who?"

"The woman at the front desk. I thought she'd have me filling out paperwork for a month."

"In the first place, this isn't our first trip to the emergency room. They have Karin's information and a consent form on file, and I told them you'd be right in to give them what was needed for Melanie. The first paper you signed was the consent to treat."

"That makes sense. Why was Melanie upset?"

"Worry that Karin would blame her."

"Not a chance. Here, let me take your place. I'm sure you want to check on Karin. They won't tell me anything."

They shifted slowly so that he was supporting Melanie; worn out from emotion, the teenager barely stirred.

Skylar got up. Aaron had admired how she'd handled the situation, but she wondered how parents managed with more than one child in the middle of a crisis. Melanie wasn't her daughter, but she'd still needed comfort, at the same time Karin was being treated.

She and Jimmie had talked about having more kids, but when Skylar didn't conceive, they'd learned he was sterile. He'd spent five minutes upset about the news, then shrugged and said that Karin was a gift from heaven and the only child they needed.

The reception desk told her Karin was back in the exam room, and Skylar walked inside to hear her daughter giggling. It wasn't much of a giggle, but it definitely qualified.

"What's this?" she asked. "Is somebody a comedienne?"

"Naw," Karin replied. "Dr. McRoth was saying it was too bad I don't play volleyball, because I could hit the heck out of the ball with a cast on my arm."

"Ohhhh, it's broken, then."

"Yup." Karin sounded philosophical about the whole thing. But then, it wasn't the first bone she'd broken.

"She has a minor fracture and it will need to be in plaster for a few weeks. It's tight quarters in here with us working on her," Dr. McRoth said. "You'd be more comfortable waiting outside while we're putting the cast on. I'll come out and talk to you when it's done."

"Are you okay with that, Karin?" Skylar asked.

"Yeah. I'm not a baby."

Skylar stepped out and rubbed the back of her neck. At least this particular crisis hadn't occurred when she had to open the Nibble Nook the next morning. She wasn't sure she had energy to deal with it at the moment.

Not that the Nibble Nook was her biggest problem…that was Aaron. She couldn't get away from how she felt about him, or her concerns for Karin. He'd changed, and he hadn't known she was pregnant all those years ago—that put a different light on things. And no matter how bad it would be for her daughter to learn the truth right now, it was also hard for Aaron not to be recognized as her father.

MELANIE HAD WOKEN up and decided to lie down on one of the couches, so Aaron was on his feet, pacing the floor when Skylar came down the hallway.

"How is she?"

"Doing well. Laughing at something the doctor was saying. It's a fracture and they're putting a cast on—don't worry, Aaron. She'll be fine."

He stalked up and down a few paces. "That's easier

said than done. And on top of everything, *I'm* the one who suggested ice-skating."

"Karin didn't break her arm ice-skating, she broke it in a parking lot. And it could have just as easily been Melanie."

"I know. That bothers me, too."

Skylar leaned against the wall. "You can't wrap them in cotton and hope they're protected. They'd just smother that way, and resent the hell out of you for trying to do it. I found that out a long time ago."

Aaron knew she was right, but the enormous responsibility of parenthood had just gotten bigger. And there was no way he could escape it; Karin had captured his heart as thoroughly as Skylar. He was going to fuss and fume and worry about his daughter no matter where he was, or how much he was allowed to see her. The same way he'd worry about Melanie…and Skylar.

Never in his wildest dreams could he have seen this coming a few months ago. He'd avoided commitment his whole life, but now his heart had made the choice. Yeah, it was a risk, but what wasn't? He didn't want to live without the three biggest loves of his life—what sort of life would that be?

The trick would be convincing Skylar.

It seemed forever before the emergency doctor came out and Aaron strode forward. "How is she?" he demanded.

The physician looked at Skylar, obviously for permission to answer, and she nodded. "I'm Dr. McRoth.

Karin has a minor injury. Nothing to be concerned about. The plaster should be dry soon, and she can go home."

Aaron wanted to deck him. *That's my kid,* he nearly yelled. It mattered that Karin was hurt, and this guy was tossing it off as unimportant.

"Maybe we should get an orthopedic specialist for a second opinion. We could go to Los Angeles or New York for one of those sports doctors who treat professional athletes."

Skylar and the doctor stared at him.

"Sir, essentially she has a greenstick fracture," Dr. McRoth explained slowly. "Very easy to treat, no complications expected. In a younger child I'd just put an elastic bandage on her arm."

"Are you an orthopedic specialist?" Aaron demanded.

"Yes."

It took some of the wind out his sails, but he squared his jaw. "I still think a second opinion is warranted."

"You're welcome to get one, of course."

"We'll talk about it later, Aaron," Skylar said sweetly. Yet her teeth were bared. "When we discuss overreacting and sounding like a jackass. If you're this way around Karin, you'll alarm her for no reason."

He shut his mouth. He knew he was overreacting, but he didn't have Skylar's years of practice as a parent to keep him grounded. Except for the tension around her mouth, she was calm and behaving like a rational person. She asked a few more questions and then nodded.

"Thank you, Dr. McRoth."

"Not at all. The nurse will bring Karin out soon."

When they were alone, Skylar planted her hands on her hips and glared. "What was that all about?"

"He was too casual about it."

"That's because he didn't want *us* to worry for nothing."

Aaron didn't know what to say in his own defense, but Karin's arrival saved him. She was smiling and chattering away to the nurse. And all things considered, she might be in better shape than the rest of them.

CHAPTER NINETEEN

AARON TOOK SKYLAR and Karin home and waited until Karin was settled in bed. She was sleepy from medication the doctor had given her and yawned as he came in to say good-night.

"I'm sorry about your arm, kiddo," he said, his chest tight.

He wanted to be a real dad and put his arms around her, assuring her everything would be all right. But being a friend wasn't so bad, either, and if he could talk Skylar into letting them become a family, it would surely work out.

"That's okay. We have gymnastics coming up, and the doctor says I can't do any. Gave me a note and everything. It's *great*."

"Oh, well, that's looking at the bright side."

"Uh-huh." She curled up on her side. "G'night, Aaron. I'm glad you're coming to Thanksgiving dinner with us tomorrow."

"Thanks, I'm glad, too. Good night."

By the time he went out to the front room, Melanie had fallen sleep on the couch. "Let her stay— you're coming over in the morning anyway," Skylar urged. "And I'll be up and down all night, checking on Karin."

"All right." Aaron gave her a quick, hard kiss and left.

He drove to the house, but when he got there and went inside, it was too empty without Melanie. The only twenty-four-hour restaurant in Cooperton was the truck-stop café by the highway, so he went there and ordered a cup of coffee.

He wanted to propose to Skylar, but she had little reason to see him as a decent husband and father candidate. His performance to date had not been stellar, and he wasn't sure she'd give him points for effort.

Of course, there was only one way to find out, and it required a leap of faith.

"Hon, you gotta have something to eat," the server said, plunking down a plate when she refilled his cup for the third time. On it was a generous slice of homemade berry pie. "Yer stomach's gonna revolt with nothing but Tad's coffee to chew on."

"Oh…well, thank you. It looks delicious."

"Day old, anyhow. We were fixing to throw it out."

She bustled away, and he smiled as he ate the pie. Throwing the delicious dessert away would have been a crime, but he doubted the "day old" part of the story was true. The server just had a kind heart with natural mothering instincts.

The thought took him by surprise. Not long ago he would have suspected her of ulterior motives.

When Aaron had consumed every crumb, he glanced

around the café. A family on the far side were the only other patrons. The father had a steaming cup in front of him, but the mother and children were just sitting quietly. The kids looked hungry, but they were well behaved.

He frowned. "Uh…ma'am?" he said when the server came by again. "That family…is everything all right with them?"

"Down on their luck, I think," she murmured. "Headed for Bakersfield. The dad's going to run a convenience store, but their carburetor went out. Our mechanic just replaced it. I doubt they got more than enough money for a cup of coffee. The cook and me wanted to give 'em a meal, but they wouldn't take it."

"I'll see what I can do. Keep the change," he said, handing her a twenty before walking across the café. "Hello, folks."

The father nodded distractedly, looking worried and focused on some internal debate.

Aaron thought hard, trying to decide the right thing to say. "I understand you're taking a management position down south. If you don't mind my asking, what's your employment background?"

The other man blinked and seemed to notice him for the first time. "Oh…out of college I went to work with a company called Wiztek Software and worked up to manager, but when they sold, most of us were laid off. It isn't easy starting over in this economy," he said dully.

"Wiztek, huh? I used to work in the computer

industry and they put out some fine software." Aaron handed him a business card. "My name is Aaron Hollister. I'm always looking for good people to work for me, and if you're interested, I'd like to interview you for a job here in town. Cooper Industries isn't computer related, but we're a good company."

"I… *Yes*. I *am* interested."

"Excellent." Aaron took out his wallet and extracted several hundred-dollar bills. "Since it's the Thanksgiving holiday weekend, I won't be in the office until Monday, but I'll pay your expenses to make it worth your while to stay until then."

"We couldn't." It was his wife protesting and Aaron saw a fierce spark of independence in her weary eyes. "We'll drive on to Bakersfield."

Aaron glanced at their daughter. She reminded him of Karin, but he'd never seen Karin with that hopeless expression, and prayed he never would.

"I'd consider it a personal favor if you'd stay, ma'am. Someone who means the world to me was injured tonight—not seriously, but bad enough. You're all tired, and I'd hate for you to risk being in an accident, especially with all the holiday traffic out there. If things work out, I'm sure you'd enjoy living in Cooperton."

"Mom, *please,*" begged the daughter.

The woman bit her lip, then finally nodded. "All right. But we'll pay you back, Mr. Hollister. Every penny."

"Just worry about getting some rest." He wrote a

note on another business card and gave it to her husband with the money. "I'll see you Monday at ten."

Aaron hurried out before they could change their minds. He didn't care if he saw the man or the money again; he just wanted those kids to have a meal and a place to sleep.

Instinctively, he drove back to Skylar's house. He parked and gazed at the front door, wishing he was on the other side of it, and wanting to be the kind of man who *should* be inside that door. Before finding Skylar again he wouldn't have even noticed a struggling family, and he certainly wouldn't have done anything for them. She'd made him a better person, and he didn't want to slide back to being cynical and alone.

Images flashed through his mind of Skylar when they were kids, and the extraordinary woman she'd become. They were different people now, and they might have failed horribly if they'd tried to make it when they were eighteen, with all of their childhood ghosts to haunt them. But now…maybe they had a chance. The ghosts were still there, but they were quieter and further away and could be dealt with.

Just then the front door opened and Skylar stepped out; she must have heard him drive up.

He met her on the porch.

"Did you forget something?" she asked, zipping up the parka she'd worn ice-skating.

Some guys declared themselves with flowers and

a ring in a romantic moment, but Aaron didn't want to waste any more time.

"No, it's just that everything important to me is right here. Melanie, Karin…*you*."

IT TOOK SEVERAL seconds for Skylar to process what Aaron had said. But when it sank in, her knees wobbled.

"Aaron, I don't… What are…?" Jeez, she didn't even know what to ask.

"I'm saying I love you and want to marry you. Give me a chance to make things right for us. I know I screwed up when we were kids."

Skylar had trouble breathing. She cast a glance at the house before grabbing his hand and dragging him off the porch and out of easy earshot.

"You're just upset about what happened tonight— give it time before you talk about marriage. Think about what it would be like introducing me to the Coopers and Hollisters. That should cool you off. Your father already knows my background, and it wouldn't be hard for your mother and grandparents to find out, as well. They'd be appalled to see me on their family tree."

Aaron snorted. "My family would be lucky to have you. And if they aren't smart enough to recognize that, then it's their problem. For God's sake, Skylar, you said it yourself, the Coopers and Hollisters are messed up. I hope you won't turn me down because of that, but I have to be honest. And my father isn't a problem anyway. He thinks you've done a terrific job with Karin—he was all for Melanie moving in here."

Skylar's jaw dropped. "Why didn't you tell me?"

"Because I'd just learned that Karin might be my kid, which swamped everything else. Put yourself in my shoes—Spence dropped that bomb as casually as he'd pop a champagne cork."

"How did he know how Karin was doing?" she asked, pressing a hand to her spinning head.

"Because he had someone check things out every few months to be sure you were all right. It was his weird idea of taking care of you both."

"Aaron, I am *never* going to understand your father."

"That's okay, neither am I."

"Not that I have anything to brag about when it comes to my own parents," she said, casting him a sideways look.

He grinned wryly. "That makes us perfect for each other—we don't have to apologize for our families. By the way, I told Spence and Eliza that Melanie is staying with me for good. I think they were relieved."

"They aren't the only ones. I felt terrible for her tonight. It breaks my heart how anxious she is to be loved."

"I'm lonely and anxious, too, Skylar."

Skylar leaned against the Mercedes and counted to ten. She'd never expected to fall in love again, especially with Aaron. And a marriage proposal? It was almost incomprehensible.

"You don't trust me," she said finally. "That's a lousy basis for a marriage."

"Hell, I've never trusted anyone. But I figured something out over the past few weeks...I've never given anyone a reason to trust *me*. It's a two-way street, and for once in my life, I want to act on faith. We'll tell Karin who I am *if* the right moment ever comes. I'll always be sorry I lost those years with both of you, but I don't have to make the same mistakes over again."

Skylar gulped.

He believes me about Karin, she realized, stunned by Aaron's raw vulnerability. She needed to protect her daughter...but it was just as bad to see him hurting. And keeping the truth from Karin would hurt.

"Think about it," she whispered. "I've seen the look in your eyes when Karin talks about Jimmie. Nothing is going to change how important he was to us. Or the Gibsons—they'll always be Mom and Dad to me, and Grandpa Joe and Grandma Grace to Karin. Do you know how difficult it would be, day after day, to be reminded that Karin doesn't know you're her biological father?"

A SURGE OF hope went through Aaron.

Skylar was worried about how he felt. Did it mean she cared...or even loved him?

Yet before he could say something stupid, he made himself consider what she'd said. Her concern was valid. It *was* hard not having Karin know who he was. He recalled his daughter's proud, happy, sometimes humorous stories about her adoptive father and tried to weigh what it would be like to keep hearing those stories. After all, she had a lifetime of memories to share.

"I'm not saying it's going to be easy," he said carefully. "But you just said something important—you called me Karin's biological father. Your husband loved her wholeheartedly. He didn't care about biology, which means Karin can learn to love me the same way, even if she doesn't know everything. We can tell her when and if the time is right."

"What if it's never the right time?"

Aaron cupped Skylar's face. The moonlight caught the sparkle of tears in her eyes, and he hated seeing them. There'd been enough tears.

"Then it's never right. Sweetheart, Karin's grief is painful, not the relationship she had with Jimmie Gibson. I'm *grateful* she had him as her dad—I only hope I can measure up. And while I can't promise to be perfect, I promise to try every day to be a better husband and father than the day before. I love you so much. Will you give me a chance and help me do that? I can't stand being alone any longer."

SKYLAR HESITATED.

Yet how could she refuse to give Aaron a second chance? She'd gotten her own share of second chances—from Jimmie and his parents, who'd taken her into their hearts without reservation, and from her sweet, smart, comical daughter, whose birth convinced her that she could be more than a messed-up girl from the worst part of town, with the worst kind of parents. Marriage wasn't easy, but neither was life. It was loving with all your heart that made it worthwhile.

"I love you, too. And we'll help each other," she promised, wrapping her arms around his neck.

"Thank God." Aaron pulled her into a kiss she never wanted to end.

"WHAT DO YOU THINK?" Melanie asked as she peeked through the curtains. "It's awful romantic in the moonlight."

Karin scratched under the edge of her cast. It was already itchy, even though it still hurt. "I think we're going to be sisters for real," she said, peeking out, as well. Her mom and Aaron were in a clinch, kissing for all they were worth.

"If they get married, it makes me your aunt."

"I'm *not* calling you Aunt Mellie."

Mellie giggled. "I like sister best. Do you mind about Aaron and your mother? You know…because of your dad?"

"A little, but I'll get over it," Karin said philosophically. And she would. Her dad had wanted them to be happy, and if Aaron made her mom happy, it would be okay.

Twenty months later...

THE GRADUATING CLASS of Cooperton High was marching slowly into place for the commencement ceremony, and pride filled Aaron as he watched his sister in her cap and gown, looking confident and happy. She'd gone from being behind in all of her classes, to a perfect 4.0 grade average in her senior year.

"Be careful, you'll bust all your buttons," his wife warned in a low voice.

"Yeah, like you don't feel the same way," he retorted.

Skylar laughed. A light breeze ruffled her dress and he put a hand over her swollen tummy. The baby was due in a month, and the wait was driving Karin and him crazy.

From the beginning he'd made it clear to Karin that he wanted to make his own place in her life, not fill the one left by Jimmie Gibson. They'd grown closer with the passage of time, but it was Skylar's pregnancy that had cemented their relationship. Karin loved that she was going to be a big sister, and along with Melanie and the Gibsons, they were a united front, trying to make Skylar rest and not overdo things.

Aaron looked around the assemblage of friends and families, still hoping to see Spence and Eliza. He'd threatened, cajoled and demanded they make it to their daughter's graduation, but good old S. S. Hollister was in Bordeaux, romancing a French actress, and

Eliza was in Japan with her husband. Flying home to the States wasn't likely.

His mouth tightened.

He could forgive Spence for missing his own high-school and college graduations; it was harder to tolerate him disappointing Melanie. As for Eliza, he'd expected better.

Skylar slipped her fingers into his hand and squeezed. "Let it go. You can't make someone change," she whispered.

True enough.

He struggled enough with changing himself. At home, with Skylar and the girls, it was easier—Skylar was his compass, drawing him in the right direction. They still fought, but making up was fun. With his employees and grandparents and the rest of Cooperton, he had more trouble.

Things were improving, though. Skylar had gotten the city council to approve his expansion plans and the new facility had been up and running for several months; it made for safer, more pleasant working conditions, and his employees seemed to approve.

As for the Coopers…at least they'd stopped serving him sherry before dinner. Of course, that was mostly because of Skylar, too. She was so forthright, his grandparents had hardly known what hit them. Despite their obvious recollection of her reputation as a teen, they liked Skylar. They just didn't know what to make of her.

He leaned over and gave his wife a long, lingering kiss, grateful beyond measure for the fate that brought him back to Cooperton. If life was about making choices, then he'd finally made the right one.

"Aaron," Karin scolded, slapping the back of his head with a commencement program. "Stop smooching and watch Mellie graduate."

"Bossy, isn't she?" Skylar said conversationally.

"Mooommmm."

Aaron and Skylar smiled at each other and obediently turned their attention forward.

* * * * *

LARGER-PRINT BOOKS!
GET 2 FREE LARGER-PRINT NOVELS PLUS
2 FREE GIFTS!

⬧HARLEQUIN

super romance

More Story...More Romance

YES! Please send me 2 FREE LARGER-PRINT Harlequin® Superromance® novels and my 2 FREE gifts (gifts are worth about $10). After receiving them, if I don't wish to receive any more books, I can return the shipping statement marked "cancel." If I don't cancel, I will receive 6 brand-new novels every month and be billed just $5.69 per book in the U.S. or $5.99 per book in Canada. That's a savings of at least 16% off the cover price! It's quite a bargain! Shipping and handling is just 50¢ per book in the U.S. or 75¢ per book in Canada.* I understand that accepting the 2 free books and gifts places me under no obligation to buy anything. I can always return a shipment and cancel at any time. Even if I never buy another book, the two free books and gifts are mine to keep forever.

139/339 HDN F46Y

Name	(PLEASE PRINT)	
Address		Apt. #
City	State/Prov.	Zip/Postal Code

Signature (if under 18, a parent or guardian must sign)

Mail to the **Harlequin® Reader Service:**
IN U.S.A.: P.O. Box 1867, Buffalo, NY 14240-1867
IN CANADA: P.O. Box 609, Fort Erie, Ontario L2A 5X3
**Are you a current subscriber to Harlequin Superromance books
and want to receive the larger-print edition?
Call 1-800-873-8635 today or visit www.ReaderService.com.**

* Terms and prices subject to change without notice. Prices do not include applicable taxes. Sales tax applicable in N.Y. Canadian residents will be charged applicable taxes. Offer not valid in Quebec. This offer is limited to one order per household. Not valid for current subscribers to Harlequin Superromance Larger-Print books. All orders subject to credit approval. Credit or debit balances in a customer's account(s) may be offset by any other outstanding balance owed by or to the customer. Please allow 4 to 6 weeks for delivery. Offer available while quantities last.

Your Privacy—The Harlequin® Reader Service is committed to protecting your privacy. Our Privacy Policy is available online at www.ReaderService.com or upon request from the Harlequin Reader Service.

We make a portion of our mailing list available to reputable third parties that offer products we believe may interest you. If you prefer that we not exchange your name with third parties, or if you wish to clarify or modify your communication preferences, please visit us at www.ReaderService.com/consumerschoice or write to us at Harlequin Reader Service Preference Service, P.O. Box 9062, Buffalo, NY 14269. Include your complete name and address.

HSRLP13R

LARGER-PRINT BOOKS!

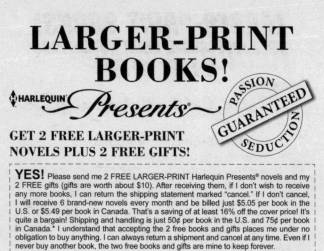

HARLEQUIN *Presents*

PASSION GUARANTEED SEDUCTION

GET 2 FREE LARGER-PRINT NOVELS PLUS 2 FREE GIFTS!

YES! Please send me 2 FREE LARGER-PRINT Harlequin Presents® novels and my 2 FREE gifts (gifts are worth about $10). After receiving them, if I don't wish to receive any more books, I can return the shipping statement marked "cancel." If I don't cancel, I will receive 6 brand-new novels every month and be billed just $5.05 per book in the U.S. or $5.49 per book in Canada. That's a saving of at least 16% off the cover price! It's quite a bargain! Shipping and handling is just 50¢ per book in the U.S. and 75¢ per book in Canada.* I understand that accepting the 2 free books and gifts places me under no obligation to buy anything. I can always return a shipment and cancel at any time. Even if I never buy another book, the two free books and gifts are mine to keep forever.

176/376 HDN F43N

Name	(PLEASE PRINT)
Address	Apt. #
City	State/Prov. Zip/Postal Code

Signature (if under 18, a parent or guardian must sign)

Mail to the **Harlequin® Reader Service:**
IN U.S.A.: P.O. Box 1867, Buffalo, NY 14240-1867
IN CANADA: P.O. Box 609, Fort Erie, Ontario L2A 5X3

**Are you a subscriber to Harlequin Presents books
and want to receive the larger-print edition?
Call 1-800-873-8635 today or visit us at www.ReaderService.com.**

* Terms and prices subject to change without notice. Prices do not include applicable taxes. Sales tax applicable in N.Y. Canadian residents will be charged applicable taxes. Offer not valid in Quebec. This offer is limited to one order per household. Not valid for current subscribers to Harlequin Presents Larger-Print books. All orders subject to credit approval. Credit or debit balances in a customer's account(s) may be offset by any other outstanding balance owed by or to the customer. Please allow 4 to 6 weeks for delivery. Offer available while quantities last.

Your Privacy—The Harlequin® Reader Service is committed to protecting your privacy. Our Privacy Policy is available online at www.ReaderService.com or upon request from the Harlequin Reader Service.

We make a portion of our mailing list available to reputable third parties that offer products we believe may interest you. If you prefer that we not exchange your name with third parties, or if you wish to clarify or modify your communication preferences, please visit us at www.ReaderService.com/consumerschoice or write to us at Harlequin Reader Service Preference Service, P.O. Box 9062, Buffalo, NY 14269. Include your complete name and address.

HPLP13R

ReaderService.com

Manage your account online!

- Review your order history
- Manage your payments
- Update your address

*We've designed
the Harlequin® Reader Service
website just for you.*

Enjoy all the features!

- Reader excerpts from any series
- Respond to mailings and
  special monthly offers
- Discover new series available to you
- Browse the Bonus Bucks catalog
- Share your feedback

Visit us at:
ReaderService.com